W9-AUG-495

THEY GOT RAIDER IN THEIR SIGHTS AND STARTED SHOOTING.

Raider spun around and returned their fire, emptying his gun. But then his horse was shot out from under him, throwing Raider off to the left. He hit hard, shoulder first, rolling over, fingers groping for his gun belt to begin reloading.

"Pink," called Greenleaf, "give it up. We're four to your one. We'll kill you. I promise."

Raider emptied his gun at them again, fumbling to reload, listening to them moving up. He got five into the chambers and slapped home the cylinder. But raising the gun, looking up to find his target, he discovered a small black hole staring down into his face.

It was the muzzle of Ben's .45.

Other Books by J. D. Hardin

The Good, the Bad, and the Deadly
Blood, Sweat and Gold
The Slick and the Dead
Bullets, Buzzards, Boxes of Pine

J.D. HARDIN

FACE DOWN IN A COFFIN

PLAYBOY PRESS
PAPERBACKS

FACE DOWN IN A COFFIN

Copyright © 1980 by J. D. Hardin

Cover illustration by V. Segrelles: Copyright © 1980 by PEI Books, Inc.

All rights reserved. No part of this book may be reproduced, stored in a retrieval system or transmitted in any form by an electronic, mechanical, photocopying, recording means or otherwise without prior written permission of the publisher.

Published simultaneously in the United States and Canada by Playboy Press Paperbacks, New York, New York. Printed in the United States of America. Library of Congress Catalog Card Number: 79-89964. First edition.

Books are available at quantity discounts for promotional and industrial use. For further information, write our sales promotion agency: Ventura Associates, 40 East 49th Street, New York, New York 10017.

ISBN: 0-872-16621-X

First printing March 1980.

1

Raider woke up to gray. A gray-shrouded, sullen-looking, cloudless sky visible outside the three upright bars of the cell window. The gray walls and floor, and the gray round bolt-head-studded door with the six-inch rectangular slot at the top. The gray faces of his three fellow prisoners of the Territory of Idaho, one of them a paler gray, the color squeezed out of his wizened features, his small button eyes darting about like a frightened hare. He was George Beckwith, a little shadow of a man who at first glimpse looked as if he didn't have muscle enough to lift a shotgun, let alone blow a man's head off with it. The law had picked him up within fifteen minutes of the deed and hauled him in front of a judge. Tomorrow morning he was to be hanged—which no doubt accounted for the man's colorless complexion, reflected Raider, stretching his six-foot-two-inch frame and yawning wide, wider, driving the last wisp of cloudiness out of his brain. He tossed off his blanket and sat up, swinging his legs over the edge of his bunk. He blinked and looked around.

The other two occupants of the cell, Ben and Charley Greenleaf, were stirring in their upper bunks, rubbing their eyes with their fists, stretching their jaw muscles. Charley cleared his throat and let the clearings fly at the barred window, falling short by no more than an inch or so and splattering the wall beneath.

"You're a goddamn pig, Charley," snapped his brother. "You know that?"

"Aw, lay off, will you, for chrissakes? I didn't do it deliberate."

Both let themselves down slowly, Ben wincing slightly as his bare soles contacted the stone floor. Raider glanced from one to the other. There was a family resemblance, but Charley was shorter, more slightly built, losing his black hair. He was constantly brushing it forward with a nervous gesture of his hand to cover the bare front of his scalp. He wore a black mustache thicker and bigger by far then Raider's own; Charley's was joined to his sideburns, covering the lower half of his face like a muffler with his deeply dimpled chin poking through the center. Charley had to be in his early thirties, while his brother was at least six years younger. Beardless and with a full thatch of dark brown hair, Ben had a homely grin permanently fixed to his face

Raider had shared the cell with the two brothers and the condemned man for a week now, enjoying every minute of it. Yeah. The cell itself was no more than fourteen or fifteen feet square; just cozy-fine for two men, but tight as a tin of fish for four. And in spite of Ben's built-in grin, he and his brother got along about as well as two scalded cats in a covered barrel. As for Beckwith, the poor bastard was so obviously suffering from just-before-the-hanging fever and was such a pitiable specimen that Raider could hardly bear to look at him. He had to keep reminding himself that the little man had nobody to blame but himself for his plight. You just don't blow another fellow's head off when an extra ace happens to drop out of his sleeve. No matter how much money you're losing.

O'Brien, the good-natured guard came by, key ring jangling. His round face filled the door opening, and the sight of his smirk, which displayed his few surviving teeth, brought scowls to everyone except Beckwith, whose haunted expression registered no response. It seemed to Raider that Beckwith's beady eyes were looking right through the guard.

"Get yourselves all gussied up and smart-looking, boys," O'Brien brogued. "Hot breakfast is waiting and apples, apples, apples."

Apples were all any inmate working outside saw six days a week, until the orchards were stripped and they got back to felling timber. Breakfast was lukewarm porridge with lumps the size of gun butts, and prison bread and coffee, hot as hell and strong enough to wrench a man's teeth in their sockets. As usual the cooks were short on sugar—probably, decided Raider, because they were holding back from the supply requisitioned and peddling it on the side. That wasn't all they cheated on, but taking everything into consideration, Boisé wasn't bad. True, it stunk continually from a blend of body odor and improperly disposed-of shit, but it was a fair-sized setup, and as well run as could be expected. In fact, it was the only institution worthy of the definition "prison" in all of the Idaho Territory, even though it had 800 men crammed into quarters for 600. Still, in spite of being able to boast a fair-dealing, hard-working warden and guards enough to keep the bullying under control, there was still too much closeness, not enough of anything and everything to go around, including liceless blankets, prison-issue clothing in decent condition, footwear—and sugar.

All day, every day except Sunday, or when it rained fit to wash away the Sawtooth Mountains, most of the prisoners were taken outside, marched to the orchards an hour away, and put to work picking and packing apples. No leg irons, no metal of any sort, but a dozen guards standing about with Winchesters, relieving their boredom by potshooting any small game that wandered into the work area.

The gang Raider had been working with—twelve men picking the apples, filling baskets, emptying them into barrels that stood on the beds of three freight wagons—included Charley Greenleaf. Raider had made it his business to become very friendly with both Greenleafs during this first week. Brother Ben was not sent out to play in the orchards, but was instead assigned to assist the doctor in the prison infirmary. George Beckwith generally went out, but prison regulations, according to O'Brien, stipulated that any man going up for execution the following day was to be confined to his cell the day and night before his last sunrise. This struck Raider as downright stupid; if anything, a man about to be hanged ought to be overworked rather than left sitting alone in his cell to search his soul and brood over his fate.

The apples smelled sweet and the guards let the men eat all they wanted, but if they overdid it and got knotted up with stomach cramps and had to stop working, they

could count on catching hell in one form or another.
Other standing rules proved a pain in the ass; you
weren't allowed to talk to the man working with you
without formally asking the nearest guard's permission,
and even if you got it, you could only talk for ten seconds or until ordered to shut up. If the guard you asked
happened to be in a sour mood or was one of the handful of sadistic pricks in blue, you were out of luck. You
also had to get permission to piss or shit and did so under the close watch of the so-called latrine guard, the
"latrine" being behind the nearest tree.

During his second day in the orchards, Raider had
earned a not-too-gentle reminder to speak "only when
speaking permission is given," as O'Brien put it. A green
fly, or something on the wing equally vicious, had stung
him on the back of the neck, he'd yelled "son of a bitch"
and turned to comment to Charley Greenleaf who was
working on the ladder next to him. A guard named
Wheatley had come striding over and without a moment's
hesitation hauled off and whacked Raider soundly across
the backs of his knees, all but hamstringing him and
bringing forth a roar of pain that made his response to
the sting sound like a whisper in comparison.

"You shut your goddamn mouth, fella," snarled
Wheatley, " 'fore I bust both your legs!"

"You motherless fuck, you ever do that again, I'll jam
that fucking iron up your ass and haul it outta your
throat!" rasped Raider, crouching and gently rubbing
the backs of his knees.

The words were out before he realized it, and no
sooner were they spoken than he cursed himself inwardly
for being so quick to beg more grief. But Wheatley and
the other guards nearby only laughed, and the job of relieving the apple trees of their bough-bending burden
went on.

The sun turned blood-red and pocketed itself in the
horizon beyond the Oregon border. The day's work had
come to its end, and the party started back. It was a tiring hour's walk for men who'd been on their feet all
day reaching and lugging and sweating. "Home sweet
home," as Charley called it, came into view, the stark,
stout-looking walls rising, dominating the landscape.

The double doors, giant-sized portals that looked much like the individual cell doors, were opened, and in trundled the wagons, the guards riding, the prisoners shuffling along behind. Two guards, including Wheatley, brought up the rear on horseback.

Beckwith looked worse than he had earlier when Raider and the others had left for work. Sweat was pouring from the man, and his eyes were white with fear; Raider could almost see his heart hammering against his skinny ribcage. It was getting on to seven o'clock. In something under ten hours, Beckwith would be dead. At least, reflected Raider, the poor bastard would be out of his misery. Counting the hours, as he had to be doing with nothing else to occupy him all day, appeared to be killing him inch by inch—a good deal more painfully than any knot under his neck.

Supper was the usual hearty meal, stew, potatoes, apples, other fruit. Christ Almighty, thought Raider, moving slowly down the line, tray in hand; as if he hadn't seen enough apples! The mere sight of the barrel at the far end of the line brought back the aching behind his knees.

The line moved on. He found himself standing opposite a light-haired, good-looking man wearing a greasy apron, a ladle in his hand. Down plunged the ladle into the pot, and into Raider's bowl spilled a generous helping of stew.

"How about a little meat in there?" he asked.

"Move along," said the ladler evenly.

"Come on, all the hell you give me are carrots and goddamn spuds!"

"I said to move—" the man began.

Before he could finish, Raider's hand had shot out and snatched the ladle. Fishing with it for meat, he came up with a chunk almost as big as a baseball. His dark eyes widened; he could feel the juices start in his mouth. But his catch never made it to his bowl. The man jerked the ladle out of his hand, and the meat tumbled back into the pot with a splash. Raider snapped. Dropping his tray, the contents of his bowl splashing on the table, he hauled back his right and smashed the ladler flush on the jaw, sending him reeling backward against the wall.

At once the dining room, hitherto filled with the dull, continuous clicking and clinking of spoons and the low rumble of conversation, came alive. Cups began beating against table tops, shouts were heard goading the two to fight. The miserly stew-doler came back at Raider with a shot to the cheek, following up quickly with another hard against his right eye, sending a set of burning needles lancing through his head. To the deafening roar of the prisoners were added the shouts of the guards as they scrambled about, trying to restore order. Raider had his enemy by the throat and was catching lefts and rights to the head as he tightened his grip. Guards came at the two of them from either side, breaking Raider's hold, backing the ladler against the wall, and pinning him there.

The warden's office was only slightly less dismal-looking than Raider's cell. It had, to be sure, the necessary furnishings, including a fairly new flat-top oak desk with enough knee room for two men between the drawer stackings, the working surface strewn with papers. The walls were bare save for framed photographs of the warden's predecessor and Idaho's Governor Neil. Both windows at the rear were barred, which struck Raider as funny; this room, with its gray walls and wearing iron over its glass, was nothing but a glorified cell.

The warden looked ancient and worn out—whether because of his job or his home life or his liver was impossible for Raider to tell; but the man seemed to be at least seventy-five. He had a hard face, one that probably had stopped a fist or two in its day, but curiously his voice was soft, even gentle in tone.

"Don't you think you overdid it a little, Mr. Raider?" he asked quietly.

"O'Toole, John O'Toole in here, if you don't mind."

"You nearly broke my jaw, you stupid fool!" exclaimed Raider's fellow Pinkerton operative and long-time partner, Doc Weatherbee, seated beside him.

"You could have given me some damn meat, you know. Try living on apples in this place and a man could shit himself to death!"

The warden grinned. "Well, at least your little disagreement gives us a chance to get together without raising any suspicions. I can't believe a single soul out there suspects that you two are working together under cover."

"If it's all the same to you, Warden, it seems to me I'm the one doing all the work," responded Raider acidly. "As usual."

Doc made a face. "Oh, for God's sake, Rade, don't waste time whining. What we want to know is, have you found out anything, anything at all?"

"Nothing worth a button."

The warden frowned. "It's not going to be easy; I told you both that from the start. Those Greenleafs are hard customers; they know enough not to spout off in front of strangers."

"I'm getting friendly with them," said Raider. "But it takes time. I sure as hell can't come right out and ask where the rest of the family's hiding out and where they've got the money."

It was not one of the partners' more complicated assignments. The case might even be described as wide open. The Pinkerton National Detective Agency listed Adams & Company, banking and express specialists, among its clients. The Greenleafs had tapped a trio of the company's offices for better than $80,000 in silver. The crimes committed, the loot seemed to have vanished like the stars in the morning, along with Ben and Charley's people, leaving the two brothers the Pinkertons' only link to the action. As luck would have it, however, Ben and Charley were behind bars not for the theft of the silver, but for manslaughter, which, at least according to Ben, came very close to self-defense in the eyes of the judge who had sentenced them. Whatever the mitigating circumstances, the killing had been heinous enough to earn them their stay in Boisé.

To Allan Pinkerton, here was opportunity dropped out of the blue. Why not install a couple of operatives in Boisé Prison, at least one in the Greenleafs' cell? It wasn't a new idea; it had been tried for, in Doc's opinion, at least four thousand years. But it had, on occasion, worked. Raider and Doc had been chosen; they were to be incarcerated and treated no differently from the other inmates. Only the warden was to know their true identities, an inspiration of Chief Pinkerton's which Raider had come to regret mightily, what with the ache that he still felt behind his knees. But had any of the guards known that he and Doc were Pinkertons, a careless wink, even the hint of a small favor, a friendly reaction of any sort could arouse Ben or Charley's suspicions.

One condition favored the Pinkertons; although the free members of the Greenleaf clan might be expected to flee the country with the silver, they probably wouldn't do so without the brothers. Such families were generally fairly close-knit organizations, even the more nefarious broods; the Youngers, the Clantons, and others had proven that. The Greenleafs on the outside wouldn't be able to break out their brethren, but if they'd found a particularly good hiding place, which no doubt they had, there'd be little need for them to pull up stakes until Ben and Charley could join them. And for the crime that the brothers had been convicted of, their sentence would amount to no more than five or six months with half of it knocked off for good behavior.

"You two should be packed away in solitary for inciting to riot," commented the warden, furrowing his forehead thoughtfully.

"What the hell are you talking about?" boomed Raider. "This big brain here held out on me—"

"So you smacked him in the jaw," the warden finished for him.

"What was I suppose to do, shake his hand and congratulate him? Besides, making it look like we hate each other could be very very helpful. Believe it."

"He's right about that, warden," said Doc, rubbing his tender jaw.

"All the same, my failure to discipline you two wouldn't look very good. Of course, there's one thing . . ." Raider and Doc raised their eyes and studied the man behind the desk, the moonlight angling through the window behind his left shoulder setting his bald head gleaming. "I could order disciplinary action postponed. The trees are still loaded with fruit; we need all the hands we can get out there, even yours, Mr. Weatherbee." He thought a moment. "I'll inform the captain of the guards that you two'll be catching yours two weeks or so from now, when the apples are in and the gangs go back to clearing the woods."

"Two weeks would help," said Raider. An idea wormed its way slowly through his mind, but he made no mention of it. The warden stood up, the two Pinkertons stood up, two guards were summoned, and Raider and Doc were led away to their respective cells.

2

"You never did tell us what you're in for, O'Toole," said Ben, fish-eyeing Raider but smiling as usual. The younger Greenleaf sat on the edge of his upper picking at his toenails with a fork sneaked out of the dining room. His question drew Charley's eyes to Raider as well.

"I never did, did I?" responded Raider, returning Ben's smile.

"We told you about us," said Ben. "And everybody knows what George there was up to. What's so special about what you done that you won't say?"

Raider sighed and moved past Beckwith, who was sitting on the cell's only stool, his hands clasped, staring blankly at the floor. At the back wall Raider reached up and took hold of the bars. The stars were bright, beautiful holes in the dark blanket of the heavens, and the moon—white, smudged with blue—hung round as a dollar in their midst.

"I got into a ruckus up Coeur d'Alene way, up in Kootenai County. Little misunderstanding with two badges."

"I mighta known you'd tangled with the law. You sure ain't the sort to take sass." Ben paused in tormenting his toenails, a broad grin spreading over his features. "Tell us about it. C'mon, we're friends."

"Not much to tell." Raider turned to face his cellmates. "They started jawing at me for tying my horse up in front of the church, which you're not supposed to do except at Sunday-go-to-meeting. My mistake was thinking they were just a couple of loudmouths finding it hard to mind their own business."

"Wasn't they wearing their tin?" asked Charley.

"Yeah, under their vests, sneaky bastards. Anyhow,

14

we got to arguing, out comes the old iron. . . . Mister, I tell you neither one of them could hit the right side of a shithouse if they were inside, drawers down. I got one in the hand, the other in the brisket."

"Did you kill him?" Ben's eyes saucered like a spooked horse's.

"You got me; I can't say. Last I heard—that is, when the judge gave me the good word—he was still hanging on. He bled like a slaughtered chicken. The other fellow, his hand was nothing, just a skinned knuckle."

"You only got to kill one to hang," commented Charley drily, nodding toward Beckwith still sitting immobile on the stool as if searching the floor for a way out of his predicament.

"He could live," said Raider. "He likely will."

"He could die, too," said Charley. "Then good-bye, John O'Toole. Mister, if I was you, I'd think about getting outta this dump."

"What would you like me to do, chew the bars out of the window and fly out over the wall?"

"There's other ways," said Charley. "Fellas bust outta places like this every day. Plenty busted outta here, you betcha." He nodded toward the window. "That wall comes flush up against the back there. Hell, you get through the bars, you could easy jump to the top o' the wall and drop down the other side."

"Can't be no more'n twenty feet," added Ben. "Into grass thick as hay in a loft."

"George'd bust outta here if he could come up with the right way," said Charley. "Wouldn't you, Georgie?"

"Leave the poor bastard be, Charley!" snapped his brother.

It was clear from their friendly tone and eagerness to talk that both Greenleafs had admired Raider's performance in the dining room. Both were quick to advise him that he'd done the right thing, that either one of them would have done the same, if they hadn't had such relatively short stretches left to serve. Raider closed his eyes for a moment and mentally reviewed the Pinkerton file information on both Greenleafs. Ben's card appeared before his mind's eye:

Name: Benjamin Greenleaf
Alias: None known
Residence: Various
Nativity: American
Color: White
Occupation: Blacksmith; suspected bank and
    express office robber
Age: 26   Height: 5 foot 11 inches
Weight: 195   Build: Husky; well-muscled arms
Complexion: Light
Hair: Brown
Eyes: Brown
Nose: Broad and flat at nostrils
Beard: None

Date and place of arrest, crime charged with, and peculiarities of body—scars, marks, etc.—followed. Then he pictured Charley's card, which had given special attention to the structure of his facial adornment.

As much as he knew about the Greenleafs, none of these details had enabled Raider to guess their intentions, at least about one thing: They wanted out of Boisé, no matter how little time, relatively speaking, was left of their sentence. On second thought, he mused, why wouldn't they want out? Stuck inside, they were holding up the whole family's works. Lucky for Adams & Company that Ben and Charley had been charged with manslaughter, which was a lot less irksome than murder. Had the two of them been hanged, the rest of the family and the $80,000 in silver would have been gone for good.

Catlett, O'Brien's nighttime replacement, came by, his scraggly-bearded face showing at the door window, his navy blue kepi sitting at a jaunty angle atop his head. Raider didn't like Catlett any more than he liked Wheatley. He had yet to have a run-in with this one, but the guard's big mouth and sadistic streak burrowed under his skin. O'Brien and most of the other guards acted halfway human. Not Catlett, though, and he lost no time in confirming Raider's opinion of him.

"Hey, George, won't be long now, eh?" the guard taunted.

"Leave him alone, Catlett," snapped Raider. "You got any mouthing off to do, give it to me."

"What are you, Georgie's big brother? That's funny, that is." Catlett chuckled, then burst out laughing. "You, of all the poor assholes in this place . . . or maybe you ain't heard?"

"What?"

"That deputy you gunned down up to Coeur d'Alene? He died last night."

"Jesus . . ." muttered Charley and Ben in unison, both turning and staring at Raider.

"You're fulla shit," said Raider.

"You wish I was." Catlett laughed again. "Mister, you'd best sit your ass down alongside Georgie there and take hold of his hand. You can see he's just chock-full o' courage. Maybe he'll pass some onto you. I wish you could see your face. Where'd the color go all of a sudden?"

"I still say you're full of crap."

"Keep on saying it, while you follow little Georgie there up the steps. Oh, not tomorrow sunup. You get a break; governor's got to sign your papers, make it all legal-like. Offhand I'd say you got at least three days afore they bust your neck." He waved and laughed and walked off.

"He's fulla shit," repeated Raider glumly.

Charley and Ben came up to him, their eyes brimming with sympathy.

"You got to get outta here," said Charley. "Three days'll go by like three hours."

"I got to get outta here, sure." Raider made fists and slammed them against the wall. *"Goddamn son of a bitch!"*

The brothers exchanged glances.

"There's a way," said Charley, "there's always a way." Beckoning Ben with one hand and taking Raider by the elbow with the other, he led them toward the door end of the cell, as far as possible from where Beckwith sat continuing to bore holes in the floor with his red-rimmed eyes. Charley lowered his voice. "Georgie there is done for. When they cut him down, they'll have the coffin waiting in the infirmary. They'll wrap him up,

dump him in it, nail down the lid, load him on a wagon
—and run him across the river to the cemetery at Morris
Hill."

"So?" Raider looked from Charley's face to Ben's and
back.

"So there's no big parade or nothing, just a couple of
old gravediggers driving," said Ben. "When they get over
the other side, the hole's already dug. All they got to
do is dump the coffin and fill in the grave, mark it with
a wooden cross . . ."

Charley interrupted. "What Ben means is that when
that box leaves here, Georgie don't have to be in it. You
follow my meaning?"

"I follow," said Raider wearily. "But tell me, how in
red hell am I supposed to get outta this cell, over to the
infirmary at the other side of the prison, and into the
damn coffin? And even if I could—and I'm not saying
for one second that's any more likely than a bullfrog
coming in a cow—what do I do with . . ." He tilted his
head toward Beckwith.

"I'll take care of that," said Ben. "You're forgetting
one important thing. I work in the infirmary; I'm supposed to be there."

Footsteps sounded outside in the corridor. Catlett reappeared holding up a bottle. All three backed away
from the door.

"Little present here for you boys," he said in a lowered
voice, glancing up and down the corridor. "Taos Lightning, the best, full bottle. She's all yours, only forty
bucks."

"Shove it up your asshole," said Charley.

"Thirty-five. This is the real stuff, I swear on my
mother's grave."

Ben snickered. "It's pig piss and puddle water mixed,
and you know it."

"How about you, O'Toole? You in the market for a
little thirst quencher? Your throat must be drying up
pretty fast."

Raider ignored him, turning away from the door. He
crossed over to his bunk and lay down on his stomach.
Jesus Christ, getting out in a pine box wasn't exactly
traveling in high style. Even supposing he could get to

the infirmary, even into the coffin. With the lid nailed down, how in hell would he breathe?

Unable to make a sale, Catlett departed with his "Taos Lightning." Ben and Charley practically hauled Raider out of his bunk and back over to the door, away from Beckwith.

"I'll put it to you straight, John." Charley licked his lips and drilled Raider with his eyes. "We can get you outta this place; we got the means. We got everything."

"Keep talking."

"Listen close. All you got to do is play sick tomorrow when you wake up. We'll yell for the guard and they'll haul you off to the infirmary."

Raider responded with a pained look. "Bullshit. Play sick how? That's such a damn old dodge. . . ."

Charley cut him off with a wave of his hand. An idea brightened his eyes. "That fight you were in at supper with the stew man. He hit you a couple of good licks alongside the head, both sides. You could wake up dizzy, right?"

Ben held up the fork he'd been using to clean his toe-nails. "I could stab your ear a little bit, just to show a few drops o' blood, like you was bleeding from the inside."

"That's a great idea!" burst Charley.

"You're not pricking me with that thing," said Raider, "not after you been picking your damn feet with it!"

"Hell, I'll wash it clean as a whistle."

"And likely make me deaf sticking me in the ear."

"I promise right hand to God I won't hurt you," said Ben, obviously, from the look on his face, eager to get at it.

"I promise I won't let him," said Charley. "Okay, you're in the infirmary and Georgie's there, too. If old Doc Pitler runs true to form, he'll be half loaded as usual. Right, Ben?"

"Drunk or sober, he won't be no problem. I'll just get him into the back room where he stores his supplies. You," he said, poking Raider in the chest with his fore-finger, "get Georgie outta the box, climb in, and pull the lid over you."

"What in hell am I supposed to do with him?" asked Raider. "Stick him in my back pocket?"

The whole idea was beginning to sound more and more grotesque. Oh, it was inviting, all right, tempting as hell; he could even put up with the ride in the coffin. But seeing the condemned man still fastened to his stool, seeing him alive and breathing, knowing he'd be dead by sunrise and having to play games with the poor bastard's corpse—just the thought of it turned Raider's stomach upside down. He'd been a Pinkerton operative for four years and time and again had been obliged to get down into the mud to work out a case, to lie and cheat and at least temporarily destroy some innocent bystander's peace of mind in the course of bringing matters to a head and closing up the case journal. But this! Jesus . . .

Ben was talking. "There's a room off the supply room with five or six new coffins stacked up in it. I'll find some fault with Georgie's and fetch out a second one. I'll lay it on the floor with the lid loose. For him."

"Ssssh," hissed Charley. "For christsakes, keep it down."

"What's the doctor going to think when he comes back out and I'm nowhere about?" asked Raider.

"That's simple. Before I take him into the storeroom, I'll make sure he's already treated you, and when us two come out and you're gone, he'll figure the outside guard brought you back to here."

They continued to work over the plan, both of the brothers coming up with instant solutions to the problems posed by Raider. Finally they managed to persuade him it would work, that between the two of them, Raider and Ben, they could make it work. *Okay fine,* thought Raider, *but what about my problems? How do I get word to the warden or to Doc?* Considering the time of night and the time of Beckwith's execution there was no chance.

"You'll be able to hear the buckboard cross the bridge over the Boisé River," said Charley. "Once on the other side, you pry the lid loose with this." He dug a kitchen knife six inches long out from under his mattress. "You knock out the two old-timers, grab the duds of one of 'em . . ."

"Then I beat it."

Charley looked at Ben with a peculiar smile, something close to a leer of triumph, it seemed to Raider.

"Yes and no," said Charley quietly.

"I figured we'd get around to that sooner or later," said Raider. "Let's see if I got it straight. You boys help me, I owe you, I return the favor."

"You got it right," said Ben. "Once you get away . . ."

"On what?"

"The buckboard mule."

"Oh, Jesus, I could make better time walking backward with a limp than up on a damn hauling mule. Mules got to be the slowest critters in creation."

"We don't give a damn how you make it," said Charley, "but you got to get back across the river and head over the Boisé Range to Pearl. It's about twenty-five miles."

"Shanks' mare. Why Pearl?"

"Just east o' Pearl you'll come to a tidy little hundred-acre spread, white house, silo, spanking-new barn. You can't miss it. That is, you hadn't better. It belongs to kin o' ours, Cousin Nat Pulford. You'll like Nat, he's fulla old Nick, just simmered down a little since his wife, Abby, passed on. He'll give you three horses and gear, a box o' dyne . . ."

"You're funning me."

"Do we look like we are?" asked Ben acidly.

Charley laid a hand on his brother's arm and went on. "You ride back here with the horses, at night, tomorrow night, that is. Get here by midnight sharp. You hoist yourself up on top o' the wall—Nat'll give you a hook and rope and saw blade, just ask him. You reach us the blade through the window there, give us ten minutes to saw through the bar tops and bend 'em down, then you go ahead and blow the side gate. I mean blow it, don't spare the sticks. Come back around; while everybody's busy at the gate, we'll be waiting for you, and it'll be goodbye, Boisé."

"You make it sound easy," said Raider.

"It sure enough is easy," responded Ben, "if you don't fuck it up."

"You two trust me to come back here after you?"

"Trust got nothing to do with it, John," said Charley. "You got to. Figure it out. If you was to get away and keep going, they'd have your pretty face on dodgers spread from St. Louis to Frisco afore the week's out. Wanted for murder. You come back for us, we ride away together, we'll take you to the greatest little hideout west o' the Big Muddy."

"Better than the Hole in the Wall down by the Powder River," said Ben.

"Ten times better. You'll be safe with us, John. On your own you wouldn't stand a chance in hell. Besides, don't expect Nat to give you a gun; all you'll get is grub, a place to sleep an hour or two, the mounts, the dyne, our saw—only what you'll need."

"The whole thing's crazy," muttered Raider.

Ben stared at him. "What's crazy about it?"

"You two sitting inside here. How could you ever set it all up, I mean with your cousin, what you'll need, all of it?"

"That's not crazy, John, that's just smart planning. We may be prisoners, but we can still send letters out and get 'em back."

"The warden or somebody reads every damn letter going and coming."

Ben nodded. "That he does, but not twixt the lines." He fished in his pocket and brought out a cheap red glass-and-brass ring. "You just show this to Nat; it was our old man's, rest his soul. Nat'll recognize it. He'll give you everything you'll need. Matter of fact, he's expecting somebody."

"Yeah," said Charley, "you. Ha ha."

"Don't look so surprised," continued Ben. "We got us a family that works together smooth as silk."

"So what it all comes down to is you get me out the hard way, I get you two out the easy way."

"You could say that. Put it anyway you want, only just don't try double-crossing us. You try going it alone and you'll likely catch lead in the back before they get around to hanging you. You can't argue that, can you?"

"No."

Ben smirked. "Besides, you don't look like the sort

who'd shove it up the asses o' them that helps you. Most fellas don't. Oh yeah, just to play it safe, you won't mind if Cousin Nat rides back with you . . . ?"

It was Raider's turn to smile. "I never thought o' that."

"You don't have to think o' nothing," said Charley. "Us two have thought it all."

3

Shortly before sunrise the cell door was unlocked and opened, a preacher and two guards came in, and away they went with George Beckwith, moaning and, struggling feebly in their grip. In a way, thought Raider, wide awake and watching, Beckwith was already dead. Raider could just picture him staggering rubber-legged up the steps, the noose, the knot, the trap being sprung, his feet dangling.

Raider still couldn't resign himself to "using" the corpse; there was something sinful about it, plain ghoulish! Doing dirty work, even to clean something up, went squarely against his grain. But if it ever came down to having to report to Allan Pinkerton that he'd backed out of the play for what amounted to reasons of conscience and Charley and Ben were sprung and they and the rest of their tribe eventually got away, there would be holy hell to pay.

He and Ben went to work, and to Raider's mingled surprise and disgust, less than an hour later he found himself lying in Beckwith's coffin, hands upward toward his face, Charley's kitchen knife in his right, just finishing prying loose a knot near his right cheek giving him a hole less than an inch in diameter through which to breathe. Lying in the coffin on the table as Ben pounded home the twelve nails one after the other had set him to trembling, chilling his spine all the way down to his ass. It was so goddamn real, so scary Nobody should ever have to lie in a coffin alive. Nobody! Ever! His heart pounded like a twelve-pound sledge, sweat burst from him in a flood, and his mind had gone to work on him, bullying him with questions. What if there was some delay in loading the thing? What if the driver got held up starting out? How long could he survive in such close confinement without air? Five minutes? Seven?

The hole solved all his problems. He had to hand it to Ben; the thieving bastard had pulled it off beautifully. And now the buckboard was through the main gate—he could hear it closing—and heading toward the river. How long a ride would it be? How did Ben expect to cover up his absence from the work detail? As far as that went, if the orchard guards were told he'd turned up sick, they wouldn't be expecting him for work. And if the day-shift guards back at the prison *weren't* told, they'd figure him to be out picking and packing as usual.

Thoughts swarmed through his head like angry bees. What was he worrying about? What if someone did discover he was missing? Whoever did would report it to the captain of the guards, who in turn would tell the warden. The warden would consult with Doc. Old Weatherbee would use his head and figure something worthwhile was up. Giving the devil his due, Doc was brainy. He and the warden would kick the thing around and likely shelve the "great escape." It could be covered up for a day and a night, long enough for him to get to Pearl and back and free the Greenleafs.

The warden wouldn't appreciate his blowing up the side gate, though. Or the Greenleafs' sawing through the window bars. But Allan Pinkerton and Adams & Company would shout hallelujah knowing that Raider'd finally gotten the ball rolling in the right direction.

Neither Ben nor Charley had given any clues to the location of the family's hideout. Raider hadn't been about to press them on that. Now, thinking back on it, sucking in the sweet morning air through the knothole, he decided he'd handled things smart as hell, playing it cool, behaving naturally, normally. Getting out had been the hard part; if the two diggers up on the seat behind his head were as old as Ben made them out to be, he could handle them. He'd have to truss them up with the reins and gag them, but they'd be all right. He'd have to ditch the buckboard and coffin someplace where they wouldn't be found for a day or so. He'd work it out.

The buckboard jounced along, creaking and swaying,

the mule just about able to get one hoof ahead of the
other. Why the hell didn't they use a horse? A horse
that he could run up over the Boisé Range and get to the
farm in a couple hours, instead of using up the whole
day. Oh, what the hell, a man can't fill every straight.
Some things had to be done the hard way.

4

Doc leaned back in his chair feeling the warden's eyes driving holes through him. The man in charge was plainly worried. He didn't know what was going on and, unable to guess, being clearly a worrier by nature, was visibly upset.

"If O'Toole . . ."

"You can call him Raider now, Warden," said Doc.

"Whatever. You really think he plans to try to spring those two?"

Now, mused Doc, you're being dense. "Why else would they help him get away? He certainly couldn't have done it without the younger one setting things up in the infirmary."

"I wired the governor. . . ."

Doc flung a glance at the ceiling and braced his arms against his kneecaps to keep from tossing his hands in the air. "I wish you hadn't."

"Mr. Weatherbee, I'm under explicit orders to keep him informed every step of the way on this business."

Doc nodded. "I can appreciate that. You've been very decent, very cooperative. Unfortunately, we have no choice but to play it my partner's way."

"You mean the Greenleafs' way."

"What I'm saying is the last thing we want is a troop of cavalry rushing over here from the federal barracks to 'help us out.' A play like that could blow this thing sky high."

The warden scratched his cheek and looked down at his desk. He picked up a letter opener and began tapping it nervously against the desk top. "I doubt that Governor Neil would do anything like that. After all, this is no Territorial problem; it's purely private."

"Promise me one thing," said Doc. "Whatever happens these next few days, please, *please* don't call in any troops. Not one man."

"Whether the army gets involved or doesn't isn't up to me." The warden was becoming embarrassed, his bald pate flushing visibly. Doc got the feeling that the man was wishing with all his heart that he'd never heard of the Greenleafs or the Pinkertons. As if he didn't have enough problems of his own!

"As I see it, this is where we stand. Somehow Raider will attempt to spring them. All I ask of you is that we let him."

"Of course. Hasn't that been the idea all along?"

"And let the three of them leave without anybody following them. Raider is a top operative; I happen to consider him the best man with the Agency. He'll know how to handle the Greenleafs, all of them."

"Single-handedly?"

"I'll be right behind them. Actually I should be getting out of here right now. I have to ready my mule and wagon and take up a position where I'll have a clear view of what goes on. Up on the bluff would seem to be the best spot."

"You mean you plan to sit up there waiting day and night until he comes back and pulls the lid off this thing? Good grief, man, you could be there a week."

"I don't think so; whatever is going to happen is going to happen soon."

Raider sat on a flat rock with his stolen shoes off, massaging his feet and looking up at the towering peaks of the Boisé Range, the purplish and reddish-brown Englemann spruce and alpine fir high up, the hemlock, cedar, pine, and Douglas fir below, and lower still, open stands of ponderosa pine mixed with crooked-trunked aspen, slender as flagpoles, their golden leaves brightened by the rays of the dying sun. He was bone-weary, but he couldn't rest until actual sundown, reckoned at about an hour ahead—not if he wanted to locate the Pulford place. Reluctantly he put his shoes back on. They were a size too big, but then the other digger's had turned out too small, and he could just picture the collection of blisters he would have picked up climbing up and down the mountains wearing them.

What was supposed to be 25 miles was already feeling more like 50. He did not count himself among that special breed proud of their hiking ability. Give him horseflesh under his butt any day. Walking was for crossing streets to get to bars or beds. Riding was a man's way of getting about. Though not for one second did he regret turning the buckboard mule loose after he'd tied up the two old-timers. The poor mule wouldn't have made it a hundred feet up the first trail, not with him on her back.

Night was coming on by the time he came hobbling within sight of the Pulford spread. Charley's description had been accurate. But no lights showed in the house and there was no answer to his knock. What should he do now? Stretch out on the veranda behind the rose trellis and nap until somebody showed? It was beginning to look as if Cousin Nat had little faith in Ben and Charley's brainstorm—if he even knew about it. Raider dug out the red glass ring, held it up, and examined it. It wasn't worth a bent dollar in his estimation. It sure as hell wasn't worth it with no Nat Pulford around to show it to.

Ignoring his aching feet, he began looking around, starting with the barn. One door was ajar. Opening it six inches more, he slipped inside. A lantern hung on a harness peg on the hayloft support to the left, the flame as low as one could turn it without extinguishing it altogether. All the feeble glow served to show was the lantern itself. He stood with his back to the door, resting and giving his eyes time to become used to the darkness. The hay smelled clean, fresh, and sweet. Glancing about, straining his eyes, he could make out gear hanging in a neat row along the wall on his right, running back to the stalls in the rear.

"Junior?"

Raider stiffened at the sound of the voice. High-pitched, female.

"Ah, no, it's . . . uh . . . ."

"Come closer. Over here where I can see your face. Turn up the lantern."

Orders were orders, and the tone in which these were delivered brooked no disobeying, no delay in compliance. He hobbled as fast as he could over to where the lantern hung, turned up the flame, and holding the lantern at eye level, surveyed his surroundings. Under the edge of the loft sat a pyramid of hay; poking out of it was a beautiful face with laughing eyes, a full-lipped sassy mouth, skin like a baby's, and hair as black as a grackle's wing pulled back and tied behind with a white ribbon. Raider swallowed. There she sat, in hay all the way up to her chin.

"You're not Junior!"

"I didn't say I was . . ."

"Who are you? What do you want?"

"I'm a friend of the Greenleafs'; they sent me. I got important business with Nat Pulford."

"Daddy's not here."

Raider's heart sank. "Where is he? He's coming back," he said hopefully.

She shook her head. "Not for a while he ain't. He's into Pearl. He went and got thrown by Tommy, swoosh out of his saddle." A slender white arm came shooting up out of the pile arcing. "Landed on his shoulder, busted it for fair. Sheila-Mae took him to town to the doc's."

"Sheila . . ."

"My sister." She stared at him. "Are you gonna stand there holding that lantern like a stone statue all night?" He slipped the wire handle back over the peg, adjusting the flame, brightening it. She had to be as naked as a new egg underneath the hay, not a blessed stitch on, waiting for "Junior." Again Raider swallowed; if her body went with her face, Junior had one helluva lot to look forward to.

"What are you staring at?"

"Nothing. Look . . ."

"What's your name?"

"Hey, don't you ever let anybody finish a damn sentence?"

"No need to swear. I asked what's your name?"

"John O'Toole."

"You a friend o' the Greenleafs? You broke out of the jail?"

"Ben and Charley broke me out." He produced the red glass ring. "This belonged to their daddy. Ben gave it to me to show your father. For proof I'm on the up and up."

"So you say."

He held out the ring. "Take it, look it over."

"What for? It don't mean beans to me. I never saw it afore."

He sighed. Damn but his feet hurt! And his stomach felt hollow as a new bucket. "Listen, little miss . . ."

She bristled. "Don't you call me 'little miss'! Don't you dare! Do I look little?" Scowling, she shot to her feet, the hay spilling down from her body. Magnificent! Breasts high and white and full as the biggest and best he'd ever laid eyes on. Skin perfect, absolutely flawless. His eyes wandered down to her navel, to her stomach as flat as a board, down to the beautiful black V of her cunt. Again he swallowed, pain filling his throat, the lump expanding and refusing to go down. He breathed deeply, sucking in the sweet smell of the hay. He could feel his cock come alive and begin stiffening, pressing against the crotch of his denims demanding room to rise and stand.

"Lady . . ."

"Lady? What's the matter with you? Ain't you never seen a *woman* afore?"

"I . . . well, sure. What in hell do you think I am? What do . . ."

"Come over here."

He almost took a step, but hesitated. Jesus Christ, what a body, the way the light hit her shoulder, bathing the front of her in brown shadow, her nipples, pink and perfect, poking straight out like the studs on a Hannibal saddle. Too much! Woman, woman, woman! Raising her arms slowly, seductively, she beckoned him to come to her.

"Listen, I came here for horses and dynamite and other stuff for the Greenleafs. I legged it clear over the Boisé Range; my feet feel like they're busted in every bone, all swollen up; I haven't eaten but blueberries since last night, I . . . Don't you have any clothes in here? A blanket maybe?"

She wasn't interested in any of it; not one word got through. Grabbing his hands, she pulled him over to the haypile. Swiftly unbuckling his belt, she got out his cock and began working it—as if it needed working. In three seconds it was standing higher and harder than the lid handle on a laundry stove, and pounding fit to shatter. Now she was standing close, pressing her breasts against him, and he could feel her nipples nail his belly. Looking up into his eyes, holding him hypnotized, a cryptic smile playing about her luscious mouth, she began massaging her quim with the head of his cock. Then with a squeal down she fell backward onto the pile, pulling him down on top of her, spreading her long lovely legs and jamming his cock into her.

"Fuck me, John O'Toole. I want to see stars; I want to see the world explode! Fuck me!"

In he drove, all the way. Her cunt was cavernous; he'd never been inside one bigger. Christ, he thought, his heart pounding, the sweat starting, a sudden surge of lust dizzying him, she could take a full-grown Red Poll bull into the damn thing! Since he was twelve years old he'd thrust his meat into quim all sizes, all shapes, all ages. And proud he was that he'd yet to lay a single woman he couldn't satisfy. He was endowed with, at least in his opinion, a cock and a half. But he had to work his balls all but off to bring this bitch to a boil, slanting, angling, driving, driving, driving with all the power he could generate. And in the process exhausting himself so completely he was afraid he'd pass out.

She loved it, every angle, every slam. She came and came, jamming her tongue halfway down his throat to duel, biting through his shirt into first one shoulder then the other, bucking like a pony with a hornet run up its ass. And yelling ecstatically, so loud she practically shattered his eardrums.

"Fuck me! Fuck me! Fuck me!"

"I am, damnit! . . ."

She quit, so suddenly it was like a switch thrown. She lay back panting, grinning she-devilishly, and pushed him upward to a kneeling position. Then she got up on her own knees, her great breasts swinging. Down came her head, her mouth trapping his limp cock, devouring it, sucking, sucking, sucking. . . .

He roared. "For chrissakes, easy, easy . . ."

His spine froze as he felt a hand on his shoulder. Her mouth let loose his cock and her head came up slowly, her huge blue eyes staring past him. Slowly he turned to look.

There she stood, the same face, same hair, even the same color ribbon. Except her charms were concealed under a frilly-shouldered calico dress with buttons down the back. She was already starting to undo them.

"It's my turn, Eloise. . . ."

5

In his years with the Pinkerton Detective Agency Raider had given his chief and all his other superiors the very best he had to offer, in courage, in sweat, in muscle. For a salary that could well be computed in cents rather than dollars, considering the hours he put in on the job. He had elevated himself above and beyond the call more times than memory could count. He had, in his own words, been "shot at and shit on" enough for any six operatives. But that fateful night in Nat Pulford's sweet-smelling barn in the clutches of the lustful twins all but cut the whole pumpkin in half. The demands the two placed on Raider's weary body came dangerously close to breaking him.

If anything, Sheila-Mae outperformed her sister, Eloise. As if all the fucking and sucking without letup weren't sufficient to drain him to death, a new worry crept through his troubled brain in the midst of the second act. "Junior" was expected; he was late, but he would show. With two pieces of ass as hot as this pair awaiting his services, he'd have to be the village idiot to waste his time on anything else. With, that is, the exception of another lay. Still, considering that possibility, Raider was hard put to imagine any woman within 900 miles capable of outfucking the Pulford twins.

Unfortunately when Junior did show up—galloping up, dismounting, and bursting into the barn—he was greeted by the sight of Eloise and Sheila-Mae down on their knees taking turns giving head to a prostrate Raider.

"What the hell!" bellowed the intruder.

Up jumped both women giggling, laughing, rushing to greet him, but he bulled his way between them, coming up to Raider still lying flat on his back, his cock rosy red and at rest in the valley of his balls, his breath coming in short, desperate pants as he struggled to regain it. Junior stood over him, feet spread wide apart, fists like two bench vises planted on his hips. He was no more than eighteen, guessed Raider, but he was six-foot-six and his shoulders, which looked at the moment to be nearly as wide as one of the doors behind him, held up arms that only a hard-working blacksmith could boast of. A low groan issued from Raider's throat.

"Who in hell do you think you're playing with, stranger?"

"Junior!" shrilled Eloise. Or was it Sheila-Mae? Not that it mattered, but clad in only their skins and hair ribbons, Raider couldn't tell one from the other.

He was upright, feeling his soles and the balls of his feet fill with pain as he restored his weight to them. Junior glared, cursed, and hauled off his left. But Raider was too fast for him. Shedding his weariness in the wink of an eye, he bought up his right to block the massive forearm and followed through with a hard left jab to the jaw. Down went Junior, the plank floor all but shattering under the impact, the entire barn shuddering.

"You motherless bastard! I ain't gonna fight you," he bellowed. "Me and you is gonna rassle. I'll snap your spine!"

"To hell with that, boy!" exclaimed Raider. "You get up, I'll put you right back down again." Confidence surged through him in a warm and welcome wave. All that height, that incredible reach, that muscle amounted to nothing at all, not with a glass jaw added to them. A stroke of blind luck, thought Raider; he could have gotten his first shot into the boy's stomach or chest, his first and only. From neck to waist he looked to be granite-hard and would have felt nothing. But under his big, surly-looking mouth he couldn't take one halfway decent punch.

Raider's threat quashed the boy's initiative with the swiftness of lightning striking. Suddenly Junior didn't want to fight in any manner; not when he could fuck. One of the two girls grabbed him from behind, and when he felt her tits pressing hard against his back, his glower gave way to an expression of sweet anticipation. Whirling, he grabbed. She grabbed for his cock. Raider turned away, buttoning his pants. The other twin came over to him.

"You all right?"

"Mmmmm."

Junior and her sister were already down in the hay and preparing to go at it. The other twin—whichever she was—put on Sheila-Mae's dress, and taking Raider by the hand, led him out. Through the closed door behind them squealing, grunting and thumping could be clearly heard.

"I can't service you, er, do, that is, you know . . . anymore, little, ah . . ."

"Ellie. Don't you worry none about me, John O'Toole. I'm feeling just fine."

"I'm starving to death, not to mention about ready to collapse."

She fed him in the kitchen, half a dozen fried eggs, fresh-baked bread with butter, peaches, and decent coffee. Back came his strength and his resolve. The drop octagon Sears, Roebuck clock on the wall over the stove threatened lateness, five after nine. Time was getting much too short; it'd take him at least two hours to get back to the prison. He'd explained what he needed and she appeared willing to cooperate, but looking at her sitting across the table staring at him hungrily, he realized that her interests lay elsewhere.

"I got to leave here by nine-thirty at the latest."

"Can't you wait till morning? You need sleep. You should see yourself, you look dead tired. You ought to take better care o' yourself."

"Yeah. But I'm sorry, I can't possibly wait until morning."

"Why not?"

"I've already said. I've got to be back by midnight. The whole business has to go by the clock."

"How about midnight tomorrow night? Wouldn't that be just as good? I mean they been in there months and months already; what's one more day?"

As patiently, as clearly and convincingly as he could, he explained the situation one more time, now and then sneaking a look at the clock, noting the speed with which the minute hand traveled down the Roman numerals on the right side. They could hear Sheila-Mae and Junior come in the front door, laughing, carrying on, the big boy evidently having shelved all his rancor against the stranger who'd beaten him to his favorite quims. To Raider's relief, though, Eloise stood up and walked him to the back door.

"Everything's out in the barn ready and waiting," she said when she returned. "You'll have to carry the dynamite in your saddlebags."

"That's all right."

"For pity's sakes, don't let your horse stumble and fall."

"You best tell him that."

"Seriously, you fall, you could blow up half the county."

"I'll be careful." He paused outside the door. "One thing more. You don't happen to have an extra six-gun and a few shells lying around, do you?"

"I think I can find something."

He practically sighed in relief. When he got back and sprung Ben and Charley and told them that Cousin Nat was laid up, that he'd never even met with him, that one of his daughters had obligingly supplied him with everything needed, adding an iron, they couldn't but be impressed. For him to come back and rescue them without Nat and with a gun had to be the best two-way way in the the world of proving his dependability.

He could hear the kitchen clock striking ten as he rode off, Eloise and Sheila-Mae standing at the open back door waving. Ellie had tried to pin him down just before she'd kissed him good-bye.

"We're doing all this for you, John."

"For Ben and Charley, too."

"Oh, to the devil with those two! What I'm saying is you owe us. So you will come back and see us, won't you?"

"If I can."

"When?"

She *was* beautiful; beat as he was, he had to restrain himself from licking his lips and grabbing her then and there. What a great, grand fuck! What a romp in the hay; double! Two trips to the stars and full rounds of the planets in two fantastic hours. Not to mention the satisfaction of a one-punch winning fight with a kid half his age and twice his size.

"I can't say for certain, Ellie. You wouldn't want me making a promise I couldn't keep, would you?"

"You never will come back." She pouted. "Not if you take to running with Ben and Charley and the rest o' their brood."

"I said if I can and I mean it. Cross my heart, hope to die." That wasn't lying, he reflected, not out and out lying.

Moments later he was galloping through the blackness, no moon, no stars—which couldn't hurt the coming midnight action any. Except, of course, if it started to rain. How in hell do you keep a lit fuse burning in a downpour?

Eloise had given him three mustangs. He'd saddled up a spotted stallion with flint-colored eyes. A fine mount. The average mustang stood fourteen to fifteen hands high; this one had to be at least sixteen. He favored mustangs. They may have been mediocre workhorses, but he was no sodbuster. Important to him was the fact that they couldn't be beat for saddle—powerful, well gaited, fast. Hell, there wasn't another horse in the whole menagerie, Arab included, who could outleg one. A handsome horse, too, just as good-looking as any Arab, with his sharp nose, high nostril, little foot, and well-shaped leg. The other two were dun-colored, with black manes and tails to match.

He'd owned other mustangs in his time, once a *grulla* as wild as the high country wind. Easiest keeping horse he'd ever had, hardy, hard-nosed, good bottom, great endurance. Mustangs were terrific fighters. Moving swiftly along, approaching the aspen and ponderosa pine woods footing the mountains, he recalled a fight he'd witnessed, crouched behind a rock, taking great pains to keep his smell downwind knowing that a wild mustang can see, hear, and smell a man further than any other creature alive.

Wild they generally ran in bunches of thirty to fifty, led by one master stallion. To hold his harem together he

had to fight every comer, every other day of his adult life.
There was always a ready opponent, usually younger. At
even a hint of aging or weakness the leader would be
called upon to mix it up, frequently in a battle to the
death. Crouching low, Raider had watched two stallions
go at it, approaching each other, forelegs high, teeth
bared, eyes wild, throwing their whole weight against one
another, the weaker, older of the two going down. His
challenger had begun hammering him with his hooves
and biting and tearing his hide and flesh off in strips.
But the loser managed to squirm out from under, gain
his feet, and run for his life. And his harem had a new
sultan, returning from chasing off the old one puffing
and proud, prepared to run all the young stallions out
of his new herd by the time they'd passed their second
birthday, even sooner than that if one made the mistake
of getting too friendly with a mare.

Raider let go of the reins and laid the flat of his hand
on his right saddlebag, then did the same to the left
one, reassuring himself that his lethal load was riding
snugly, safely. Climbing and descending with two horses
in tow promised to be no easy chore, especially at night,
more especially on a no-light night like this one. It was
the little things underfoot that neither he nor the horse
could see that worried him. Nothing spooked any horse
quicker than a quiet thing moving toward him. He would
jump and toss his rider and break both their necks at the
soft rustling of a rodent or a snake in the grass or a twig
falling too close to his ear, while a buffalo bellowing its
loudest or a locomotive roaring by rarely turned his head.
Courage he had in abundance, the inbred courage to face
anything he could see or hear and handle, but anything
small and sneaky . . .

"Don't let anything happen, Lord," said Raider aloud,
raising his eyes to the black heavens. "Not tonight, not
with this load."

6

Picking his way carefully up, over, and down the mountain, Raider made extremely poor time, losing, by rough estimation, at least an hour and a half, possibly closer to two hours. That obviously shot midnight all to hell. He could almost hear the Greenleafs cursing him up and down for a traitorous son of a bitch, a friend-fucker first class. But blowing Charley's deadline didn't make a helluva lot of difference, other than getting their danders up. Now that he thought about it, he felt a twinge of regret at having turned down Eloise's offer to get a good night's sleep before starting back—though how much sleep she and Sheila-Mae would have let him get was debatable. Face it, you just can't fly up and down a hill the height of the Boisé Range, with or without a load of red sticks.

Thunder had accompanied him down the near side, and time after time lightning ripped the sky, turning Idaho and nearby Oregon momentarily powder blue. If only the damn rain held off, thought Raider. But with his luck it wouldn't. And didn't. He was three hundred yards from the wall, galloping at a good pace, when the storm hit. And it hit hard, a full bucket turned upside down obscuring sight of the prison, reducing the visible lights to tiny orange dots.

Wonderful! Jesus Christ! The dynamite and coil of fuse were dry under the bag flaps and would remain that way as long as he kept his hands off the straps. What was he to do, pull up a safe distance from the rear wall and wait out the deluge? Or mount the wall, pass the saw through—which would at least let them know he hadn't double-crossed them—then make a stab at blowing the gate? One sure thing, he couldn't ride in too close, black sky or no. He was too close already. Swing-

40

ing about, he made for a stand of trees. Passing in the saw posed no problem, but he'd be taking an unnecessary risk waiting out the storm. It could last until daybreak, which would kill the whole scheme until the following night. Would that be bad? Could be. Very. Twenty-four hours' delay or close to it could screw things up four different ways.

First off there was Doc. His partner had to know long before now that he'd gotten out. The wandering mule, the buckboard, the two old-timers, all must have been found by this time. At that, all Doc needed to know was that John O'Toole hadn't gone out to pick apples and hadn't come back to his cell from the infirmary.

He touched the inside of his right ear where Ben Greenleaf had drawn blood with his fork. More blood than he'd needed to draw, Raider had argued at the time. The wound had clotted; it was sore, as such a tender spot might be expected to be. Sore, but not nearly as painful as his cock and his balls. He'd need a week and a half to recover from those twins.

He hauled up and dismounted, patting his horse affectionately on the neck, feeling the scar bump across the gristle where whoever had originally captured the stallion had creased him with a single shot, stunning him so that he would fall and could be secured with hobbles. He tied the stallion to a tree and, taking down the coil of rope with the grab hook tied to one end from the pommel of his saddle and the saw blade out of the saddlebag, he started down the gentle slope toward the wall. Following the initial downpour, the rain seemed to be letting up, temporarily to be sure, as if the cloud sending it earthward were expanding before once again contracting, squeezing like a sponge, and dropping the next bucketful. Raider stopped and surveyed the area, finally fixing on a bluff close by, the highest point overlooking the prison. He stared, straining his eyes, unable to believe what he saw. Lightning fractured the sky. Perched on the summit of the bluff was a familiar-looking wagon, with what appeared to be a mule covered with a rain blanket standing patiently in the shafts. The driver's seat, exposed as it was, was empty; no glow showed through the bonnet. Thunder growled and shook the world.

"I'll be damned."

Sore feet, aching ankles, and all, he ran toward the bluff, scrambling up the side, pulling himself along bush after bush with his one free hand, gaining the top gasping, ready to collapse. Stumbling up to the tailgate, he fell against it, draping his forearms over it for support.

"Doc!"

"My camera's broken," said his partner, without so much as a half grin at the sight of him. "Shot. Looks like no pictures for this Case Journal."

"What in red hell are you doing up here?" inquired Raider.

"Waiting for this moron I know to show, what do you think? Well, are you just going to stand there? Don't you even have sense enough to come in out of the rain?"

After helping Raider up over the tailgate and sitting him down on a crate of Hooker's Wigwam Tonic, Doc dropped down onto a box of Samaritan Nervine. Raider filled him in on all the important details while he changed into his own clothes, shivering with the cold, drying himself off as best he could with a blanket.

"You'd better give some serious thought to going to work," cautioned Doc. "You've less than four hours until daylight."

"Let a man catch his breath, will you?"

Doc brought his face up close to Raider's and lit a match. He had, noted Raider, exchanged his prison-issue gray for a fancy English worsted brown suit, the jacket with four buttons down the front.

"Good Lord, Rade, you look terrible."

"I had a run-in with an old friend. . . ."

"Mister, you need a good night's sleep—in a pair of loving arms."

"I do like hell!" snapped Raider. "Don't talk to me about women."

"What's the matter with women all of a sudden?"

Raider softened his tone. "Nothing. It's just that we got a tough piece o' work cut out for us. At least I do. I can't afford to think about anything else. Hey, put out that fool match, will you?"

Doc fished an Old Virginia cheroot out of an inside pocket, lit it, and waved out the match.

"I need my poncho," said Raider.

"It's with the blankets and the rest of your gear behind that stack of Dr. John Bull's Compound Cedron Bitters." He indicated. Raider donned his poncho.

"Now give me your Diamondback."

"The devil I will. You're wearing a gun, what do you need with mine?" Doc puffed, the orange end of his smoke pulsing. "Besides, you keep telling me a thirty-eight's worthless, not a man's gun. And your own forty-four's around here someplace."

"Use your head, Doc. I get together with those two Greenleafs, I can hardly show two guns." He patted the holster filled with Peacemaker given him by Eloise. "This baby they can see; I can't show my own along with it, too. But that little playtoy o' yours I can hide inside my shirt or someplace. I mean you don't think Ben and Charley are gonna let me keep this Peacemaker. . . ."

"What you're saying is you hand it over to them voluntarily before they demand it. Gesture of good faith."

"After they demand it. I got to be nice, but natural-nice, not ridiculous."

Doc got out his .38 Diamondback pistol and handed it over. Reluctantly. "You'd better get a move on. Use the other side; there's a winding, gradually rising trail. How do you think I got Judith and the wagon up here?"

"Five more minutes." The rain was coming down again, drumming against the bonnet over their heads. "We got problems, Doc. Getting the saw into them won't be anything. Keeping the fuse lit in this downpour so I can blow up that side gate to distract the guards looks like the longest shot in the book to me."

Doc pondered this. "How about if you keep the sticks, the fuse, and all inside the saddlebag. That way they wouldn't get wet."

"I could do that, I suppose, except I'd have to cut down to a real short fuse, like an inch."

Doc handed him his penknife. "So what, you can run, can't you?"

"Shit, I can barely walk. How do the outside guards time out? Sitting up here, you've got to have noticed."

'They won't give you any problem. Most are no different from soldiers or deputies, ready to sneak out of duty every chance they get. Only greenhorns take every order seriously."

"You're not answering my question."

"I haven't seen a single guard along the rear wall all night. I can't see the side gate from here."

"I'll just have to take my chances."

"It should take you ten seconds at most. Just lay the bag against the gate, loosen the flap belt a notch or two, stick your hand with the match under the flap . . ."

"Do you mind not telling me how to do my job? Spare me that brilliant fuckin' mind o' yours half a shake."

"Just trying to be helpful."

There was something bothering Doc. Raider sensed it, and identified it specifically when the conversation got around to pursuit. Raider and the two Greenleafs would be traveling ten times as fast as Judith, Doc's mule, pulling his apothecary wagon.

"You've no idea where you'll be heading?" asked Doc.

"You guess. I can't begin to."

"That's too bad."

"What did you expect them to do, draw me a map?"

"Judith and I will just have to do the best we can. When I lose sight of you and can't hear your hoofbeats anymore, I'll hang a couple of bulls'-eye lanterns under the seat; they'll light the way ten feet or so ahead of Judith so I can follow the mess you make in the mud. I'll do my catching up during daylight, when those two will have to lay low. If they have any sense, that is."

Raider sighed discouragedly. "I hope. They claim their family's holed up waiting for them in the best hideout there is. If you fall too far behind, how in hell will you find it?"

"I will or I won't. If I don't, you don't have any backup."

"How about stabling Judith and this foolish rig; just stick 'em back where you had 'em, and put in for a mount?"

"No."

"Stubborn as usual, eh?"

"Careful, not stubborn. Number one, this foolish rig,

as you call it, is an excellent cover. I can drive up to any door in the West, introduce myself, and break into a sales pitch. This time around I'll have to disguise myself, to be sure; all the same I've got to go with my little girl and my wagon."

"If we don't stop till we hit Texas and I never see you again, do me a favor. Think about me once in a while. Did you remember to report to the Agency?"

"Have you ever known me to forget?" Doc pushed forward toward the front of the wagon, set aside a large box, and pulled a twenty-inch-square section up out of the bed, bringing with it battery jars, a transmitting apparatus, and a receiver. "I could use some blue vitriol, but what's left should last out the week."

They talked for a few more minutes, covering everything that seemed important, before Raider straightened his poncho and climbed back down over the tailgate. They shook hands.

"Lead them around the left rear corner there," advised Doc pointing. "I'll be behind those pines over to the side there."

"How in red hell are you ever gonna keep up with us?"

"Cross your fingers, Rade. It's got to stop raining sometime."

"Maybe where we're heading it's not even raining," said Raider morosely.

"So you'll leave tracks in the dust, three sets. Stop worrying, get going, and good luck."

7

Traveling as straight as a crow on the wing, the two Greenleafs and their Pinkerton companion headed south, picking up the Snake River, which was already somewhat swollen by the downpour, and following it under the shadow of the Owyhee Range down to near Garnet. They covered at least fifty miles, estimated Raider.

The "rescue" had come off far easier than he would ever have imagined it could. The dynamite—twenty sticks dry in the saddlebag—blew up the gate and ten feet of wall on either side of it. Ben and Charley had dropped down from the top of the rear wall, having cut their way out with the saw "easy as slicing cheese," according to Ben. Mounting up, away they'd galloped. Not a shot, not a yell, not even sight of a guard for a sendoff. The storm volunteered timely cooperation, the rain coming down in sheets as the three riders hurried on. Ben's response to Raider's question as to how hard it had been to saw through the three bars were the only words exchanged until Garnet came into view, a miserably dilapidated-looking brood of low-lying buildings emerging from the blackness. By now the rain had begun to let up. The horses were well winded, lathering, losing it to the downpour; Raider was beginning to feel that the long stretch at breakneck speed was taking its toll on his stallion, stinging his lungs, and if they didn't at least slow the pace it could easily burst his heart. They pulled up.

Here by Garnet the Snake twisted off in an easterly direction, skirting the Plains bearing its name beyond, findings its way between the Big Hole Mountains and the Caribou Range toward its source in Yellowstone Park near the continental divide.

But Ben and Charley seemed to have lost all interest in following the river. Ten miles ahead lay the confluence

46

of Wickahoney Creek and the Bruneau River. According to Charley, that was where they'd be heading once their mounts had caught their breaths.

"With a little luck we should make at least forty miles more afore daylight."

Raider groaned inwardly. Those forty miles, he knew from his wanderings, would bring them to a spot where the Bruneau forked east and west. At the gait they'd been going, Doc had to be well behind them. But the hand would be all over for this Pinkerton before the first up card showed if the three sets of tracks he seemed so certain he could find and follow, regardless of how far back he fell, got washed away, or if the three of them hit on a stretch of shale, or crossed the Bruneau even before reaching the fork—which, now that Raider thought about it, would be the smart move, assuming anyone saw them leave and other pursuers besides Doc were on their trail.

It was getting hairier and hairier by the mile. Hadn't he told Doc to turn Judith and the wagon in for a horse? Didn't it always turn out like this? When Raider really needed backing up, the backup was back up the line so damn far that Doc needed a goddamn crystal ball and six platoons of cavalry to find him!

"Goddamn son of a bitch!"

"What's biting you, John?" asked Charley. "We got away clean as a boiled shirt, didn't we? What's to gripe about?"

"My feet, that's what's to gripe. They're killing me. When's the last time you legged it up and down a mountain?"

They had dismounted in a grove of cottonwoods by the river bank and let the horses wander down to drink. Raider leaned against a tree trunk yawning. Nearly twenty four hard hours without so much as sixty seconds' sleep was beginning to get to him. Charley came over and patted him on the shoulder.

"You did a great job, partner, every step o' the way. Give us the whole story what happened. How's old Nat?"

"I never laid eyes on the man." Both men stiffened. He explained.

"How are the twins?" asked Ben, when he had finished. "Us two haven't seen 'em in a long time. Must be seven, eight years back; ain't that so, Charley?"

Charley nodded. "Running around in them little starchy pinafore dresses, in pigtails, cute as new buttons. Always giggling. They must be grown up some by now."

"I would say so," said Raider drily.

"That's a shame about Nat, getting thrown by his horse," reflected Ben, "but he sure did right by us with those three." He nodded toward the mustangs.

It stopped raining. Raider took off his poncho, revealing the Peacemaker given him by Eloise. Both men's eyes lit on it in surprise.

"Why, you sly sidewinder," ventured Charley, his tone jocular. "You never mentioned she gave you a gun."

"I asked her for it," said Raider. "I figured at least one of us shouldn't be riding this run bare-hipped."

"You figured right," said Charley. Reaching out, he unbuckled the gunbelt.

"What are you doing?"

"I'll wear it."

"Suit yourself." Raider shrugged, as if he couldn't have cared less.

Ben stared at him curiously. "Eloise only gave you one?"

"It's all she had, or so she claimed."

"That's strange," said Charley, running his hand over his beard. "Nat generally has a dozen guns lying around. Still, one's better than none, eh, partner?" He smiled and surveyed Raider. "Hey, with that poncho off, I see you got yourself a mighty fine fit o' clothes from one o' those gravedigger fellas. Mighty fine."

Raider stiffened. He'd been in such a breakneck rush to get out of his wet borrowed duds and into his own— his black Stetson, fringed buckskin jacket, new denims, and old Middleton boots—it hadn't even occurred to him that clothing with such a perfect fit would arouse suspicion. Nor had it occurred to Doc, who usually thought of everything.

"Charley," he said wearily, "I get the feeling you want to get something off your chest. That you don't trust me from here to that tree, never have, never will. No matter how hard I bust my balls for the two o' you. You got me out, for which I'm grateful, but no matter what you thought of my chances riding lone, I could have kept right on going with all three o' those mounts. West, east, down this neck o' the woods . . ."

"John . . ." began Charley.

Raider cut him off with a wave, scowling, the resentment building in his voice. "The man wasn't even home. I had to ride back to the prison as we planned all by my lonesome. I didn't have to, but I did. And got you two out. It wasn't all that hard, but it could have been; I could have got myself grabbed red-handed and boom back in the jug, with the cork in and somebody fat sitting on it. Lucky for me it was raining like hell and those two gate guards were fucking off someplace under cover. Lucky for me, lucky for you boys. So she gave me a Peacemaker and I didn't hand it over soon as you hit the ground. So what? Do you figure I was trying to hide it or something?

"I thought I was being counted into this ride, that you trusted me. Like I trust you. But now that you get me thinking about it, I really have to be some kinda four-square, twenty-four-carat asshole to think we fit together. It's plain to see we don't, so I'll just mount up and ride out. Good luck, I hope you make it."

He started down the bank to fetch his horse. Both Greenleafs came after him.

"John, take it easy," whined Ben. "Charley didn't mean nothing."

"I didn't, I swear I didn't," said Charley with pain in his eyes. "We're beholden to you more than anybody we've ever been beholden to in our whole lives. We're powerful grateful, I mean powerful."

He was beginning to look and sound like a pulpit pounder bent on swaying his flock to his point of view on a point of Scripture. Raider was hard put to keep from laughing aloud.

"We don't want to lose you now," interposed Ben. "We need you as much as you need us. If you can shoot as good as you ride and fight, brother, you are found gold. Stick with us; I'm asking you man to man."

Raider stared at them for a determinedly long moment. Then, shrugging, he turned back toward the trees.

"I'm beat to boots. How much further to this world's greatest hideout of yours?"

A test question. They passed. "Not far," said Charley, "just down over the border to Niles Peak country."

Raider was tempted as hell to demand that the Peacemaker be returned to him—as Doc would put it, a gesture of faith—but resisted the urge. Asking to wear it, practically ordering Charley to hand it back over, would only flip the coin, make it look as if he didn't trust either of them.

They recovered their horses from the water's edge, mounted up, and climbed the bank. The rest stop had lasted under half an hour, more like twenty minutes. Unless Judith had sprouted wings, thought Raider, drawing the mustang's head southward and heeling him forward, Doc and his damn apothecary wagon were forty miles behind.

And would be a hundred behind by the time they reached their destination! Why didn't the educated bastard ever listen to him? Just once! Trailing his two companions, he sneaked a feel of the .38 Diamondback shoved into his belt under his shirt.

Thank the Lord for it. . . .

8

They reached the fork before sunup, taking the west water, skirting the Shoshone Indian reservation in Duck Valley, and continuing on toward the border of Nevada. Raider rode in the rear, a deeply troubled man, his back drenched with sweat, his mouth dry, his hands clammy in the chill air of the oncoming dawn. He had been thinking about his clothes; Ben Greenleaf had nailed down the lid of his coffin, had been present when it was loaded into the buckboard, had probably helped to load it. How could he possibly fail to notice what the driver and his companion were wearing? He'd have to be blind not to see that neither one had on any kind of Stetson. Their jackets might've been black, but not with fringe on the sleeves, and even if they had similar denims and boots, what good was that when the hat and jacket were different?

How in red hell could he and Doc have been so short-sighted? It was such a simple-minded mistake. All because he'd gotten soaked to the skin coming within sight of the prison and was shivering his way into a promising case of pneumonia. But that wasn't the only distraction; the real trouble had been that they had so much to discuss, so many decisions to make in so little time.

Maybe he was blowing it up all out of proportion. Maybe Ben never even noticed what the gravediggers on the buckboard were wearing. Maybe.

Thinking about clothes, neither brother seemed to care less that they were still wearing Boisé Prison issue from shirts to shoes. Evidently, reasoned Raider, they figured that riding over the desolate tableland of the Great Basin, cluttered as it was with buttes and mesas and isolated mountain ranges, they could spy anybody coming their way at a distance and could easily cut off

51

into the nearest ravine or pass or pull up behind any decent-sized outcropping. Charley, who time and again took the lead when the trail narrowed, kept them fairly close to the west fork of the Bruneau. Eventually he led them across it. Great, thought Raider, as they sloshed through the swirling water, that clinched it. Now even the fish wouldn't be able to follow their tracks!

They rode and rested, letting the horses nibble grass and drink, more and more sparingly as the sun's heat increased in intensity. No rain had fallen here, not a drop in weeks. All things considered, Doc's beard would reach his knees, Judith would pass on, and the wheels would fall off his wagon before he'd ever catch up.

Damn! If only Charley wasn't dead set in riding straight through to the hideout. If only . . . what? They stopped and corked off for three hours within sight of a settlement so that he might sneak into town and grab the law? Maybe send a telegram to Wagner in Chicago? With what? Some pipedream. Vera Cruz would be lying under three feet of snow before these two ever tossed a chance like that into his lap.

Crossing the border, they sighted Niles Peak dead ahead, and early in the afternoon, with Raider's stomach growling for something more nourishing than what little saliva he was managing to send down, Charley and Ben cut away to the right, putting Niles Peak atop Raider's left shoulder and sending all three of them scrambling up a shale-strewn trail to a narrow opening beckoning between walls that seemed to lift halfway up to the solitary cloud in the sky almost directly overhead.

One behind the other they filed through the opening and came finally to the entrance to a mine that looked to Raider as if it hadn't been worked in twenty years. Two crossed weather-punished boards barred the entrance; a third board, about the length if not the thickness of a railroad tie, hung from a single rusty nail on one side. Branded on it were two words, now all but obliterated by time and the elements. Leaning his head to one side Raider read:

"New . . ."

"Glory," said Charley.

"Home at last," observed Raider drolly.

"Almost, not quite," said Ben. They dismounted, Ben moved the crossed boards blocking the entrance to one side, and they led their horses into the blackness, Ben "closing the gate" behind them. The adit was dry as a tomb; it led down and down into an overhead stope, like an old-fashioned Mexican silver mine, as resealed by the light of Raider's last match left over from blowing the side gate. When the match died, they resorted to feeling their way along the walls. Remarkably, despite the mine's age and long period of neglect, every timber seemed to be still in place. As they proceeded onward, feeling their way, gaps appeared, passageways branching off left and right into other stopes. The air was warm and stuffy, getting closer and closer. They turned a corner left, leveling off, turned right, and came to light showing fifty feet ahead. Moments later they emerged into the sunlight onto a knoll surrounded by rising red stone like the bottom of a crater in a volcano. Squatting cozily in the center of this crater was a miner's shack twice the size of any Raider had ever seen, nearly as big as Nat Pulford's farmhouse. From the outside it looked about ready to topple over: The door hung from two hinges, but in the curtained windows the glass panes appeared intact, and although it was late in the season, flowers were set out in boxes under each window, blue lupines and red and white phlox. A small barn, sturdier-looking than the house but badly wanting paint, stood close by; and there was a corral occupied by six horses.

"Home at last," said Charley, grinning at Raider. "Now you can say it, partner."

Before Raider could comment, two men in their shirtsleeves came around the side of the house, whooping loudly as they recognized Charley and Ben, waving and coming toward them on the run. Raider saw at once, in their facial structure and the way they carried themselves, that both were family. The front door opened, revealing a red-haired man with a face that looked as if he'd been standing too close to a fire. He stood aside, giving way to a woman.

Out she came. She was short, dumpy-looking, her pudgy hands and forearms white with flour up to her elbows; her five chins were separated by lines arcing upward across, stacking their way to a thin-lipped, mean-looking mouth—which instantly lost its meanness, the corners pulling up into a beaming smile. Her nose was mashed, flattened like her sons' at the nostrils, and her gray eyes peered out from under heavy, swollen-looking lids. She wore her iron-gray hair pulled up all around her head to the top and there fixed in a bun. It lay like a coiled baby rattler, thought Raider.

Everybody was shouting at once, the red-haired man, who followed the woman outside, the loudest of all.

"My boys, my babies," the woman shrilled, "my sweet lovin' darlings come home at last." She waddled forward, her flour-covered arms reaching out for them. Embraces, kisses, everybody talking, carrying on. Old home week. Raider stood back near the exit of the mine, holding his horse's reins and consciously feeling the .38 snugged into his belt under his shirt, well to the right so that his jacket, even though open, covered the slight bulge.

Mrs. Greenleaf broke away from Ben and Charley and came forward, her smile fading, curiosity displacing it. "Well, now, who do we have here?"

"Take off your hat, John," said Charley. "Show 'er."

Raider tensed. Instinctively he felt trouble coming on, swiftly, like the rain hitting the night before.

"Take it off, John," said Ben.

Raider obliged. "Pleased to meet you, ma'am. O'Toole's the name, John O'Toole."

He had lifted the brim of his Stetson and with it the shadow covering most of his face. Mrs. Greenleaf gasped.

"Surprise, surprise, maw!" burst Charley. "It's him. Look, look at that face. It is him. No mistake."

She stared at Raider, her eyes widening, her chins slowly sagging. "Heaven preserve us. . . ."

"It is," insisted Charley. "Eyes black as coal, his face, the shape of it, the 'stache, his mouth, his chin. Just look at that chin. . . ."

"I don't believe my eyes," said Mrs. Greenleaf in an awed tone. "Lydell . . ."

"Yes, Maw?" The taller of the two who had come out from behind the shack took a step forward.

"Go inside into my bedroom and bring out the picture."

"Right." Lydell turned and started toward the door, then froze at the sound of Raider's voice.

"Hold it. Everybody, get 'em up. High!" Like a snake striking, his hand whipped out the .38. Backing toward the exit, he waved it slowly from side to side at the six people staring at him. Mrs. Greenleaf gasped but held her ground. The others began backing off, spreading out, forcing Raider to widen the slow sweep of his weapon.

"Freeze right where you are!"

Both orders, to reach and to freeze, were ignored. Mrs. Greenleaf had yet to budge, but the five men facing Raider continued backing away, fanning out toward the sides of the knoll.

"Easy, John," said Ben tightly, "we wouldn't want to see you get hurt."

"*I said freeze!*" Raider aimed between Charley and Ben and squeezed the trigger. It locked. He pulled and pulled, cursing, and they, everyone, broke into wide grins.

"Having a little trouble, John?" asked Charley. Out came Eloise's Peacemaker. "Try this one, I think it works. Let's see." He sent a slug singing past Raider's ear and slamming into the rock behind him. Raider threw away the .38. Mrs. Greenleaf gestured to Lydell. He nodded and went back inside.

9

Doc managed to stay on the trail of Raider and the Greenleafs past Garnet, down to where the Bruneau forked. The fact that the rain had let up and stopped was a considerable help: Three sets of tracks bunched fairly close were now visible along the east bank of the Snake. Doc let Judith travel at her own pace but without stopping. Nor did she seem to want to. Like all mules, she was strong and boasted the endurance of a mustang. Although nature had denied her anything close to a mustang's fleetness, having been called upon to pursue Raider on horseback many times before, she seemed to sense the urgency of the run and put forth her best efforts, without any need for the reins against her flanks.

But as they reached the point where the Bruneau forked, the tracks following water all the way vanished abruptly over a rocky stretch. Suddenly Doc found himself without a clue as to which fork the trio had taken. Stopping for the first time since descending the bluff behind Boisé Prison, he got down from his seat and inspected the area. There were no tracks. It had stopped raining north of Garnet; now he took off Judith's blanket and got back up on the seat, spreading it over the top of the wagon so the sun would dry it.

"East or west, little girl?" he asked, getting back down a second time and curling his fingers behind Judith's ear, a gesture of affection she was especially fond of. "West or east?" He might as well toss a coin, he reflected. As far as that went, the trio could just as easily have broken away from the river and run directly east or directly opposite across it in the direction of Duck Valley.

No, that didn't make sense. Why follow the Snake River down as far as Garnet, if that were the case? Why not angle either east or west from Boisé rather than head south?

"Judith, which fork? Which way did Rade go?" he asked.

If she knew, she wasn't telling. Digging a silver dollar out of his vest pocket, Doc flipped it and caught it.

"Heads east, tails west."

He sighed. A college-educated man, he was by nature logical, a realist in everything. Heads or tails was not his usual method of arriving at a choice of any importance. He flipped his fist over and opened it on the back of his right hand, disclosing Liberty seated, surmounted by fourteen stars. Heads.

Pocketing the dollar, he climbed up onto his seat and with a flip of the reins and a tug on the left one, steered Judith east.

Approximately fifteen miles from the west fork of the Bruneau, Raider found himself standing surrounded by menacing stares, Mrs. Greenleaf eyeing him balefully. Lydell had returned with a pencil drawing mounted on cardboard and handed it to his mother. She stared at it in silence, then lifted her eyes to Raider's face. Down to the drawing, up to his face. A look of pure loathing spread across her features. She handed the drawing to him.

"Is this supposed to be me?" he asked quietly, recognizing himself instantly.

"It's you." The others closed in for a look, Charley and Ben coming up on either side of him.

"Clear as a tintype," murmured Charley confidently. "Mister, we spotted you the minute you walked into the cell. Isn't that so, Ben?"

Ben nodded. "Right off the bat. I confess it was all I could do to keep from blurting it out."

Raider handed the picture back to the woman. "I've never laid eyes on any of you before." He glanced from face to face. "Not before you two back at Boisé . . ."

"I believe that to be the pure truth," said Mrs. Greenleaf icily. "We're not claiming you have. But you sure enough laid eyes on the gentleman who drew that picture, Mr. Charles W. Carroll, these boys' loving daddy, my husband, bless his soul and body and rest 'em. You, Mr. Pinkerton, shot and killed Mr. Carroll in an Oregon Short Line baggage car nearly four years back. Shot him down in cold blood. He lingered for three days and died in a hospital bed in Blackfoot. Barely conscious long enough to dash off this picture."

"You seem very sure that's me."

"It's you all right." The boys nodded; the decision was clearly unanimous.

"You said Carroll . . ."

"That's right, Mr. Charles Wilfred Carroll."

"You're all Greenleafs."

"My maiden name. My husband's name became so besmirched, dragged through the mud from one end of the Territories to the other, buried under lies and exaggerations, I was forced to change our name. Never in history has an innocent man been so vilified, crucified." Up came her flour-covered hands slowly, her forefinger pointing straight at him. "Not that I blame you for that. All you did was murder the poor dear man."

Raider's mind flew back over the years. Carroll . . . Carroll . . . Oregon Short Line . . . baggage car. There'd been so many train cases, so many baggage-car holdups, attempts. . . . The Oregon Short Line. Four years ago. In his mind's eye an Agency Case Journal popped into view. Carroll, Charles W. Carroll, train robber, bank robber. His eyes drifted to Ben. His imagination put a mustache on him, black speckled with gray, Charles W. Carroll.

She was right. He'd shot him all right. Riding alone in the car ahead on the way to Blackfoot, he'd been approached by the conductor. Together they had run back toward the baggage car reaching it just as the safe blew, the explosion rocking the car, all but derailing it. Out came his .44, the conductor jerked open the door and stood aside, and in he'd rushed. The car was blue with smoke. Carroll was crouched in front of the blown safe gun in hand, the baggage clerk standing face to the corner like a schoolboy being punished by his teacher, only his hands were high, his palms flat against the walls. Carroll turned at the intrusion, bringing up his iron. Both got off their shots almost simultaneously. Carroll's chewed away a chunk of the door jamb by Raider's left ear; his own shot caught Carroll full in the chest.

"Look at his face, Maw," said Charley. "He remembers, don't you, John?"

"What's your real name, John?"

"What difference does that make?"

She shrugged. "Suit yourself." She sucked her teeth and, eyeing him, began wiping her hands on her apron. "All the same, you are a Pinkerton. I'll just call you Mr. Pinkerton, how's that?"

"He's a Pink, all right," said Ben. "You wouldn't expect us to get anything but the best to help us bust outta that prison, would you, Maw?"

Everybody laughed except for Charley who had retrieved the .38 and was studying it.

"Where'd you pick this up, John? Not up to Nat Pulford's. He wouldn't give room in a drawer to a little old toy like this."

Raider paid no attention to him. Suddenly his thoughts were flying back to Doc. Not with any idea that his partner might ride up, surround the place with fifty men, charge in, and save his skin. Rather he was thinking that even if by some miracle Doc had been able to stay on their trail, he'd never find this spot in ten thousand years. Not without a hot air balloon and a damn telescope!

He could thank Allan Pinkerton for this; it was all his idea. Put a man in with the Greenleafs, he'd said, a first-rate operative, somebody with good hearing who knows how to handle their sort. He'd handled them all right, and every step of the way they'd been laughing up their sleeves at him. Being tabbed for a bullet in the head was bad enough, being made a laughingstock into the bargain was a little too much. Raising his eyes to the crown of peaks surrounding the knoll, he sighted a bird high up, floating effortlessly on the breeze, which eased it over their heads and out of sight.

"All right, boys," barked Mrs. Greenleaf, "let's show our guest inside. Maybe he'd appreciate seeing some more samples of Daddy's drawings. As you can see, Mr. Pinkerton, he sure was some fine artist."

"Mrs. Greenleaf, if it's all the same to you, I'd prefer we cut the clowning and get down to cases."

"What ever are you talking about, Mr. Pinkerton?"

"It just so happens I didn't shoot Mr. Carroll in cold blood; it was a simple case of him or me. I caught him in the act of robbing a safe. . . ."

Out flew one white hand, slapping him soundly across the cheek. "Don't you dare say such a thing, you filthy-mouthed liar. Don't you dare in front of his proud sons!"

"How'd you like it if we started out busting both your hands," said Charley through clenched teeth. "Fix 'em so they match your sore feet?"

"Mmmm." Raider shook his head disconsolately. "I can see there's no sense me trying to tell you anything, ma'am. Seeing as you got it all worked out by yourself four years back and been holding it inside ever since. Still, I'd be obliged to you if you'd let me say one thing."

"Say it, as long as it doesn't besmirch Mr. Carroll's good name." She flipped up one hand, urging him to get on with it.

"If you think killing me in revenge is going to help the situation any, solve anything, you'd best think again. There happen to be operatives on the trail following us down from Boisé. . . ."

"You're a goddamned liar!" snapped Ben.

"Let him talk!" exclaimed his mother, "and mind your foul mouth. Go on."

"And other lawmen, even troops if necessary, following them. Not to rescue me, not at all. They're after that Adams & Company silver you stole. And they'll get it. You got my word on that."

"Well, now, I purely appreciate your confiding in us like that, Mr. Pinkerton. But I wouldn't count on any peace officers or soldiers or any o' your detective friends catching up with us. We don't plan on being around here long enough for them to get close."

"Yippee-yay!" Lydell whipped off his hat and tossed it in the air. "Heading out at last! Sonoita, here we come!"

"Tonight," said Mrs. Greenleaf smirking at Raider. "And you, Mr. Pinkerton, are coming along."

"You'll make one fine hostage, Mr. Pinkerton," said Charley.

"Now that that's settled, do step inside and have a look see at Mr. Carroll's work. You really should show some interest in a man who reaches up from the grave after four long years and catches you by the collar."

10

The sun was rising, graying the creosote bush and mesquite-cluttered area, the brooding hills gradually shedding their darkness. A mile down the east fork of the Bruneau the shale gave out and mud reappeared. But no tracks, not a sign anywhere on the ground that anyone had passed through. Perhaps, mused Doc, they'd cut away from the river at some point behind him, to head even more sharply east.

Once Raider and the brothers rejoined the family, the chances were excellent they'd light out for Mexico, heading for the nearest border crossing. Doc pulled Judith up and got out his maps. From where he sat, the nearest crossing point was just above the Gulf of California, east of the Baja. The shortest distance between two points. The problem was, as logical a destination as the crossing point seemed, he hadn't any idea where the family would be starting from. Blind luck could place the hideout south of Boisé, precisely the way he was heading, though shortly the east fork would be pushing him further and further to the left. As for the Greenleafs' hideout, he had to assume that they had selected it and holed up there *before* Ben and Charley were arrested and confined. After all, the crime that all the Greenleafs were suspected of was the string of Adams & Company robberies, not Ben and Charley's slipup.

This meant that Boisé had no relationship, no connection whatsoever, with where they were presently hiding. The absence of any hoofprints clinched it for Doc, that and Judith's evident reluctance to keep up the pace she had sustained since starting out. All the way down he'd been reminding her to "find Rade, find Rade." Now something in the way she slowed, as if she were deliber-

ately holding back, suggested not that she was tiring but
that she simply had no faith in the route dictated by the
toss of the coin.

Over the course of their long association Doc had developed great confidence in Judith's instincts. Putting
away his maps, he turned her around and headed back
the way they had come.

The river was swollen from the night's downpour and
there was no bridge, but crossing the fork would be easier
than crossing the broader mainstream up above. Doc
crawled back into the wagon and piled his blankets and
other unprotected things on top of crates, getting them
up as high as possible. Lastly he turned up his telegraph
equipment, removing it from its compartment in the
wagon bed and placing it in his junk box under the
driver's seat.

The reins wrapped tightly around one wrist, both
hands gripping the brake, he started Judith down the
bank into the river. The muddied waters careened by,
but fortunately for the two of them the fork proved surprisingly shallow, the water coming up only as high as the
wheel hubs, piling against the right ones and slipping
through the spokes. In answer to his urging Judith gave it
everything she had. When they'd reached the other side,
Doc jumped down into the knee-deep shallows, climbed
out, and helped her haul the wagon up the bank.

Pouring the water out of his boots and wringing out
the bottoms of his trouser legs as best he could without
removing them altogether, he resumed the chase, heading Judith westward, reaching the west fork shortly, then
turning south. He studied the ground in front of them,
now and again glancing across the water in search of hoofprints. But the vegetation clustered along the right bank
made it almost impossible to see any open ground beyond. As it had along the east fork, the shale was thin-
ning, promising to give way to mud at any time now. But
even before this transition took place, Doc spotted something that raised his heart and his hopes.

"Judith, Judith, will you look at that! Look, little
girl. . . ."

Droppings directly ahead of them. Fresh, not yet

dried and moldering away under the glare of the sun. Someone had passed this way the previous night. Whether it was Raider and the Greenleafs was arguable, but common sense suggested this was probably so. And when the shale gave out and tracks appeared, well battered by the rains but faintly recognizable, Doc whooped again.

Two hours later they crossed the border into Nevada.

The shack inside was as neat as fence pickets in a row, with an enormous circular rag rug on the floor, cheap furniture, a well-polished bull's-eye mirror over a set of four matching carved-back six-spindle chairs lined up and a couple of saddle-seat curly birch rocking chairs drawn up by the windows, all of which were draped with white chenille curtains. The walls on all sides were adorned with mounted drawings, mostly of faces. Charles W. Carroll, safecracker, husband and father, had no mean ability when it came to reproducing a face on paper, mused Raider, letting his glance drift from likeness to likeness.

"A talented man, wouldn't you say?" Maw pressed her homely face too close to Raider's shoulder. He resisted the impulse to back away, to put a couple of feet between them. "Land sakes, I'm forgetting my manners, Mr. P. Charles, you and Benjamin are just as lax. Introduce Mr. P. around, why don't you?"

"Sure, maw," responded Charley. He indicated Lydell and the fourth brother, the first to greet them when they emerged from the mine. "This is brother Lydell and brother Dewey-Blair. And Mr. Red Hair there is our cousin, Raymond Clapp, joined us up from Lubbock."

"Maw!"

A female voice called from behind a closed door off to Raider's left.

"What is it, darling dumpling?" asked Maw.

"Maw, who's out there? Open the door. Maw, Maw?" It was a voice naturally turned to a nagging pitch, too nasal to be melodious, to insistent to be ignored. "Maw, maw!"

"Coming, Bertie darling." Mrs. Greenleaf turned to

Raider radiating a proud smile. "My daughter, Albertina. She woke up this morning feeling poorly. Been asleep most o' the day."

Raider put an expression on his face in reaction to this that silently proclaimed that he couldn't care less, but darling dumpling's mother took no notice. Moving to the door, she opened it. Standing practically in the center of the room Raider had a good line of sight into the bedroom. Lying in bed, the covers pulled up snugly to her chins, was one of the ugliest females he'd ever used his eyes on. By comparison, her mother looked like the Jersey Lily. Her daughter's face appeared to have been molded out of bread dough, a careless, a poor effort. Albertina Greenleaf had the family nose, but nothing like her mother's piercing, heavy-lidded eyes. Albertina's eyes were those of a sick cow, two-thirds the size of pool balls thrust only halfway into her pudding face. Her brown hair, identical in shade to Ben's, was plastered to her forehead by sweat, and her complexion was a sickly flush, pink threatening to deepen into red. One fat forearm, then the other, emerged from under the covers.

"Maw, who's that man? Maw, Maw?"

"Hush, darling dumpling."

"Maw, I'm sick. My throat's burning up, Maw. Who's that man, Maw?"

"A friend come to visit, Bertie. Mr. . . ."

"O'Toole," interjected Ben. Everyone moved toward the door, as if Queen Victoria had awakened in her royal bedchamber and her court was assembling to pay its respects. Mrs. Greenleaf preceded her boys into the room, waving them away with her hand behind her back and closing the door in Charley's face.

'Ever been to Sonoita, John?" asked Ben, coming up to Raider.

"No."

"It's not much," said Charley, eyeing him coldly. Long gone was the friendly tone both brothers had affected in the cell and on the way down. "Then again, you won't be missing much. I mean it's a little hard to see anything from inside a coffin, isn't that so?"

Everybody in the room was smirking at him. The

bedroom door opened and Mrs. Greenleaf reappeared looking apprehensive.

"Why bother with a coffin?" asked Raider. "Why not just put a bullet in my back and dump me in the nearest ravine?"

"Because that's not the Christian way, Mr. P. You are a Christian, aren't you?" She gave him no time to answer, running right on. "*We* are; you'll be buried proper, though face down."

"How come face down?" asked Lydell, his face going even blanker than usual.

"Face down is for cold-blooded murderers, son. So that their eyes look down to the fiery pit, not up to heaven like decent folks. Boys, your sister's sick. She's burning up with fever. Her throat's as raw as a busted boil, poor little thing. If you'll excuse me, Mr. P., boys, I'll go into the kitchen and fix her a potato. I only hope I can get it down her. I wish to heaven I had some catnip; there's nothing better for bringing a fever down, though potato's good, too. One o' you fetch a napkin from out the cedar chest and drench it with water to lay across her forehead. Poor child!"

"Are we gonna be able to pull out tonight like you planned now?" asked Charley.

"I'll go ready the wagon," said Dewey-Blair. Cousin Raymond stepped forward, wordlessly indicating his willingness to help.

"Not yet," said Maw, "we'll wait till sundown. She's best off lying in her bed there. If we can get her fever down . . ."

Raider was taken out to the barn, tied hand and foot, and left sitting against the back wall. Unlike Ned Pulford's barn, this one stunk to high heaven, as if the Greenleafs had deliberately brought their mounts inside to relieve themselves. So powerful was the odor that his eyes began watering. He was exhausted, barely able to keep them open, and speedily decided that there was little to be gained by so doing. Maybe, he thought, if he slept a couple of hours, he'd wake up and they'd all be dead, or gone, or this whole mess'd turn out to be nothing but a bad dream. He laughed brittlely. Thank you,

Allan Pinkerton, for four years, enough scrapes with more people in more places from the Mississippi to the Coast, from border to border, to fill a wagon with case journals. All come down to this, one last long ride, a bullet, a box, and an unmarked grave somewhere in the vicinity of Sonoita, wherever the hell that was. Face down in his coffin.

Casting a last look around him, taking in sight of the gear draping the walls on both sides and picks and shovels and other mining equipment leaning against them and scattered about the dirt floor, along with upwards of twenty bales of hay, he sat and, slumping over on his right side, fell asleep.

He dreamed of a bar in a fair-sized town constructed by his imagination, black batwing doors, brass rail, full-width mirror, a crowd, plain and pretty scantily clad females, a redhead coming up to him. He bought her a drink to match her own. Her hair turned to blond. It made little difference, it wasn't the part of her that was attracting his attention. He bought her another and it turned black; her face changed along with it, her lips becoming fuller, her mouth more inviting, her breasts bigger, exposed more at the top, almost down to her nipples. The bar, the crowd, all of it disappeared, and they were in bed, naked as two shoats. She was working on him, readying him for the big plunge, his cock willing, growing and stiffening, becoming twice as big as it ever had. Man oh man! Her wide eyes widened even more at sight of it. . . .

Out of nowhere came a fist punching him hard in the shoulder.

He came awake. It was no fist, but Ben's boot kicking him into consciousness. Light showed through the cracks between the wall planks. From the brightness it appeared nowhere near sundown.

"No sleeping on the job, John," said Ben. Lowering himself to his haunches, rocking slightly, bringing his face up close, he smirked at Raider. "You really made a mess o' this one, didn't you?"

"We'll see," said Raider thickly, his brief sojourn in dreamland furring his tongue, raising his thirst.

"Albertina's sick, real sick. We're going nowhere tonight. Sorry about the delay." Raider strained his ears. The muffled sound of a hammer pounding came through the wall at his back. "Know what that is? Dewey-Blair. He's some carpenter. Guess what he's making."

"How about a little grub?" asked Raider.

"Sure, we don't aim to starve you to death. Like I told you back up the trail, we need you. You got nothing to worry about, John, not until we come within sight o' the Sierra Madre Occidentals." He laughed and clapped Raider good-naturedly on the shoulder. "Man, if I was you I'd sure enough feel foolish as the goat that fell down the well. I figured you Pinkertons were trained, keen-eyed types, able to spot a flimflam from six miles off. But you didn't suspect a damned thing, did you? Not for one second."

"Not one."

"Terrific. Either you're bone stupid or me and Charley are smart as whips." Again he laughed, but quickly sobered. "Poor Bertie, you should see her; she's so sick she can't talk. Lydell's riding all the way to Cameron to fetch a doctor."

"Won't that make a problem for you?"

"How's that?"

"What do you plan to do, bring him in here, let him treat her, then ride back where he came from? Or gun him down?"

"That's up to Maw. Listen, hear that sawing? That's Dewey-Blair."

"You people are stark, staring crazy, you know that? There's wanted dodgers out on your mother and the rest o' you all over the territories."

"You bet. But no pictures, not even a rough sketch. Oh, they'll be getting 'em out on me and Charley, but if Lydell brings a doctor in here, we'll just make ourselves scarce, that's all."

"I'll just bet you will."

"It really ain't much o' your business what we do, is it?"

"How about that grub?"

Ben began untying his feet. "I ain't about to wait on you; you'll have to come in and get it. Pot luck."

The sawing stopped and Dewey-Blair went back to hammering. They headed for the kitchen, Raider with his hands tied in front of him a step ahead of Ben, boiling slightly under his breath. Damn dumb owlhoot; he sure had his nerve winding up a man's dream in such a rotten way!

11

The day was well into afternoon when Doc stopped Judith, unhitched her, brushed the dried mud off her legs, and got out her feed platter. He mixed two heaping handfuls of bran in with a mound of clean oats and set it under her muzzle. She ate greedily, as usual, and drank while Doc took her blanket, by now thoroughly dried out, down from atop the wagon bonnet, folded it, and put it away. Then, climbing back inside the wagon and moving crates and boxes about, he found the unmarked one he was searching for and set it on the seat beside him. He got out a battered wooden-framed mirror and studied his somewhat haggard-looking features in the glass. Then, poking about amid his collection of mustaches and beards, he came up with a matching pair, the beard a sharply pointed and decidedly European-looking van dyke. He daubed both with spirit gum and carefully secured them to his face. Locating a pair of silver-rimmed spectacles to his liking, he perched them on the bridge of his nose, then surveyed his handiwork. He looked ten years older, but very distinguished, extremely so considering his whereabouts and his profession. Divested of Judith and the wagon, strutting down a corridor in the Massachusetts General Hospital, where he had had his appendix removed some years earlier, he would have easily passed for a visiting Viennese surgeon. Allen Pinkerton was very high on disguises; Allan Pinkerton, decided Doc, not for the first time, was very astute.

Disguising himself fulfilled a purpose other than merely relieving his loneliness and boredom. Ben and Charley Greenleaf had passed him in the chowline many times back at Boisé Prison. One or the other would be certain to recognize him if and when he caught up with the trio and a confrontation developed. He could only hope it would develop somewhere, sometime in the near future; although before it did, he and Raider would have to send out a call for reinforcements.

He wondered how Raider was doing, whether or not the tracks Judith was following had as yet stopped anywhere. His partner had been on his own many times in the past; he was resourceful, tough, and wise to the ways of types like the Greenleafs. Doc had boundless faith in him, but he wished he could find him. Them. And soon.

Judith had finished her food and water. Doc backed her into the shafts, hitched up, and on they rolled. There was no indication that any rain had fallen since they'd crossed the border; quite the contrary, the ground here looked as if it hadn't been touched from the sky in months. Apart from being arid, this place had far less vegetation than there was further north, the land sunburned and rocky and ravined, as if Nature had collected all her loose bits and pieces of mountains and hills, buttes and mesas and gougings in the earth, and scattered them willy-nilly throughout the Basin.

Running out of tracks a second time earlier in the afternoon, he had stopped, gotten down, surveyed the area, and spied the rocks climbing the river bank opposite. Forcing them to cross the west fork as they had the east.

Ahead Niles Peak thrust itself boldly into the bright blue sky. Approaching him from the base of it was a cloud of red dust. A rider appeared, the first human being Doc had seen since losing sight and sound of Raider and the Greenleafs just south of Boisé. Closer and closer came man and horse. A big bay stallion, a fine-looking, wide-chested animal. A big man astride him, his round face carrying a flowing mustache, the ends bent back around his cheeks, the front of his hat brim pushed upward by the wind. Doc slowed Judith and stood up, waving to the man to stop. He waved back, but did not stop. He thundered by, his dust following him, beclouding Judith, reaching Doc and settling down over the two of them. Turning, Doc followed him with his eyes. He seemed to be slowing; he was. He came barreling back, pulling up alongside, the stallion's head rearing, the creature blowing hard.

"I just wanted to ask you," said Doc, affecting a slight French accent. "Have you perhaps seen . . ."

"Are you a doctor?"

"I . . .why, no, not exactly."

"What do you mean, 'not exactly'? Are you or aren't you?"

"As you can see from the inscription on the bonnet of this wagon, I'm an apothecary, a pharmacist. Drugs, nostrums, homeopathic medicines are my business. Health restorers . . ."

"You'll do."

"I beg your pardon?"

"Mister, doctor, whatever you are, I got a little sister back there who's sick as a dog. Been throwing up, running a red hot fever, throat raw. She needs tending to bad."

Doc stiffened. "I'm sorry, sir. As I told you I am not a physician. I . . ."

Once again he was interrupted. But it wasn't words that stopped him this time, rather a .45. Jerking it from its holster, the stranger leveled it at Doc's chest and cocked.

I already told you I got me a very very sick baby sister." Doc stiffened a trifle more, bringing the short hairs at the back of his neck to life. The muzzle of the gun turned away from his toward Judith's head. "One more word and I put two right through your mule's head. Then you'll have to take her place between the shafts and pull this rig home. Got it?"

"Got it. Lead the way."

"No you don't." He reached out and fanned Doc for a weapon. "I'll just hitch my horse onto your tailgate and ride up there in the sky with you. You stand up and hold 'em high so's I can see you from the back, got it?"

"Got it."

Seconds later, his .45 still filling his right hand, he climbed up alongside Doc. Nudging him in the ribs with the muzzle of the gun, he scowled. "Get going, straight ahead. And pull her right when I tell you."

"Got it."

"You tryin' to be funny?"

"Nothing of the sort."

Flapping the reins over Judith's back, Doc urged her forward. Less than an hour later, having covered close to five miles without any additional conversation whatsoever, the man with the .45, in the interim returned to its holster, pointed to the right.

"Cut over there. Those sheer cliffs. See that opening?"

"Yes . . ."

"Drive right on through."

Doc did as ordered. They emerged from the passageway to sight of the mine entrance, crossed boards lying on the ground in front of it. Glancing about, he spied a pile of support timbers wedged between the rocks to the right.

As he left Judith and the wagon, out came the .45 again, the man motioning Doc to precede him into the mine. He struck match after match as they walked through and eventually reached the knoll. Doc stopped short, surveying the scene with mouth agape, sufficiently surprised to momentarily drop his newly acquired accent.

"Well, I'll be . . ."

A man was coming out of the barn to the left of the shack. It was, noted Doc at once, Charley Greenleaf; that distinctive design of facial hair he'd recognize anywhere. Charley waved.

"Lydell!"

"Charley, this here's the doc. Gonna fix up Albertina."

Doc sighed. "I've already told you . . ."

"Shut your mouth and get on inside." He lowered his voice. "And see you keep that big mouth o' yours clamped shut tighter'n a trap. You don't say you're not a doctor; you got the medicines and stuff and you sure as hell look like a damn doctor, so that makes you one. Got it?"

"Got it," said Doc wearily. He groaned under his breath. His "patient" could very likely be dying; if this were so and he was unable to avert the inevitable and at least begin to restore her to good health, he might just as well lie down right here in front of the door and invite either of these two to put a bullet into him.

Lydell knocked, then opened the door. "Maw, it's me, back with the doctor."

Relief spread over the woman's face as Lydell introduced them, Charley coming up behind and closing the front door. Doc shook Mrs. Greenleaf's outstretched hand.

"Pleased and purely relieved to meet you, Doctor . . ."

"Phillipe D'Ascoygne," said Doc graciously. High time for a change in attitude, he reflected. His. Time to begin performing, putting on the best show he could—authority, professionalism, confidence. With any luck he just might be able to bluff his way through. The one who'd kidnapped him had mentioned sore throat, fever, vomiting. Maybe the girl had nothing more than a head cold compounded by an upset stomach. A dose of Doctor Folger's Ready Relief Remedy and a teaspoonful of Dobermann's Homeopathic Specific Number K-15 would help. At least they wouldn't hurt. Here and now, with the chips down, the pot right and the cards about to be shown, he was forced to admit that he had about as much genuine confidence in the efficacy of anything he could produce from the back of his wagon—pill, powder, or liquid—as Raider did. Speaking of Raider, where, Doc wondered, had he gotten to? Or rather what had they done with him? Had they done anything? Was he even here? Had he made it this far? Charley's presence confirmed that he and Ben had, but what about . . . ?

"Won't you kindly step this way, Doctor Coin?"

"D'Ascoygne, madam."

"Of course." Mrs. Greenleaf beamed. She was, at least up to now, clearly impressed with him. "The patient's right in this room, poor darling dumpling. In all her seventeen years I've never seen her so sick."

Into Albertina's room they sallied, Mrs. Greenleaf shutting the door in Charley's and Lydell's faces. Doc all but gasped at the sight. A great lump of young woman was bent over the side of the bed dry-heaving, aiming at a basin, whining loudly between surges. Her mother ran to her, bending, lifting the basin and holding it under her chin as the girl straightened up.

"Who's that?" Her voice was a hoarse whisper escaping her throat, causing her no small amount of pain, from her expression. She raised her plump hand as if it weighed 200 pounds and pointed.

"The doctor, darling dumpling, come to make my precious all better."

Doc had wandered halfway into the room and was standing about three feet from the bedside behind Mrs. Greenleaf. Disgusted by sight of his patient, he shifted his eyes to the window looking out upon the rear of the barn. Sitting on two sawhorses was a coffin without its lid. He could see the handle of a saw leaning, poking above the edge, the blade standing on end. His heart thumped in his chest like a steam hammer starting up. Rade! Good God Almighty!

He wasn't dead, he couldn't be. On third thought, he all-too-easily could be; they just hadn't gotten around to laying him in his box yet.

"Doctor?"

Mrs. Greenleaf's voice drew his attention to her and her daughter, by now having given up trying to empty the empty. One look confirmed that she was obviously running a high fever. Her cheeks were flushed and her face and neck beset by the beginnings of a rash. It sure looked like scarlet fever.

"Open your mouth, please, my dear," said Doc.

She refused to, clamping her flat lips tightly together.

"Open it, Bertie; he has to see your throat, precious."

She opened her mouth, suspicion creeping into her huge round eyes. Her throat was on fire and her tongue swollen. He felt the glands under her jaw; they were swollen.

"Does your tongue taste funny, my dear?" he asked. She nodded. "Stomach sore?" Another nod. He straightened up. It was scarlet fever. He needed no medical training to diagnose it with certainty. He'd had it himself when he was twelve or thirteen. Thinking back on it, he could almost feel soreness starting in his throat. It was, he recalled, one decidedly uncomfortable affliction. How long had it taken to run its course? A few days, a week? If he could only remember how long his mother had kept him out of school. Four or five days, at least. Trying his damnedest, he was still unable to recall exactly how long. But there was one thing he had no need to recall. Scarlet fever was highly infectious; the whole family could be coming down with it!

"What is it, Doctor?" asked Mrs. Greenleaf.

"Scarlet fever."

"Oh, my precious, my darling Bertie!" Down on her knees she fell, flinging her arms out across the girl's stomach. Albertina winced and tried to give voice to her pain, but could not. Instead, as her mother began carrying on like a lunatic, she began to whimper, tears filling her eyes, sliding down her rosied cheeks.

"Here, here, here, there's no need for that," said Doc taking hold of Mrs. Greenleaf's shoulders and helping her to her feet. "She'll get well, I assure you. With proper treatment, plenty of rest, and strict attention to diet, she should be good as new in two or three weeks."

The woman sobered abruptly. "That long?"

"Maybe less, maybe less. Now, if you two will excuse me, I'll go back to my wagon and get the proper medication." He started for the door, but Mrs. Greenleaf beat him to it, whipping it open and calling out. "Lydell, Charles, anybody, come here!" Lydell, Charlie, and Ben appeared, all three wearing quizzical looks. "Lydell, the doctor's going back to his wagon to get the medicine. You go along and give him a hand."

"Sure, Maw."

"That won't be necessary," said Doc, hopefully. "It'll only take a few minutes; I'll be back before you know it."

"Maw says I go, I go," said Lydell.

Doc shrugged. "Whatever you say."

Covering the distance between the front door and the mine passage exit, Doc looked around in hopes of spotting Raider. But there was no sign of him. Hopefully he was still alive, as well as could be expected, and tied up in the barn, rather than already dead and lying in there or elsewhere waiting to be dumped into the coffin. Why a coffin? What had happened? Had he accidentally betrayed his identity? Never. Nobody, certainly not Raider, could be that careless with his life on the line.

"What are you looking around for?" asked Lydell.

"Nothing in particular, just admiring your place. Most unusual location. One would never dream . . ."

"Yeah. Let's just get a move on. What's ailin' Albertina?"

"Scarlet fever."

Lydell blanched as if he'd heard bubonic plague. "Damnation, you sure? A hundred percent sure?"

"I am."

"How in hell can you be? You're no doctor . . ."

"I am now, Lydell, now that you told your mother I was. No mistake, it really is scarlet fever. You could catch it; all of you could."

"You got anything for it?"

It was, reflected Doc, little more than a glorified sore throat and an intensely bad cold, the combination bringing on the swelling, the rash, the upset stomach and fever. As such he would treat it.

"We'll see," he said.

As they reached the wagon, Doc saw Judith nibbling bunch grass and ran up to stop her. "Don't touch that, little girl, not a bite."

"Never mind her," said Lydell. "A little grass can't hardly hurt a damn mule."

"She happens to have a very sensitive digestive tract; I'm extremely careful about what she eats."

"Good for you, but right now just get inside there and find what you need for Albertina."

Doc got out his copy of *Ruddock's Stepping Stone to Homeopathy and Health* and his *Dr. Hezekiah Stringle's Family Physician* and browsed through the paragraphs in each volume dedicated to scarlet fever. Then he availed himself of a bottle of Dr. Folger's Ready Relief Remedy and two bottles of Dobermann's Homeopathic Specific Number K-15. Down on his knees on the twenty-inch square of the wagon bed under which lay the secret compartment containing his telegraph apparatus, put back after crossing the west fork of the Bruneau, he began silently pleading with the fates for an hour. One hour to get away, though on second thought he recalled that he hadn't passed a settlement of any size since Garnet well over the border into Idaho. And not one telegraph pole since Boisé. The Great Basin, at least this part of it, was, ostensibly and unfortunately, one of the least livable, most conscientiously avoided areas for settling in all the Territories. This realization brought home one undeniable fact.

If Raider was in their clutches, so was he. Only one card was left for the two of them. A queen. Albertina.

12

Doc tended to Albertina as if he were ministering to a sick cow, while Mrs. Greenleaf hung over first one shoulder then the other, hovering like the Grim Reaper.

"If she does as she's told and tries to sleep, it would be all for the best," observed Doc.

His eyes roamed the room. On a window sill he spotted a familiar-looking weapon. His .38. He quickly shifted his glance to a picture on the wall to avoid arousing the woman's suspicions.

"What about the rest of us, Doctor?"

"*Pardonez-moi?* Er, I beg your pardon?"

"Scarlet fever's catching. Shouldn't we be taking medicine to keep from getting it? I never have had it, and I've been in with Bertie off and on all day."

Doc stared into the woman's heavy-lidded eyes; there was worry there, genuine concern. The girl would recover, if she took her medicine and stayed in bed and they didn't do anything foolish with her, like loading her onto their wagon and leaving. So they were stuck for the rest of the week, at least; if he could get out, get away, get to the nearest settlement or even a railroad, he could hook up and send for help.

Of them all, he had the mother off balance; he had to keep her there.

"Quarantine would be advisable," he said.

"Quar . . . ?"

"Keeping the child in strict isolation. Have any of your sons been in the room?"

"No."

"Good, keep them out."

"What about me?"

"You've already been exposed." He paused for effect. "Somebody will have to give her her medication."

79

Again he paused. Her worried look indented itself more deeply. "My dear Madame Greenleaf, what I am trying so inarticulately to say is that if you haven't caught it already, you probably won't. And if you have, being near her won't make any difference, will it?"

"Land o' Goshen, I know I got it! I must have . . ."

"Not necessarily. You could be immune. But there's something else."

"What now?"

"You must keep a sharp eye out for any change, anything that looks like the onset of complications. Rheumatic fever, acute nephritis . . . It's imperative that whatever strikes be treated, preferably with Restitone Compound."

"Couldn't you give her some now? That way you could stave it off, the complications.. . . ."

Doc shook his head, his face as solemn as the grave. "I wish I could. Unfortunately, I don't have any Restitone."

"Then we'll have Lydell or one o' the other boys ride into Cameron and fetch some. Res . . ."

"Restitone. I'm afraid it's not that easy. Restitone comes in no fewer than eight different compounds, each one slightly varied from the others. What amounts to eight different medications for eight different complications."

"Great day in the morning!"

"As a trained physician I would have to select the correct one, possibly two or even more to combine in a mixture. Very carefully measured proportions, of course."

"Of course."

Her expression betrayed her mounting confusion. She wasn't all that stupid, he decided, but she was under a strain, and he was moving too fast for her. He repeated what he'd said.

"As I said before," he went on, "I would have to go myself to obtain the correct compounds." He glanced out the window. Evening was coming on, the knoll darkening perceptibly. *"Mon dieu!* It's already dark out. I shall go right away, come right back, instruct you, and be on my way."

She shook her head. "Sorry, Doctor, you won't be able

to do that. You'll have to plan on staying over until Bertie's all better."

"See here, I have to get back to Salt Lake City. . . ."

"Salt Lake City's gonna have to wait on Bertie, I'm afraid."

The door opened. It was Ben. "Hey, Maw, guess what Charley and Dewey-Blair and I found in the back o' this fella's rig."

He stood aside revealing the other two standing side by side. Doc could feel the color drain from his cheeks. Charley was holding his telegraph set. Holding it, lifting it to eye level, and letting it drop with a crash. Dewey-Blair showed his Pony Premo Senior camera and likewise smashed it.

"Hey!" burst Doc.

"Charles, what in thunderation . . . ?" his mother asked him. All three came in, leaving the rubble where it had landed, Doc eyeing it and suddenly feeling slightly nauseated.

Ben leered at him. "Maw, that was a telegraphing set he had hidden in the bed o' his wagon."

"You idiots!" burst Doc. "Imbeciles, morons! How dare you destroy my property?"

"Calm down, Doctor," said Charley evenly. "You'll notice I call you doctor 'cause you call yourself that. Is that what you really are? I look at you, I listen, and mister, there's something awful familiar about you."

"Charles!" snapped his mother. "What are you carrying on about?"

"What do you think, Maw? What's a doctor or patent medicine drummer, or whatever he is, doing with telegraphing equipment?"

"And this forty-four . . ." Dewey-Blair held up Raider's .44, which he had neglected to take with him leaving Boisé, and which Doc had left in the wagon.

Clenching his teeth, he speared each of them in turn with his eyes. "Of course, I have telegraph equipment, you imbeciles. How else am I to keep in contact with my suppliers? What do you think I do when I run out of something I need, stop off at the nearest drugstore?"

It was precisely what he did do, though not as far as any of this rabble was concerned.

"I don't see anything wrong in a man carrying a gun," said Mrs. Greenleaf. "Give it here." Dewey-Blair handed it to her. "Riding around this neck o' the woods, it seems to me what with Indians and wild critters and wilder people any man'd be a fool not to travel armed."

"Absolutely," said Doc.

She nodded. Then handed Raider's Colt back to Dewey-Blair. "Though you won't have any need for this for a spell. We'll protect you."

"Are you giving me to understand that I am your prisoner?" asked Doc.

"Not at all," responded Mrs. Greenleaf. "You're our guest, until Bertie's on her feet again fit as a fiddle. And anybody else who might come down with the scarlet fever."

"Then what?"

"Then you'll be free to leave."

Charley's inability to suppress his grin was all the confirmation Doc needed. As if for one minute he'd ever dreamed they'd eventually let him go.

"With your permission, I should like to go back out and see to my mule," he said quietly.

"By all means." She waved her arm grandly. "Benjamin'll go with you. Then come back and we'll give you some good home cookin'; I baked bread today, crusty and sweet as a nut. We'll find a place for you to sleep, too. We got all the comforts here."

"Tomorrow morning I shall have to ride into Cameron for the Restitone Compound."

"I was about to mention that," she said. "One of the boys can ride with you. That way, you see, you won't get lost coming back."

13

At nine that night Doc was handed a blanket and escorted to the barn by Charley.

"You intend to make me sleep with horses?" he asked.

"The horses we keep in the corral. Only thing in the barn is a jackass, two-legged." He laughed uproariously, unlatching the door and ushering Doc inside. "Be smart and don't try anything funny during the night. One o' us'll be out by the passage through the rocks to the mine entrance keeping his eyes peeled for anybody wandering in. He'll just as easy see you trying to wander out."

The sound of the latch dropping into its notch behind Doc restored memories of the metal doors at Boisé. The moon was out, sending pale blue rails through the cracks.

"Goddamn! *Goddamn!*"

Doc gasped. "Rade . . . is that you?"

"Goddamn!"

"Ssssh, keep it down."

"Keep it down, he says." Raider emerged from the darkness in the rear. "So you walked right into it, eh? Eyes wide open. Christ Almighty, I mighta known this would happen."

"Calm down, Rade, it gets worse. They found everything, my telegraph equipment, your forty-four . . ."

"What about my Winchester?"

Doc brightened. "Hey, that they didn't find! They searched the wagon, but they didn't look under the bed. They couldn't have."

"Did they find the disguise box?"

"Would I be here now if they had? They'd have shot me on the spot."

"Don't bet on it, I'm still alive. They need hostages; two are better than one." Each filled the other in on what he knew.

"Whatever we do," declared Raider in conclusion, "for chrissakes, don't let 'em know we know each other."

"Rade, do I look stupid?"

"You sure do, with those specs and all that fur on your face. You look like a horse's ass."

"Thank you. Seriously, we've got one chance, a fairly slim one. I get to go into Cameron tomorrow morning; one of them will be coming with me, obviously, to make sure I come back." He explained his Restitone ploy.

"What in hell is Restitone?"

"Nothing, Rade, a name made up on the spur of the moment. The problem is I could probably lull whoever goes along into believing I'm perfectly harmless. Then when he gives me an opening, going or coming back, I can overpower him and get his gun."

"Speaking of guns, I really got to congratulate you on that world-famous thirty-eight Diamondback o' yours. When I really needed it, it came through like a damn Gatling at a massacre. It jammed on me, Mr. Weatherbee, the damn trigger wouldn't even come back. Don't you know you're supposed to test-fire a weapon every so often to make sure it works?"

"Sorry."

"You're sorry. That's great. You can't believe how worried I was that you wouldn't be."

"Let's get serious, Rade. I was saying I can probably surprise him and disarm him, but then what? The rest of you will still be back here. If he doesn't show up, if I show up without him . . ."

"Why in hell would you do a dumb thing like that? You get outta here, you stay out."

"What about you two?"

"Two?"

"Judith, and now you."

"Forget about Judith; this bunch aren't about to take their tempers out on a dumb animal, not with all they got cooking. If you can get away tomorrow, get. If they can't move the girl for a spell, you'll have time to round up two hundred guns. Bring the damn army. This place is a bottle; cork up the entrance and you'd have to be a bird to get out. You'd have 'em cold."

"I still don't like the idea of leaving you and Judith behind."

They discussed it, keeping their voices low. As dangerous as it might make it for Raider it appeared, after lengthy examination, that Doc's disarming his escort to Cameron the next morning was the only worthwhile strategy available. In addition to Raider's vulnerability, there was one other flaw. Albertina. In spite of the girl's condition and Doc's earlier warning that she shouldn't be moved if it came down to her health against everybody else's, "Maw just might order them to pack up and get out."

"She's weak now, but she's big enough and rugged enough to throw it off in two or three days," said Doc, "maybe less. Or at least show marked improvement."

"I don't know; her mother's batty about her. Darling dumpling precious. I can't believe she'd risk moving her. Besides, there's one thing you're overlooking. They know I'm an operative, but they don't suspect you. If you were to light out, they'd figure you were only trying to save your hide."

"You're right. . . ."

"Of course. For you to come riding back here with a crowd would be the surprise o' the century to them. How are you planning on taking whoever goes along with you? Listen, just talk his ear off, get on his gun side, and grab."

"We'll see. If I can't pull it off before we get to Cameron, maybe I'll get a break while we're there." He grinned. "Maybe make a break."

14

"It shouldn't take you two over seven hours," said Maw. "No cause to rush it, just keep a steady pace going and coming back."

Charley nodded. He, his mother, and Doc stood by the corral. The sun had risen, the crown of peaks above them blocking out sight of it, but the whiteness of the sky betraying its appearance. Doc looked on in silence as Mrs. Greenleaf handed Charley money and, turning him away, whispered something to him. Doc threw a look at the barn. Raider was still asleep, at least had been, when he himself was awakened by Charley and taken away for a look at his patient and for breakfast. Darling dumpling's rash was blossoming gloriously, the thickly set red spots spreading to every generous part of her. It would reach its most severe stage by nightfall, reckoned Doc, and by the following morning begin to fade. The day, the hour it vanished completely he, Doc, would be finished, his role performed, his usefulness at its end. He had to get away today, before, during or after Cameron; it would be, he reminded himself, his first and last look at the outside world before joining Raider on the condemned list.

Charley and he led their horses through the passageway into the adit and out into the open. Judith stood patiently in her shafts. Doc, leading one of the mustangs Raider had brought down from Nat Pulford's farm, walked toward her.

"Mount up and let's get outta here," said Charley.

Doc ignored him, reaching Judith, petting her. Mounting, Charley came pounding up to him.

"Give me a couple of minutes. I want to check one last time and see if there might just be some Restitone." Charley stared blankly. "Medication for your sister."

"That's the stuff we're riding all the way to Cameron for?"

Doc nodded. "Cross your fingers, we may not have to make this long ride after all."

"That wouldn't bother me none. Take a good look."

Charley dismounted and set about replacing the crossed boards over the entrance to the New Glory. Doc set a platter of oats and her water bucket in front of Judith, optimistically anticipating that he would not be coming back for a while, then went inside the wagon. Charley, Ben, and Dewey-Blair had done a thorough job of ransacking the interior; boxes and crates were overturned, their contents dumped, bottles and pasteboard boxes and tubes scattered about.

"Mon dieu, what a mess! Savages!"

"Cut the whining, just find what you're looking for."

Doc did, a box filled with loose samples of dozens of different products. He poked about among them and found an unlabeled bottle no larger than his little finger a quarter full of a clear liquid. Uncorking it he sniffed it, grinned satanically, replaced the cork, and pocketed the bottle. He then went about straightening the mess left by the Greenleafs.

Charley's face showed over the tailgate. "Find it?"

"No."

"Shit. Come on, let's get moving." They mounted their horses. Doc gestured, inviting Charley to precede him. Charley shook his head. "You lead the way. And see you stay to my left when we get outside, away from my gun side, understand?"

Doc nodded.

Outside the cliffs the sun was busy drenching the broad valleys, the volcanic cones, the sand dunes, the heights and the ravines. The thousands of square miles surrounding them sloped gently eastward. It was a land so wide, so boundless it stretched a man's mind; the glare, the dryness, the stillness, the desolation and sterility and the endless clutter of sagebrush and creosote bush suggested another planet, a place closer to the sun than earth, where no man lived, only small burrowing creatures—gophers, mice, kangaroo rats, ground squirrels, pygmy rabbits.

Three and a half hours to Cameron, starting out retracing their route northward, then cutting east, eventually to lose Niles Peak behind them. Doc rode up front, his horse loping effortlessly. It had been weeks since he'd been in a saddle; he vastly preferred his plank seat behind Judith. By sundown, wherever he'd gotten to, he'd be feeling this day's ride.

Where would he get to? Out of Cameron and north, back up into Idaho to Burley, the nearest town of any size. A good site for a rendezvous; he could contact William Pinkerton at the Denver Office. In thirty-six hours he could have fifty men to lead back to the knoll. This thought warmed him. Once he got clear of the man behind him neither he nor any of the rest of his tribe would expect him to come roaring back with half a hundred guns. He could only hope they wouldn't destroy his wagon. And leaving Judith in their clutches troubled him as much as his leaving Raider.

Charley came up alongside him. The wind reshaped his beard, reddened his cheeks, and brought tears to his eyes.

"We'll be getting there middle o' the morning. We'll go straight to the drugstore. We'll get what you need, we'll head back. We got no time for lollygagging, Maw's orders."

"I haven't been on a horse in ages."

"You're riding fine."

"I'll need a few minutes to stretch my legs before starting back."

"Sure, a few minutes. Just don't forget one thing, you and me will be sticking together close as skin when we get there, side by side at that drug counter."

Doc nodded. He faced the wind, but could feel Charley's eyes burrowing into him; he turned to face his stare. "What's the matter?"

"You sure we haven't met afore? Someplace, maybe over to Utah at Cedar City near the Escalante?"

"I'm sure," said Doc, returning his stare unblinkingly through his spectacles. The sight of Charley's beard and mustache reminded him that he, too, was wearing such adornment. He hadn't shaved, they hadn't given him time to, and running his hand over his face, he could feel his natural stubble starting.

The first hour's ride from the hideout took them well past the spot where Lydell had abducted him, mule, wagon, and all. The road swung sharply to the right and they followed it, still side by side, Charley more talkative than Doc had ever imagined he would be, or wanted him to be. He crowed and crowed about "the family"; Doc closed his ears as best he could and for the tenth time reexamined the situation. Had he thought of everything? There wasn't all that much to think of; Albertina still remained their main hope. As long as her scarlet fever held out, her mother and the others would stay put. And Raider would be safe. Until they crossed the Mexican border actually, but there was no way he could let things get that far.

They rode on, stopping once only to rest the horses, to let them drink from a creek and munch on blue-bunch wheat grass. The sun rising in front of them shed its glare down upon a settlement, ripples of heat rising from the road and setting the clutch of buildings wavering before Doc's eyes. Charley pointed.

"Cameron."

The streets were dried mud liberally laced with wagon tracks, the wooden sidewalks bleached by the sun, the buildings all wooden, clapboard and plank, so dried out and with so little space between them a single match might have destroyed the entire town.

They tied up in front of the store. A huge square sign above the entrance proclaimed:

BOB BOLTON & CO.
Drugs
and
Medicines
and
Dealers in
Fancy Articles
and
Perfumes
Trusses, Braces, etc.

A gray and bile-green-striped awning shaded the front door. Doc stretched, groaned slightly, and as decorously as he could separated the seat of his trousers from one sweating and sore cheek, then the other.

Inside was, thanks to the awning over the door and the absence of windows, as dark as pitch to the two men coming in out of the glare. Both quickly became used to the gloom, and Doc surveyed the ten-foot-high shelves on all sides filled with neatly arranged bottles and boxes. The names were familiar, a powder or pill or teaspoon or tablespoonful of something for every known ailment and not a few unknown, products of overly fertile imaginations. Ostensibly, whatever your affliction—harelip, cross eyes, club foot, club hand, stiff joints, weak joints, malfunctioning hip joints, disorders, paralysis, diseases of the eye, the ear, the nose, the throat, the womb, of every anatomical area—Bob Bolton & Co. could provide you the cure.

In addition there was a counter devoted to "fancy articles," mostly brush and comb sets, mustache cups, razors, mugs, and shaving brushes, as well as perfumes. Trusses, shoulder braces, leg braces, neck braces, and knee braces hung from the top shelves, and one corner of the ceiling was festooned with crutches and other aids to ambulation.

An elderly man wearing too little white hair on his head and far too much muttonchopping his cheeks confronted them.

"Morning, gents, what's your pleasure?"

"Do you have Restitone?" asked Doc straight-faced.

A puzzled expression seized the older man's face. "Res . . . ?"

"Generically the homeopathic species Q-424, Q-428, 429, and 30."

"Yes, sir."

He climbed his ladder to the nearest top shelf, pushed aside a line of braces curtaining the boxes, and brought down all four specifics.

"That'll be sixty cents." Charley paid him. "Anything else?"

"No thanks," said Charley.

"You sure?" We just this morning got in a shipment of Wordan's Catarrh Cure."

"No thanks," said Charley. They had started for the door.

"And Swayne's Ointment. Greatest treatment on God's green earth for acne, blackheads, and pimples. You fellows have children?"

"No thanks," said Charley. They had started for the door.

"If you can spare a few minutes, it'd be my pleasure to demonstrate our new Wilcox Electric Belt. Guaranteed to ease the discomfort of rheumatism, lumbago, sciatica, kidney complaints, lame back. Light as a feather; you don't even know you got it on."

Outside they unhitched and climbed onto their horses. Swinging about, Doc's eyes strayed across the street to the Elko County Bank, next door to the Silver Spur. A lanky farm boy, resplendent in bib overalls and straw hat came staggering out, heading up the sidewalk.

"I could use a drink," said Charley behind him. "How about you? We made good time coming up; it seems a pity to get here, stay three minutes, and start back. Besides, the horses could use a breather."

Doc never said a word. They went into the Spur, Charley strode up to the mahogany, bought a one-dollar bottle of Melchor's Rye Whiskey, set it and two glasses given him by the barkeep down on a table, threw his left leg over his chair back, and sat. Doc sat, much more gingerly. Charley poured for the two of them.

"You a drinking man, Doctor?"

"I seldom indulge."

"You ought to, you're missing something special."

There were few patrons present at such an early hour. Three men stood at the bar, from their slouches over it and the way they gripped their drinks, habitués, decided Doc, men who drank by the clock in their throats rather than the one on the wall. Two others sat at a table in the rear going over papers of some kind, one of them reading and signing, reading and signing. A girl came drifting toward Doc and Charley, her blonde hair piled in ringlets from one ear to the other, her face pretty but overly made-up and rapidly going to sag and lines. There was, however, nothing sagging up front. She supported her breasts proudly, with blatant vanity, not supporting them actually as much as displaying them.

"*Mon dieu,*" gasped Doc.

Charley turned to look, a long, appreciative stare. She smiled, patently accustomed to such spontaneous admiration. Out of Doc's pocket came the little finger-sized bottle he had brought from his apothecary wagon. Under the table, out of the girl's sight, he pulled the cork and concealing the bottle in his fist, added a few drops of its contents to his own drink. It was back in his pocket in a second and a half. Charley's eyes remained riveted to the girl, rising reluctantly to her face. Coming up to them, she curled one arm around his shoulder.

"I'm Ernestine. You're . . ."

Charley leered. "Charley."

Doc rose from his chair, his hand atop his curly-brim derby set alongside the bottle.

"Doctor Philippe D'Ascoygne."

"Doctor? My, my. And French, too . . ."

At once her arm and her attention deserted Charley in full favor of Doc. This Charley did not appreciate. She had barely begun falling all over Doc when he issued a curt order:

"Beat it, woman, we got private business to discuss!"

"Well, pardon me, I'm sure." Pouting, she raised her breastworks another two inches, swung them dangerously close to Charley's head, and strutted off.

"Goddamn shemales, always poking their noses in where they're not wanted," he said glumly. He emptied his glass. "Drink up, we can't hang around here all day."

Doc lifted his glass to his lips and tasted it. He grimaced.

"What's the matter?"

"It tastes . . ."

"Tastes just fine to me, mighty fine."

"I told you, I rarely indulge."

"That's your problem. Give it here." He downed it in one gulp. "No sense wasting good liquor." He got to his feet, filling his own glass a second time and hurling it down. Then corking the bottle, he shoved it into his back pocket.

"Let's go."

They went. They reached the batwing doors and stepped outside; Charley stopped, teetered slightly, swallowed hard, looking painfully confused, and sank to the boards in a heap. Doc never broke stride, never looked back.

Untying both horses, he started off trailing Charley's behind him. Good old choloroform, colorless, odorless and disguised by rotgut, tasteless. Next stop Burley!

He passed the first intersection and the second and last, glancing down one side, then the other. He caught a glimpse of the Western Union office one door down on the left. He went on his way, thinking about it, seeing it reappear in his mind's eye, envisioning the interior. Pulling up, he wheeled about and galloped back to it.

Inside a man the size of a nine-year-old boy wearing an eyeshade and matching green garters on his sleeves, tobacco stains blotching his shirt front, approached him, elbowing the counter.

"Morning."

Doc waved. "How long will it take to get a message through to Denver?" he asked, picking up a pencil stub and starting to write on the yellow blank pad.

"Got to go through Salt Lake City," said the man, crinkling his small chin, pausing, pondering. "Not long, maybe a hour. Depends on Salt Lake City."

As he listened, Doc's pencil never stopped. He put down rough directions to the split cliffs using Niles Peak and the sharp turn in the road east to Cameron as reference points, estimating the distance from the turn to the swing right toward the passage between the rocks as "15 miles plus." He cited his needs, established Raider's plight, and named the Western Union office in Burley as the assembly site. He finished up with a few words stressing the urgency of the situation.

No time to encode. Just get it on the key.

"Here we are," he said, proferring the message. The clerk was reaching out to take it from him when his apparatus behind him came to life. He paused.

"Hold it just a shake, message coming in."

Doc groaned. "Can you hurry it up, please?"

"No, I can't; you'll have to ask the fella at the other end."

The message coming in was mercilessly long, the clerk filling three-quarters of a page on a pad three times the size of the telegram in Doc's hand. Finishing, he rose and returned.

Doc was handing it over when the door burst open. The clerk's hand froze in mid-air as he looked up. Doc turned to look.

It was Charley, wringing wet, boiling mad. Out shot his hand, snatching the paper from Doc.

15

The muzzle of the Peacemaker hard against his back-bone moved Doc down the alley.

"Hold it right there," said Charley.

Doc turned to face him. "Do you mind if I lower my hands?"

"You bet I mind. So you're a Pinkerton, eh? We seem to be collecting you bastards by the barrelful these days. I oughta gun you down right where you stand!"

"That'd be pretty stupid."

"It'd be pretty damn satisfying." He cocked his gun.

"You fire that thing, they'll hear it from one end of this town to the other. They just might grab you, Charley. What would you tell them? Besides, aren't you forgetting Albertina? She needs me."

"The hell she does. You're no doctor!"

"I'm as good as. And better than most, if I do say so. Wait and see, you get back home tonight, don't be surprised when your mother tells you her fever's down and the rash and sore throat are starting to go away. Can I ask you a question? How in hell can you drink chloroform, faint dead away, and less than fifteen minutes later walk in on me big as life? Mister, you're a medical marvel."

"Simple. Some slobs dunked me in a horse trough. I woke up and threw up. All over the steps o' the Silver Spur. Finding the horses was the only thing that took any time."

"Even throwing up, you still shouldn't be . . ."

"Shut up."

The muzzle found Doc's stomach and pressed even

harder than it had against his spine. Charley was examining him.

"You don't smell very good, Charley," said Doc, re-
coiling in disgust.

"I told you shut up. Take off your specs." Doc failed to
move fast enough to suit Charley, who jerked them off his
face and threw them to the ground. Then grabbing the
end of his mustache, he stripped it off.

"Hey, damnit!"

Off came his van dyke in identical fashion. Doc let out
a howl, rubbing the sting out of his chin vigorously.
Grabbing his wrist, Charley pulled his hand down. Rec-
ognition flooded his face.

"You! I knew there was something about you. The
chowline back at Boisé. You and O'Toole had a row over
meat. Let me guess, okay? He was bunking in with us,
everything he heard he passed on to you, and you got it
outside. Am I right?"

"Sorry, Charley, regulations forbid me to divulge the
Agency's methods to outsiders."

"You're a barrel o' laughs, you know that? Okay, let's
go get the horses and get outta this place. I'm taking you
back; it's gonna be up to Maw what we do with you."

"You won't do anything with me, friend, not as long as
your sister's bedded down with scarlet fever. You try anything and your mother'll break your neck."

"We'll see, Pink. When she finds out you're as phony
as a wooden duck, it just might be your neck she'll break.
Maw got two strong things going for her; she got no
sense o' humor and a temper like a stepped-on wildcat.
Move."

Charley was right about one thing; his mother turned
out to be somewhat less than overjoyed upon being told
that the doctor treating her darling dumpling was a Pinkerton operative. The confrontation took place in the
front room. It began with a slap in the face. Doc's.

"You filthy liar; you dare pass yourself off as a doctor!
My precious in there could be on her deathbed and you
pretend to treat her. . . ."

"Don't be ridiculous!" boomed Doc, deliberately jettisoning his accent. This unexpected outburst startled the woman so he was able to add a few more words. "I didn't pretend a thing; I treated her according to prescribed medical procedure. It's in my medical books, and I followed it to the letter."

"You're a fake! Charles . . ."

"Yeah, Maw?"

"Go find Lydell; he's to blame for this. He ought to have the stuffing whaled outta him." Charley started out the door grinning. "Fast as you can, you hear?"

"Answer one question," said Doc. "Is Albertina better or is she worse since we left this morning? Never mind, I'll see for myself."

She stepped in front of him blocking his way, holding her arms out, a martyred expression seizing her features.

"Don't you dare set one foot in there!"

"Maw? Maw, who's out there? Maw . . . Maw!"

"It's only me, precious."

"I hear a man's voice. Who is it, Maw? Maw?"

"Her throat sounds a hundred percent better," observed Doc in a confident tone. "Not nearly so gravelly. Tell me it doesn't sound better. . . ."

"It seems better," said Mrs. Greenleaf, lowering her arms.

"Has her rash started to fade? If it hasn't, it will shortly, before tomorrow morning."

"It's hard for me to tell, looking at her all day." The woman's change in attitude toward him was so abrupt and so thoroughly unexpected, he was hard put to restrain himself from laughing out loud. The fact that there was very little left to laugh about helped discourage him from doing so.

"Let's have a look."

She opened the door. Albertina was sitting up; her rash was indeed fading. Her bovine eyes had lost their dull look and were on the verge of sparkling.

"Who . . . ?" She paused, tilting her head, puzzled. "It's you, Doctor D'Ascoygne, without your glasses and mustache and stuff. . . . I thought I heard your voice. I'm better, aren't I, Maw? Tell him, tell him, aren't I? My throat doesn't hurt hardly half what it did last night and this morning. . . ."

"Hush, darling dumpling, you mustn't overwork it. Lie back down, precious, and let Mother tuck you in."

"I'm sick o' lying in bed. Can I get up? Can I, Doctor? Say I can, please. I want to. Can I? Can I?"

Seventeen, thought Doc, with the brain of a five-year-old, the personality of a bucket of hog sloppings, and the face and body of a . . . He thought briefly; there was nothing to compare either of them to. They were unique.

"Doctor?" asked Mrs. Greenleaf as Albertina continued to wheedle.

It was all he needed to persuade him that he was back in her good graces. Doctor Weatherbee, thank you. He ignored her.

"Be patient, my dear," he said, patting Albertina's hand in kindly fashion. "Stay in bed until tomorrow, at least. If you get up too soon, you might have a relapse, you might get sick again." He snapped his fingers. "We wouldn't want that to happen, would we?"

"Doctor knows best," said her mother.

"Let's have a look at your throat," said Doc. She couldn't open her mouth fast enough for him. Down inside it was still red and raw looking, somewhat swollen, especially the uvula, soft palate, and tonsils. "That's a good girl. Mmmmm, coming along nicely. We won't be needing the Restitone after all."

Getting up from the side of the bed, he waved and smiled and went outside with Mrs. Greenleaf. Lydell had come in and was waiting, looking more sheepish than his usual stupid, nervously working the brim of his hat in a circle through his fists.

"You wanted to see me, Maw?" he asked.

"No, I do not. Get back to what you were doing. I want those wheels greased proper, dripping with it. We got a long trek ahead o' us."

"Maw!" snapped Charley indignantly. "You told me to . . ."

"You go along with him, Charles. See that the two o' you make a decent job of it."

"Maw . . ."

"Out!"

"Well, now, Doctor," she said in a ladylike tone.

"There's a pot boiling on the stove. Would you care to join me in a cup o' camomile tea?"

"I'd be delighted to, Mrs. Greenleaf."

He wasn't as delighted as he pretended. A glimpse through Albertina's window and the sight of a second coffin on top of the first, both carelessly covered with a sheet, prevented it.

16

Promptly at nine that night Charley once again escorted Doc to the barn. While they were covering the short distance from the house, the Pinkerton's thoughts raced ahead of him. He could picture the look of disappointment on his partner's face. He knew it well, for he'd seen it many times; it was usually accompanied by a grayish tinge to Raider's skin. At that he probably already knew that Charley had not come back alone. Raider could easily see what was going on outside through any one of a dozen spaces between the side boards.

"Remember what I told you last night, Pink," said Charley as they approached the barn. "One of us'll be on guard out by the passage near the entrance to the mine all night. My shift tonight."

"Don't fall asleep."

"I never have. We got too much at stake here."

"So it seems."

Charley grinned. "That's some walk you got there. You look like you're ninety years old. Little sore in the cheeks?"

"A little."

At the sound of the fumbling with the latch Raider came to the door and was standing there when Charley opened it. He already knew, Doc could tell by the sour look on his face and the total absence of surprise.

"Seeing you two are bosom buddies, I won't bother introducing you," said Charley laughing. He continued to chuckle as he closed and latched the door and walked off to work.

Raider wandered to a bale of hay and sat down heavily, his back to his partner.

"Aren't you even curious to know what happened?" asked Doc.

"What's the difference? Is your excuse gonna change anything?"

"I wasn't about to make excuses," said Doc, bristling. He felt rotten, and limp with nervous exhaustion. "Crushed" described it better, he thought. To come so close, to within five minutes of getting away. To blow it. And he had; that he could scarcely deny. He never should have stopped at the Western Union office in the first place. Once back up on his horse pulling Charley's behind him, he should have hit stride and kept going; played it safe, played it smart. To compound his misery the soreness afflicting his butt was worsening rapidly, becoming so painful, his cheeks so sensitive he couldn't even stand up straight.

Raider heard him out, playing priest to confessor. Doc had bungled things so badly it almost seemed he had to spill his guts out or die. To allay a conscience became almost as painful as his hind end.

"Funny," said Raider in a tone as hollow as a reed, "I always figured you for smart. With all your education, your book reading . . ."

"Don't rub it in, Rade, okay? I admit it was stupid of me."

"For this there's got to be a stronger word than stupid."

"He drank chloroform. It had about as much effect on him as if I'd watered his whiskey. When I saw him walk up to that counter I was absolutely thunderstruck. I couldn't believe my eyes."

"The hell with it, all of it; it's blown and that's all there is to it. All it does is make things a helluva lot tougher. And settles it. We're getting out tonight. There's a full moon; it can hurt us, but it can help us, too."

Bracing his hands against the end of the hay bale, Doc let himself down to his knees, slowly, painfully, grimacing every inch of the way. Then he leaned over the bale to rest on his forearms. He sighed heavily.

"Rade, I hate to say it, but I'm not going anywhere. I can barely walk, forget ride. You might just as well ask me to fly."

"Who's fault is it? A full-grown man belongs up on a horse out here, not a dumb apothecary wagon, not any kinda wagon. Not unless he's past seventy-five. You're outta shape so we're stuck here, is that what you're trying to say?"

"I am not out of shape!"

"Doc, I don't care how you ride, but you're going to. Maybe like a jockey, with your ass up and the wind to cool it. If it's any consolation, my dogs ache just as much. I'd like to see you climb a damn mountain shanks mare, walk fifty miles . . ."

"Twenty-five."

"Whatever. It wasn't the distance, it was the climbing."

"All right, all right. Let's not waste time arguing over trivialities. Have you thought about how we're going to work this?"

"What else do you think I got to think about sitting in this stinkhole all day, all night? I've worked out a way to get by your friend Charley out by the split. That's not the hardest part. The horses are gonna be the problem."

"How? The corral is full of horses, the saddles sitting on the fence. . . ."

Raider shook his head and hissed in exasperation. "Like I said, you don't ride, you don't know beans about horses. You and your goddamn mule. Doc, there's got to be eight or nine mounts in that corral, with only two of them mares. Those three mustangs I brought down from the farm near Pearl are all stallions."

"What's the difference, stallion or mare?"

"Didn't those college professors o' yours ever tell you? At night a mare won't make a sound, unless she's spooked or attacked or something. But a damn stallion will whinny at anything."

"Is that true?"

"No, it's a goddamn lie. Why do you suppose the Comanches are so partial to mares? What I'm trying to say is it's gonna be some job trying to cut two horses outta that pack without the others raising a fuss."

Doc thought a moment. "What if we let them all out? Just let down the bars and let them wander. Then grab the two closest to the mine and lead them out."

Raider shook his head. "No good. Wandering around they'd maybe not whinny, but you'd hear their hoofbeats, especially if one or two got over onto that flat rock on the far side o' the shack. If just one o' those crazies wakes up, we'd never even make it into the mine passage."

"We have to have horses."

"We wouldn't get two hundred yards without 'em. Besides which, when the sun comes up, that Basin out there gets as fierce as the damn Mojave. And it's one helluva lot bigger."

"Two hundred thousand square miles, Rade."

Raider unfolded his plan step by step. Few of the steps appeared any less perilous or dependent on some degree of luck than the others. The most dangerous aspect of all continued to be the horses. Raider would have loved to take every one of them along, but this could create a racket that would raise the dead. Unfortunately for Doc, he added, now that Raider had thought it over for the dozenth time, they could not risk bothering with saddles. After cutting out two horses, their only stop on the way out would be to collect Raider's Winchester from underneath the wagon bed.

As for Charley on guard out by the wagon, Doc wasn't all that enthusiastic over his partner's suggestion for how to deal with him. But unable to come up with a better idea, he grudgingly went along with Raider's.

Raider cautioned, "We take care of Charley and while I'm getting the Winchester and the shells, you get some oats outta Judith's bag. Just a handful to quiet the horses when we take 'em. After everything's in shape outside, one of us'll come back."

"What you mean is the other should stay outside so he'll have a chance of getting away . . ."

"Even if whoever comes back for the horses blows it," Raider said.

"I'll come back. I'll be very careful. I'll take two, feed them to keep them quiet and . . ."

"*I'll* come back."

"Rade . . ."

"I'm not gonna argue with you. You've already blown this thing twice."

"How the devil do you figure that?"

"Once for me, once for yourself. First you gave me a gun with a busted trigger. I could've held 'em off and been long gone before you even got here. I coulda ridden back and intercepted you."

"Let's not cry over spilt milk."

"Which could turn out spilt blood if we're not careful and goddamn lucky."

"How do we get out of this barn? Wait, I gave you my penknife to cut the fuse for the dynamite you used to blow the gate."

"I still got your knife."

Doc stood up, painfully, tentatively rubbing one cheek, then the other. "Hand it over." Opening the knife, he slipped the blade between the barn doors edge up, reached the outside latch bar, lifted it, and pushed open the door.

The knoll was bathed in moonlight.

"It's the daughter we've got to worry about waking," whispered Doc. "The head of her bed backs up to the right rear corner of the corral. The mother has a room in the back, off the kitchen. The sons are in a small bunk room out back. Albertina's been dozing off and on all day; she could be wide awake now."

"I don't give a shit. Nobody's claiming this is gonna be a snap. Let's go."

Like two wraiths loosed from a tomb they slipped silently across the open space in front of the house to the mine and into the passageway. Feeling their way along in darkness, they eventually came to within sight of the entrance, the crossed boards that were blocking it clearly defined by the moonlight.

Doc moaned plaintively. "Rade, I can't go another step; the pain goes all the way down to my ankles."

"Stop bellyachin', goddamnit! You'll go, you'll walk twenty-five miles over a fucking mountain if you got to. Just grit your teeth."

"Sure. I wonder where he is out there?"

"Who cares? We're not going to him, he's coming to us." They moved to within ten feet of the crossed boards, Raider in the lead. Reaching back, he stopped Doc. "Get down on your belly."

"I'll try."

"Do it!"

"Sssssh."

Doc got down; Raider moved up to the boards. Tipping them over, he backtracked and threw himself flat to the side and just ahead of Doc. They froze. They could hear Charley curse and mutter outside, and come clomping up. Still bellied down, they began inching backward as he approached, gun at the ready, stopped at the entrance, then came inside a few steps. Raider and Doc held their breaths.

"What the hell . . ." muttered Charley.

He stopped less than two yards from the top of Raider's head, the Pinkerton's right cheek hard against the floor of the mine. Failing to hear anything, Charley began slowly, backing away.

Raider cursed under his breath. *Turn, goddamn you, turn.* Near the entrance Charley did so at last. Tensing, Raider sprang to his feet and threw himself down the passageway. Charley reacted to the sound, and started to turn, bringing his gun hand back around. He never made it; Raider slammed into him knocking him flat, the .44 flying out of Charley's hand and falling outside in the grass. Two hard lefts to the jaw finished him.

Doc came up as Raider regained his feet. "What in God's name did you do that for?" he asked breathlessly. "I thought you were going to wait until he put away his gun so he'd have both hands free to put the boards back in place?"

"What's the difference, it worked didn't it?"

"Just don't do it again, Rade."

"Do what?" he asked, removing Charley's gunbelt and buckling it on.

"Change tactics spontaneously."

"Oh, knock it off with the big words, will you? Find his piece, I'll fetch the Winchester and the shells. We got tracks to make."

Moments later, his pocket bulging with the box of shells, his hat half filled with Judith's oats, Raider was on his way back to the corral, wearing the Peacemaker, leaving the rifle with Doc, when Charley stirred and groaned. Doc shifted the Winchester to his left hand and bent to deliver a hard right to Charley's jaw. He stopped groaning and lay still. Raider nodded approvingly and went on into the mine.

"Good luck," called Doc.

"Fuck luck, just pray."

"I'll pray I'm going to be able to get up on the horse."

Raider didn't answer, didn't hear; he half ran down the passageway, sliding his free right hand along the wall, coming out onto the knoll and stealthily approaching the corral. A ticklish business this, he thought worriedly. One whinny or clop of a hoof, a rail slipping from his grasp as he removed it—any sound could wake the girl. And in ten seconds she'd wake the whole crew!

Setting down the oats, he moved to the corral. He took hold of a top rail, his eyes glued on the shack. He was sweating furiously by the time he'd gotten all three rails down and laid them aside. Not one of the nine horses had moved a muscle. Sucking in the chill night air, filling his lungs and letting it out slowly, he muttered under his breath. It failed completely to relax him, to loosen the tightening knot of his nerves.

The saddles were lined up along the top rail to his right, and further along lay bridles. So far, so good as it had been, he was tempted to steal time and gear both horses once he got them out. His eyes strayed to his hat with the oats on the ground. Filling his right hand with some, he set the hat back about fifteen feet from the fence, returned, and began feeding the horse closest to him, a stallion, one of the mustangs. The mares stood at the back, just his luck. The stallion practically took his hand off in his eagerness for the feed.

"Fuck it." Leading the animal to the right, he bridled and saddled it, tightening the cinches, finishing up. Then he tied it to a post.

By the time he was done the other horses had discovered the opening and were starting out, lured by the scent of the oats. He got hold of another stallion, but a third followed before he could get the top rail back up into place. The uninvited one went straight to the hat, leaving him with nothing to give the second horse.

If it objected and whinnied in protest, he was dead. By some miracle it did not, instead sidling up beside the first horse in friendly fashion and obligingly standing stock-still while he put on a bridle and saddle. The odd horse had by now finished eating and was wandering off toward the barn, probably, attracted by the odor of the hay bales, thought Raider, although how it could smell hay over the stink was more than he could fathom.

He wished to hell he could lure it back into the corral, but was reluctant to try. Luck had been with him so far; why press it by lingering any longer than he had to? After tying the second horse's reins to the first's saddle horn, he retrieved his Stetson and led them slowly, carefully, quietly to the mine. The second horse was almost inside when the stray turned his attention to the activity. Raider stiffened and froze as it came prancing over to join them.

Jesus, if that doesn't wake 'em, nothing will!

He hurried down the passageway to the adit, the stray following them, its curiosity aroused. To hell with it, he thought, if it woke 'em, it woke 'em. There wasn't much he could do about it. An idea flashed across his mind. Hurrying down the adit, he reached the entrance and found Doc pacing nervously near Judith, Charley still lying in the grass, out.

"Thank God, I was beginning to think something went wrong back there."

"It turned out easy as picking apples."

Doc turned to Judith. "I hate leaving her here with this tribe of crazies, Rade. They'll shoot her out of spite. . . ." He stopped and stared with a puzzled expression. "Why three horses?"

"Nothing. Never mind." Dropping the horses' reins, Raider ran to the stack of support timbers wedged between the rocks on one side. They were piled ends out to a height of about fifteen feet. Climbing up, Raider began pulling off the top ones and flinging them to the ground.

"Rade, what the hell are you doing? We've got to get out of here!"

"We're gonna block that entrance, just the cross-beams, the longer ones."

"That'll take an hour."

"I don't care if it takes till sunup, it's worth it. God-damnit, don't just stand there, help!"

Clenching his teeth, fighting back the pain, Doc bent to pick up one of the timbers.

"Oh, man . . . ohhhhh."

"Never mind, I'll do it myself. You just stand in front o' that entrance and aim the Winchester down the adit.

If you hear anything, I mean *anything*, start blasting."

Doc started to say something, changed his mind, and did as he was told, raising the rifle, pointing it into the mine.

"This is crazy, we should be getting out while we can."

Having tossed down a couple of dozen cross-beams, Raider got down and began stacking them up; sealing up the entrance.

"Crazy your ass."

"Don't talk about my ass," said Doc.

"Remember what I said last night about this place being a bottle? We'll I'm corking it. If we were to leave it open we'd lose 'em for sure. They'd run to God-knows-where."

"To Mexico."

"Yeah, but how, which way? It'd take fifty men, a hundred and fifty spread from Texas to California to cover all the roads."

The beams were a good four inches wider than the entrance at each end when laid down crosswise. An even dozen stacked up created a wall that came within two inches of the top. The thirteenth sealed the entrance completely. Now, as Raider pointed out, any of the timbers would do just to bulk up the wall, add weight to it so that the Greenleafs would need a battering ram to break through. He worked feverishly, like a man possessed. Doc, no longer required to stand aiming down the passageway, worked like a hundred-year-old invalid. The three liberated horses ignored the operation and busied themselves foraging. Charley, still unconscious, lay on his back, the moonlight bathing his expressionless face. By now the wall was three timbers thick.

"Two more stacks oughta do it," commented Raider, pausing to catch his breath and surveying their handiwork. "Three would be perfect. They'd need a herd o' stampeding steers to push through." He went back to work.

"I've been thinking, Rade."

"That's bad."

"Seriously. How about if you light out for the Idaho border, for Burley up through the Goose Creek Mountains? As soon as you get there, you wire the office in Denver for reinforcements."

"And what are you gonna be doing all this time?"

"I'll follow you with Judith and the wagon."

"Doc . . ."

"Hear me out. If we leave her, if they don't shoot her, she could die of thirst. With us blocking up the entrance like this, they're not going to be able to get out to feed and water her."

"Yeah, I didn't think about that."

"I'll follow, only I'll cut over to Cameron. I'll stable her and the wagon, then head on up to Burley and join you."

"We can leave the stray and tie one o' the others to your tailgate."

"Right. You'll have to wait in Burley until you collect everybody anyway; I'll be there long before that. I'll check in at the Western Union office."

"Okay. Just be sure . . ."

It was as far as he got. Awakening and rolling over on his stomach, Charley hauled out a gun. And fired. Doc grunted and caved in, his knees bending, falling forward, his hand flashing to his left shoulder. Raider drew and fired simultaneously with Charley's second shot, the slug whistling past Raider's hat brim as he started to fall. The fact that Charley had been trying to support his weight on his elbow and shooting too hastily at the same time was all that saved Raider.

The one shot he himself got off did its job—with a generous helping of blind luck. The slug hit the ground three feet in front of Charley, kicking up dust as it ricocheted straight up into his face.

His grim look exploded, a bursting flower of crimson. Raider ran to him, reaching down, rolling him over on his back. The shot had blasted his face halfway back into his head. Raider swallowed hard and looked away . . . at Doc, down on his knees, grim-faced, refusing to fall forward, his hand still clutching his shoulder, slender stripes of blood showing between his fingers.

"Doc!" Raider caught him as he started to fall forward.

"I'm all right, I'm all right."

"I can see that. Jesus Christ!"

"I'm all right."

Raider unbuttoned Doc's jacket and, easing it open, examined the wound. The slug had traveled straight into muscles and meat. Whether bone was broken or not was impossible to tell.

"That's in there, Weatherbee," said Raider solemnly. "She's gonna take some deep digging." He whipped out his neckerchief and folded it into a pad, placing it over the wound and closing and buttoning Doc's jacket to hold it there.

"Give me a hand up, Rade."

"Listen . . ."

"Please. If I get up on my feet I'll be okay."

Raider helped him up. "Hurt bad?"

"Like a son of a bitch."

Doc rarely swore. It brought a smile to Raider's face. "You bastard." He began fanning his partner's pockets.

"What are you doing?"

"Looking for your penknife; I'm gonna have to dig that slug outta you."

"Like hell. Let it stay. I can put up with it for as long as it takes me to get to Cameron and a doctor. Just answer me one question."

"Yeah?"

"Where did he get a gun?"

"It was inside his shirt. . . ."

"That's not what I'm talking about and you know it!"

Raider cast his eyes down sheepishly, then glanced at the corpse, the gun lying in plain sight between two clumps of grass where Charley had dropped it.

"It's . . . it's your Diamondback."

"I thought you said it jammed on you."

"It did." Raider groaned wearily.

"The last I saw of it, it was lying on the windowsill in the front room."

"He was the one who picked it up when I threw it away. I remember him asking me where I'd got it. He must have fixed whatever was wrong with the trigger."

"Oh? What makes you think that?" Doc scowled and winced.

Raider ignored him. The horses, frightened by the exchange, had reared and backed off, as far away from the combatants as they could. They had been standing frozen but now, sensing that the fireworks were over, returned to their nibbling. Raider went back to the wall, finished it, and, tying one of the horses to Doc's tailgate, helped him up onto the wagon seat.

"If that horse didn't wake 'em clopping over from the barn, those three shots sure will," said Raider. "Aren't you glad now we closed up the mine?"

"We needn't have gone to all the trouble, wasted all this time. We should have used our heads and pulled the entrance upright supports loose. Collapsed the ceiling."

"It never would, that overhead stope is solid rock."

Raider dug out a blanket, folding it neatly and slipping it under Doc's upraised cheeks to soften his seat. Muffled voices could be heard on the other side of the wall. He paused to listen, then retrieved the Diamondback, handing it up to Doc.

"They're up and about, Doc. Let's go. See you in two days."

"You take the Winchester."

"You. I won't need it; I'll be riding straight through. Are you gonna make it?" He handed him the box of shells.

"I'll make it."

They took off, leaving Charley's corpse, the battered, unrecognizable front of his head upright, the stray horse quietly nibbling grass beside him, the muffled voices inside the adit dying away.

17

Raider rode hard, heading northward for the Idaho border, his mind brimming with worry. Doc was so sure he'd make it; not if he bled to death along the way he wouldn't. If Cameron had taken him three and a half hours by horse, he wouldn't reach there before sundown the next day by mule and wagon. But it would have been a waste of time to try to talk him out of it.

Getting away from the Greenleafs counterbalanced his concern over his partner; leaving them corked up was the best idea he'd ever had. Oh, they could get out if they kept at it with axes working full time; with two of them to a shift, it'd take 'em most of the day. They could blow away the wall, of course, but dynamite would be pretty risky in such a close, confined space. It just might bring the ceiling down, solid though it appeared. That would solve one problem only to create another. Somebody had to survive who knew the whereabouts of the loot.

If the wall held for two days, for even thirty-six hours, he might be able to get back in time with enough men to take the whole tribe for keeps.

Climbing up on the timber pile, he'd discovered their wagon parked behind it, just barely able to fit into the space. It was nearly as big as a prairie schooner, size enough to pack three or four thousand pounds with ease, with four horses up front. They'd probably hide the Adams & Company take in the wagon bed when they took off.

If they were able to. Ducking lower, he heeled the mustang, urging it to greater speed. How far to Burley, he wondered. Maybe a hundred, with the last fifty or so over the border into the Goose Creek Mountains no easy traveling. And at this rate the horse would be puffing hard by the time they got there and started climbing. He slowed a trifle, then more, then pulled up. He'd been riding at least an hour, maybe more. The horse could use a breather. He got down, letting the reins go, letting it wander off a few yards. It stopped, tossed its mane, whipped its tail, and glanced back at him as if to ask Who are you? Where'd you come from? What's your hurry?

Funny, he thought, you run into a strange horse and ride it hell-bent-for-leather into the night—what runs through its head? Owning it, riding it day after day, man and horse got used to one another, took each other for granted; but this business of strange two legs climbing up on strange four legs must mystify. Small wonder most horses didn't just up and run off, back to the wild, to freedom, to no more saddles, no more spurs, no more strange two-legs.

He whistled. The horse, tail to him, wheeled about and came trotting back.

"You're a good fella, you know that? You never made a sound back there, did you?"

Turning his attention to the cinches, he loosened them a notch and was restrapping when he stopped suddenly. A low rumbling sound, came from somewhere out there in the darkness. The Basin at night, even with the moon full, especially so, resembled a giant's graveyard, with tombstones in all shapes and sizes. The sound came closer. It was from the northeast . . . hoofbeats. Finishing up the saddle, he mounted swiftly, swinging left, westward, booting flanks, bolting off.

But whoever it was had spotted him. They took up the chase, got him in their sights and started shooting. He ran a zigzag pattern, which slowed him noticeably but kept away the lead. A half-mile ahead the spine of a seemingly endless stretch of hills thrust itself moonward. If he could reach it, he could lose them.

Lose who? The Greenleafs. Who else would come at him shooting? Who else would know it was him out here? How in the hell had they gotten out so soon? Lead whined by, snapping against the rocks ahead. How? A piece of ice found the nape of his neck and moved slowly down his backbone. There couldn't be another way out. Impossible! They must have blown away the wall. But to be ahead of him at the pace he'd been setting . . . it was unbelievable!

It wasn't them, it couldn't be. Jerking out the Peacemaker, he turned and returned their fire, emptying the gun. Damn, what had ever possessed him to turn down Doc's offer of the Winchester? One of the last things he'd done was hand him back the box of cartridges he'd stuffed into his back pocket earlier.

He was in among the rocks now, the horse nimbly picking its way, the lead continuing to pursue him. A bullet struck a rock alongside him, ricocheted, and hit the horse squarely in the flank, driving it to the left so hard it all but unseated him. Down it went, throwing him off to his left. He hit hard, shoulder first, but luckily squarely into a thick patch of grass. Rolling over, his fingers groping for his gunbelt, he began reloading, then blasted away at the shadowy figures coming at him. Just in time to slow them up and send them hurtling down from their saddles seeking cover.

All four.

"Pink," called a voice he immediately recognized as Ben Greenleaf's, "give it up. We're us four to your one. Hey, Pink, O'Toole, do you hear me? We'll kill you, I promise."

Letting him run on, Raider reloaded again, then answered with a single shot.

"Come and get me, Ben," he called.

"Have it your way."

His horse lay off to one side, motionless, but breathing audibly, a long ways from dead, voicing no pain, more shocked than hurt, he guessed. Whatever its condition, it was useless to him; this was down-on-your belly, man-against-men time. Lousy odds, rotten. If the four of them had the brains of an ore-cart jackass, which at least Ben did, they'd spread out and come at him from 180 degrees. Just the way they'd done it back on the knoll.

Ben, Lydell, Dewey-Blair, and Cousin Raymond.

"Son of a bitch!"

As if his previous thought had been reached aloud, they responded. He couldn't see thanks to the abundance of rocks, but he could hear them scampering to either side.

"Pink? O'Toole?"

"Yeah?"

"What happened to Charley? How'd you get the drop on him?"

"He fell asleep."

"You lie in your goddamn teeth, he'd never . . ."

"You want to shoot it out, or you want to chat?"

He was answered immediately. A volley came spitting at him, the lines of fire now fan-shaped. He flattened out, suddenly wishing he were a crab, able to burrow into sand in six seconds. He still couldn't believe what was happening; not that he needed a slug through the forehead to prove it wasn't all a bad dream. If they didn't know what had happened to Charley, they couldn't have come through the wall. There had to be another way out of the bottle. Possibly even more than one. They'd bragged about what a tremendous hideout it was. It wouldn't have been so tremendous if all it had was one way in, the same way out. No, that type of setup was a mixed blessing at best. But the same setup, with a secret exit to boot . . .

A hat rose on the right, head and shoulders. Bringing up his gun, he fired twice. A roar of pain and a string of curses followed . . . and another volley. He emptied his gun a third time. But they were counting, or at least one of them was. Fumbling, struggling to reload, listening to them moving up, he managed to get five of six cartridges into their chambers and slap home the cylinder, but raising the gun and his eyes to go back at it, he discovered a small black hole staring down at him, the muzzle of Ben's .45.

"You bastard, you hit Cousin Raymond side o' the neck; he's bleeding like a stuck sow. Up on your feet and let's go." Reaching down, he snatched Raider's gun from his hand, jamming it into his belt. "You're only half o' what we're looking for."

18

"How come you and your sidekick didn't stick together?" asked Ben, who managed to stanch Raymond's
bleeding with his neckerchief. He and Raymond were
taking their captive back toward the hideout, Raider was
forced to share Raymond's mount, and could feel Raymond's eyes burning into the back of his neck. It was not
the most pleasant feeling; it stirred suspicion that at any
moment the wounded red-haired one might decide that a
dead Pinkerton was preferable to a captive Pinkerton.
His mind on death, Raider thought of Charley. Wait until
they found him. It promised to be an interesting next few
hours. Anytime now they'd be bumping into Doc. With
his left arm useless, hurting as he was, in any gundown
he'd be about as useful as a wooden chief.

"I asked you a question," said Ben tightly. "How
come?"

"Oh, we had a falling out. We do every now and then.
He goes his way, I go mine."

"So where's he heading?"

"West. Over to the Cascades. He's got family there."

"Is that a fact? You're fulla bullshit tonight, aren't
you? Tonight and every night."

Raider wondered if by some miracle Doc had hurried
Judith just enough to reach the turn and head eastward
toward Cameron. Losing Lydell and Dewey-Blair—Ben
having sent them further north to look for Doc—helped,
but not much. Ben was healthy and Doc was anything
but. And this was the only road worthy of the definition
through this part of the Basin.

Within half an hour it turned out, not unexpectedly,
that Doc had not pushed Judith, not enough. Up she
strolled, the wagon clattering behind, Doc dozing at the

reins. Ben chortled with glee, slapped his thigh, and yelled victoriously—bringing Doc to life.

"Reach high, Doctor," yelled Ben. Up came Doc's right arm.

"I'm hit in the shoulder," he called. "I can't raise my left."

"You fucking raise it or I'll blow it clean off!"

"Hold it!" shouted Raider. "He's telling the bald truth. He got winged. The slug's still in there."

"What'd you do?" asked Raymond from behind, "shoot him when you two had your falling out?"

"Don't be stupid, Raymond," said Ben impatiently. "They didn't have no falling out. How you doing?"

"I'll make it." Raymond growled in disgust. "Shit, I musta lost me a gallon o' blood. Your maw better let me be the one to finish this bastard off when the time comes, else I'm leaving. Fuck Sonoita, I'll damn well head back home to Lubbock!"

Ben laughed. "Relax, cousin, I'll put in a good word for you. Just toss down your iron, Doctor."

Down came the Winchester, clattering to the ground. Raider stifled a sigh of relief. Quick thinking, partner.

"What about the .38?" asked Ben. "Charley had it on him. I know he did, he showed me he'd fixed it. Back just before supper."

Down it came.

"That better be all you're carrying."

"It is."

Ben dismounted to retrieve the weapons, pausing and looking at Raider, then back at Doc.

"Can I lower my arm now?" asked Doc.

"Sure. Let me tell you two something. I hope for your sakes you didn't hurt Charley none. You harm a hair o' that boy's head and Maw'll boil you alive. Charley, he's the apple o' her eye, first in everything, number one . . . Raymond?"

"What?"

"How about riding on back the way we came, catch up with Dewey-Blair and Lydell, and tell 'em we're all wrapped up."

"To hell with that. I feel shitty. All I want is something for the pain, a bandage and some shut-eye. No need to go chasing after them, anyhow. When they don't catch up with him, they'll sure enough turn round and come back."

It was more common sense than Raider would have ever given Raymond credit for. The only one dumber than the Greenleafs' redheaded Lubbock cousin, as far as he'd seen, had to be brother Lydell.

"Turn around and lead us back," said Ben, retrieving the weapons and remounting his horse. He gestured to Doc.

"If you think this night's work is gonna get you anything. Ben, you're outta your head," said Raider.

"Oh, come on, Pink, don't go back into that crap tune o' yours about other operatives on the trail, troops and all after the Adams loot. Don't waste your breath. Just turn it off and ride right up where you are now, where we can keep an eye on you."

"Sure. Just answer one last question. How'd you get out?"

"How do you think?"

"There's a way out through one o' the side stopes?"

Ben laughed. "Something like that. This boy's getting smart, eh, Raymond?"

"Yeah. Real smart for a dead man."

19

Charles Wilbur Carroll, Jr., the apple of his mother's eye, lay in one of the coffins built by his brother, Dewey-Blair, and intended for use by another occupant. Charley's hands were crossed at his chest, and over his mutilated face a damask napkin had been neatly laid. Man-in-coffin lay on his bunk, and on the floor at both head and foot sat candles. Mrs. Greenleaf occupied a rocking chair, rocking furiously, keening loudly. With her behind the closed door was Albertina, all but completely recovered.

She was, Doc had earlier concluded, as strong as a draft horse. Between her mother's wailings, while the older woman refilled her lungs for the next lamentation, the younger whimpered continuously, evidently not needing to take a breath. The two sounds in combination were perfectly awful, mused Doc, listening outside, sitting in the first chair in the row against the other side of the wall in the front room. A kerosene lamp spread an eerie glow about the room.

Raider was outside with Judith and the wagon. Under the eye of Dewey-Blair, who with Lydell had fulfilled Raymond's prophecy and returned to the hideout after searching a few miles north of where the four had taken Raider. Fifteen minutes before Ben and his redheaded cousin with their two prisoners had come back and found Charley's body. Ben had gone absolutely wild, and it was all Raymond could do to keep him from shooting both Raider and Doc.

Raider had been put to work at once clearing the timbers from the entrance to the mine and pulling down what remained of the pile wedged between the rocks to enable the Greenleafs to bring out their wagon.

This, among innumerable other thoughts, muddled

119

Doc's mind as he sat listening to the bereaved in the bunk room behind him. Raymond, under the circumstances unable to get either his aunt or Albertina to tend to his wound, had taken care of it himself. Since he couldn't sleep in the bunkhouse, he had wandered off to the barn. Ben and Lydell stood in the front room, both patently in shock, their faces expressionless. Neither seemed even aware that Doc was sitting there, his derby on his knee.

Doc's rear end ached dully, and his shoulder was on fire. It hurt like hell; the clavical was broken, the trapezius muscle ripped, the brachial plexus nerve parted. At least that's what it felt like to Doc. Any movement, even breathing, seemed to increase the pain. The slug had to come out, the bone had to be set—and soon. As it was, his shoulder would never be the same again, always sore, stiff. He could easily lose the use of his left arm entirely. Unfortunately, his dilemma was the last thing any of the Greenleafs was concerned about. If they chose to ignore Raymond's wound, he could hardly expect them to attend to his. Not that he particularly wanted their ministrations. Given the opportunity, even if Charley were still alive, Mrs. Greenleaf would have spared him no pain digging the slug out. Doc recognized a bloodless human when he saw one; there was something in the eyes, the set of the lips, a built-in indifference to anybody's suffering but her own and her loved ones'. After all, how many mothers did he know who led their brood about the territories robbing people?

"I wish we were outta this place for permanent," said Lydell quietly. "It's starting to get a stink about it makes me sick to my stomach. The stink o' death."

Ben glared. "Shut up."

"I just said."

"I heard. Listen, if you got nothing to do but stand around, how about seeing to bandaging Raymond's neck?"

"Why don't you?"

"Goddamnit, go do it! Lying there in the barn, he's liable to roll over, that wadding against the wound fall off, the wound open up again and bleed him to death in his sleep."

"All right." Lydell yawned and stretched.

"Goddamnit, go do it!" repeated Ben. "There's old sheets in the bottom drawer o' maw's chiffonier. Pad the wound, then maybe you'd best make a sling 'cross his chest." Ben indicated on his own. "Tie it under his arm."

"Okay."

Lydell went into his mother's room, came out with an old sheet, and left. The muffled keening and whimpering let up for a long moment. Doc could hear mumbling. Presently the door opened and Albertina appeared. Her rash had all but vanished, but the departure of the disease did nothing to improve her appearance. Staring at her Doc, decided that she could still lay claim to being the ugliest female child ever brought into the world. Behind her, her mother resumed her keening, her chair rockers grinding away at the floor as she tipped back and forth.

"Ben, Maw says for you to call Lydell and Dewey-Blair and bring the other one here."

"Tell her I got to wait till Lydell comes back from tending to Raymond."

Albertina turned away, then back. "She says go get them now."

"Take that one with you out to the wagon," shrilled Mrs. Greenleaf. "Do as your told, Benjamin, else I'll hide the daylights outta you!"

"Yes, Maw, right away. On your feet, Pink."

Doc winced, reaching for his shoulder as he stood up slowly. Albertina studied him pityingly, then, to his surprise, approached him.

"Does it hurt bad?" she asked solicitously. He almost shrugged, catching himself just in time, then settled for a nod. "I'm awful sorry, Doctor."

"What are you calling him 'Doctor' for?" snapped Ben irritably. "He's no more a doctor than I am."

"He cured me!" She patted Doc's hand. "I am truly sorry. I'll speak to Maw, she knows all about shooting wounds. She'll fix you up proper."

"Yeah," laughed Ben, "she'll fix you up real good. Get moving."

Doc felt shaky—a combination of loss of blood, pain,

and sheer exhaustion—but there seemed little point in complaining to a man whose brother he'd shot. As good as, in Ben's eyes. At that, none of the Greenleafs appeared curious as to which of them had actually done the deed. Obviously, both being Pinkertons, both were guilty.

Doc preceded Ben at gunpoint through the mine out into the open. He stopped short, gaping and gasping at the sight that met his eyes. Dewey-Blair was sitting on the ground, a Winchester, probably the Agency-issue rifle, balanced across his knees. Timbers were scattered about. The stray horse was long gone. Raider was up in the wagon, the canvas cover removed and lying on the ground in a heap. With the bows exposed Raider was busy dropping crates and boxes over the side, working slowly, mechanically.

"Rade, for God's sakes, what are you doing?"

"What in hell do you think he's doing?" asked Dewey-Blair. "He's getting rid o' your junk, making room for our goods."

"You don't have to smash . . ." began Doc.

"Shut up!" snarled Ben, "afore I belt you one."

"Orders are orders," said Raider quietly, pausing to wipe his brow with his neckerchief. "I tried to tell him . . ."

"*You shut up, too!* Just keep dumping that junk. We need that mule and wagon." Walking over to where a number of crates lay, some burst open, Ben began kicking one after another, smashing bottles and pasteboard boxes, scattering them. The wagon was almost emptied; the timbers blocking sight of the Greenleafs' own wagon were still piled high.

"What's up?" Dewey-Blair asked Ben.

"Maw wants us all in the front room."

Dewey-Blair got up, dusting off the seat of his pants. "How's she taking it?"

"Real bad. How are any of us?"

"Ain't that the truth." Dewey-Blair turned to look up at Raider dropping the next-to-last box over the side. "If I told you once, I told you ten times, you don't drop 'em, you throw 'em." Raising the Winchester, he pulled the trigger, sending a shot whizzing by Raider's ear. "Come on down here afore I put one through your face like you did poor Charley."

With the exception of Raymond, tended to by Lydell and drifting back into a fitful sleep according to him, everyone assembled in the front room. The door to the bunk room opened and Albertina and her mother came out. Mrs. Greenleaf looked appalling, her eyes blood red and wild-looking, her face as sallow as a corpse's. To Doc she looked like a lunatic on the verge of an outburst. Understandably, she was taking it hard. What was unfathomable to him was the fact that it was such a shock to her. Why was it people who lived by the gun never seemed to consider that doing so increased the odds in favor of an early death for them and those who shared their activities?

"Close the door, precious."

Albertina obeyed. Ben brought up the other rocking chair for his mother, but she waved it away, without taking her eyes off the Pinkertons.

"You heartless scum, you slimy crawling vermin!" Her lower lip quivered, she sniffled and put on a grief-stricken expression. Ben and Lydell hurried forward to support her as she threatened to fall. She caught herself and pushed them away. "I'm gonna ask you a question, you two are gonna answer it. Truthfully. I want to know which of you killed my boy."

"I did," said Doc tersely.

"He's a goddamn liar!" burst Raider. She slapped him hard across the face.

"How dare you take the Lord's name in vain in front o' my little girl? *I want the truth!*"

Ben cleared his throat. "Maw . . ."

"What?"

"The big one did. I'd bet my life on it. It has to be. Charley's forty-four and the Colt Diamondback are the only two weapons been fired. Charley had the Diamondback inside his shirt; I saw him stick it there." He nodded toward Raider. "That one took his .44. And shot him with it. Shot a man with his own gun, lowest o' the low. . . ."

"I shot him," said Raider.

"You sound proud o' yourself, mister," Maw said venomously, her lips stretched tautly over her teeth, her eyes wild. Doc's glance drifted to the window. The darkness was fading. In less than half an hour the sun would be coming up—the eye of the Great Spirit, the Cheyenne called it. To look upon what?

"You murdered my husband, you murdered my boy," Mrs. Greenleaf went on. "You deserve to die a hundred deaths, each one more painful than the one before. It crushes my heart to know you can only die once." She turned slowly to Doc. "You'll see to it."

"I beg your pardon?"

"Are you deaf and dumb? He'll be stood up against the side o' the barn and from twenty paces off you'll shoot him. Ex-e-cute him. The good Lord above has ordained it; an eye for an eye, a tooth for a tooth. Two lives for two. He comes first." She looked out the window. "I said the good Lord has ordained it and he has, there's your proof. Dawn is for dying. He who lives by the sword dies by the sword. Violence begets violence, murder begets retribution; in keeping with the will o' Almighty God. The sacrifice o' the wicked is an abomination to the Lord; but the prayer of the upright is his delight. Wickedness is the seed and violence the tare, fire and brimstone, death and destruction to them who would offend the eyes o' Jesus. Who will die? Who shall be doomed but the guilty, the miscreant, the murderer? The blood, their hands dripping with it, blood of innocents, blood of godly souls. Listen . . . sssh, this is the hour, this the time of . . ."

"Maw . . ." interrupted Ben, staring at her with anxious eyes.

"Silence! The Lord has spoken; His will be done. The Devil is downcast into the fiery pit and will burn through all eternity. Destruction shall be to the makers of iniquity." She had raised one arm; now she lowered it slowly, her huge eyes blinking, her breath coming in short gasps, her face white.

"Justice, justice . . ."

The silence in the room was an enormous block of ice fitting neatly into it. She was staring at the rug at her feet. And everyone else was staring at her.

"Blue, yellow, rose, purple, lavender, green . . ." She

was pointing out the colors. Ben moved to her, taking her by the shoulders.

"Maw, it's okay. You want to sit down?"

She nodded. Lydell brought up the rocking chair, setting it in front of Raider and Doc. She sat slowly and began rocking, her eyes flicking from one to the other Pinkerton. She touched her forehead with her fingertips, as if trying to remember something.

"Yes, yes. All right, you two, I want the truth. Which of you murdered my boy? Which of you pulled the trigger?"

Ben pointed at Raider. "He did, Maw; killed Paw, killed Charley."

"Lydell, Dewey-Blair." They came to life. "Go inside and fetch your brother. Carry his coffin outside and set it against the side facing the barn, upright, so his dead eyes can see the retribution of the Lord. Justice served."

"Maw . . ." began Dewey-Blair.

"Go do as she says!" rasped Ben. "You help, Lydell. While you're in there, snuff out them candles."

20

The bowl of the sky poured pale gray down upon the knoll, a color befitting the occasion. Raider's hands were tied behind his back as Ben marched him to the barn, stood him against it, and covered his eyes with a blindfold.

"Wake Raymond," called Maw to Ben. With the others, Doc among them, she stood at the front door. The coffin leaned against the side of the shack, the napkin removed from Charley's gory face, the features, except for his mouth, indistinguishable. Maw took pains to keep Albertina back so that from where she was standing she would not see the revolting sight. Raymond came out of the barn with Ben, rubbing his eyes, yawning, stretching his left arm. Lydell had bandaged his wound just as Ben had instructed him. It pained Raymond nonetheless; his grimace betrayed it to Doc. Dewey-Blair handed Doc the Winchester.

"Take your time, Mr. Pink, you can do it with one shot. Even with one arm you can."

Accepting the rifle, Doc tossed it away. "Forget it. I won't do it; nobody's going to make me."

"Don't bet on that, Doctor," said Ben tightly. He drew his gun. "Pick it up."

Doc sighed and picked it up. Ben snatched it from him and shoved his pistol against his belly, cylinder first. Reluctantly, Doc gripped it. Ben then moved around behind him and, levering a shell into position, brought the Winchester's muzzle up, setting it against Doc's neck at an angle.

"Raise up the pistol and take aim. I'm gonna count to three and you're gonna fire. If you don't, I will. I'll splatter your brains all over this knoll. And if you miss him, I'll shoot. You put all six into him."

Doc swallowed; his mouth felt like gun cotton, his throat constricting, closing so tight he could barely breathe. The pain of his wound seemed to dull as his mind riveted his concentration on the agony of the moment.

He couldn't do it; before he pulled the trigger he would die himself. Raider was the last human being on the face of the earth he could kill. They were brothers, closer than brothers. Together they had stared death in the face a hundred times, had saved one another's life time and again. If they wanted him dead, they'd have to kill him themselves. There was no way they could make him do it.

He had brought up the .45 and was staring down its length, finding Raider in the sights, feeling a wave of nausea rise in his stomach. Ben pushed the muzzle harder against his neck. It was ice cold.

"One . . ."

Slowly Doc lowered the pistol.

"Two . . ."

"No!" screamed Albertina. Lunging forward, she pushed Ben away. "He won't do it, can't you see? He won't! You can't kill him . . ." Teetering on one foot, succeeding in keeping his balance, Ben stared, unable to believe she had interfered. She threw her arms around Doc at his chest, hugging him to her protectingly. "You can't, I won't let you. I love him, I love him. Maw, make him stop. Maw, Maw, please, Maw . . ."

Mrs. Greenleaf came forward, her ashen face coloring in embarrassment.

"Now, now, Bertie, precious darling dumpling, you mustn't!"

"Make him stop, Maw." She set her jaw determinedly and glared. She stood with her back to Doc's, her arms behind her holding him protectively. "You shoot him, you got to shoot me, Ben. So there!"

"Maw . . ." said Ben, his tone pleading.

"I mean it!" shrilled Albertina. "I'd rather die than see him killed. I rather, honest. Maw . . . Maw . . ."

Ben and the others began grumbling and flashing dirty looks at Albertina.

"Quiet!" screamed Mrs. Greenleaf, visibly upset. "Everybody shut up. Bertie . . ."

"Cross my heart and hope to die, I won't let you do it. I won't! I won't! I won't!"

"Boys, into the house. You too, Raymond." Mrs. Greenleaf snatched the .45 from Doc and tossed it to Ben.

"But, Maw," he cried, "this ain't right. Albertina, you're just being goddamn foolish!"

His mother slapped him, the sound ringing across the knoll. "Filthy mouth! How dare you use such language in front of your little sister!" Spinning him about, she pushed him toward the door after Lydell, Dewey-Blair, and Raymond, who were already slowly on their way inside.

"I've changed my mind," she said acidly. "You don't shoot him. He's to live. You both do for now." She glanced from Doc to Raider still standing motionless blindfolded, his back to the side of the barn.

Albertina began jumping up and down, clapping her hands, her pigtails swinging. "Oh, Maw, thank you, Maw. Thank you, thank you, thank you. I love you." She threw her arms around her mother's neck and kissed her. Then she kissed Doc.

Mrs. Greenleaf smiled indulgently. "You go inside with the boys, darling precious. We'll be right along."

"But Maw . . ."

"What now, darling dumpling?"

"He's got a bullet wound."

"In the shoulder, I know."

"You got to take the bullet out. You can. Please, Maw."

Mrs. Greenleaf threw Doc a venomous look. His heart sank. The girl was right, *somebody* had to take out the slug, but a knife in the hand of this lunatic . . .

"I'll take it out," said Mrs. Greenleaf.

"Thank you, Maw. You see, Doctor, you're gonna be all right. Maw's gonna take care o' you."

"Oh yes, precious, I'll take care o' him. And his friend, too."

Albertina waved and skipped away, turning at the door, throwing a kiss to her mother and one to Doc. How, he wondered, could she look more revolting with a smile on her face than without one? To Raider's red hell with her looks; suddenly she was a raving beauty, a goddess, Lillie Langtry, Lillian Russell and the Garvey sisters, the most beautiful whores in the West, rolled into one. She'd saved Raider's and his lives—for the time being at least.

Mrs. Greenleaf turned back to him. "Go on down there and undo his wrists and take off his blindfold. Then the two o' you carry my boy's coffin into the barn and set it on a bale."

Doc nodded. He'd manage somehow, one-armed. Somehow it seemed neither the time nor the place to remind the woman that he was wounded.

21

Cousin Raymond was first in line for treatment. His wound, although bloody, had turned out to be much less serious than he had led himself and everybody else to believe. Rebandaged and dismissed by his aunt, he went with Raider out to the mine entrance to overseer the Pinkerton's efforts to removed the timbers concealing the family wagon. Albertina was sent back to bed.

The gray light of dawn filled the front room as Mrs. Greenleaf went to work. Ben, Lydell and Dewey-Blair stood about scowling, still disgruntled by their sister's untimely emulation of Pocahontas.

"Lydell," said Mrs. Greenleaf rolling up her sleeves, "there's a knife on the windowsill over the sink pump. The coals are still hot in the stove. Hold it over them till it turns red, then bring it in here."

Doc sighed. "Mrs. Greenleaf . . ."

"What?"

"Do you happen to have a bottle of spirits lying around? Just a swallow would do, anything . . ."

"Sorry," she said crisply, "I don't abide liquor, don't allow it in my house."

"Then would you have a short stick I could clamp down on?"

"No need. Just clamp your jaws tight together. You can take a little pain, can't you?" She smiled icily. "Benjamin, Dewey-Blair, take off his jacket and vest and shirt."

"That's all right, I'll do it," said Doc.

"You just stand stock-still, if you know what's good for you. Get at it, boys. We can't take all morning for this."

"You could cut it away," said Doc hopefully. "I don't care about the clothes."

"Why ruin a perfectly good jacket and shirt? That

blood'll wash out in cold water. Now stop trying to hold things up. Boys?"

They took off his jacket, vest, and shirt with about as much consideration for his wound as they might have shown to a corpse. In removing his shirt they managed to tear the clotting, so that blood surfaced and coursed down his bare chest in slender rivulets. Maw held a folded napkin against the wound to stanch the flow.

"Sit down in the rocker. One o' you two fetch the broom from the kitchen and slide it under the front rockers. I want him tilted back so's I can work proper."

The broom handle was placed holding the chair angled back. The lamp had been turned out, but at his mother's insistence, Ben relit it and stood beside her holding it so that the light fell on the wound. His scowl, as well as his brother's, had given way to a smirk.

"Lydell, what's keeping you?"

"Coming, Maw."

He appeared in the doorway holding a six-inch knife. Doc suppressed a groan.

"Well, don't just stand there, dimwit, give it here!"

By now sweat was glistening all over Doc as he watched her accept the knife, saw her eyes narrow evilly. He wished to God she hadn't sent Albertina back to bed. Had the girl stayed to watch, though it probably wouldn't have lessened the agony to come, her mother might possibly go in a trifle more gently. His chief worry was that when he passed out, as he had every intention of doing, the woman or one of her sons would impulsively jam the knife into his belly. The mere thought made him wince; he could imagine the blade driving into him.

"Hold still!" snapped Mrs. Greenleaf. Since taking the knife from Lydell a change had come over her. Holding it up to the lamplight, studying it, she seemed fascinated by its sharpness. Doc closed his eyes and fought back a shudder. No, he thought, not that, not now. She had put on quite a performance earlier, putting into words her convoluted logic, misquoting scripture, carrying on like a madwoman. Her face, her eyes, looked now exactly like they had then.

"The sword of the Lord and of Gideon! It shall cut the bonds of the righteous. Gideon be praised, rise up and slay thine enemies. Conquer the Midianites. But beware . . ."

Doc opened his eyes slowly. Her sons were staring at her. Lowering the knife she glared at them and at him. Then she swung out her hand, slicing the air, back and forth, sending all three back one step.

"Careful, Maw," said Ben.

"The Lord comes to judge you, the quick and the dead. Are you ready to be judge? Are you pure of heart? Of spirit? Charles! *Charles!* You come when I call you. . . . Mind your mother!"

"Charley's gone away, Maw," said Dewey-Blair quietly.

Doc swallowed hard and started to get up. Lydell and Dewey-Blair grabbed him, holding him down.

"They're against us, all of them, the unrighteous, the heathen, the Devil and his armies. Be vigilant, wary. Else your lives will be forfeit. Forfeit . . . forfeit . . ."

Her voice trailed off repeating the word. She lowered the knife to her side and lowered her head, staring blankly at the rug. Then she touched her forehead lightly with her fingertips. Ben came up to her, taking hold of her shoulders.

"You okay, Maw?"

She said nothing for a long moment, then barely above a whisper: "Hold him, Lydell, Dewey-Blair. Don't let him move an inch. Hold the lamp up, Benjamin. I need all the light."

She went in. Too hard. Doc yelled; there was no way he could stifle it. Not so much as a blink of her eyes betrayed that she heard him. She had moved the cloth to one side to get at the wound; Lydell pulled it from under her free hand and, holding it by the ends, whipped it into a gag, drawing it over Doc's mouth and pulling it tight.

She was digging for the slug now, probing, finding it with the knife tip and beginning to excavate around it. Doc lifted his eyes to the ceiling. His agony was a fist gripping his entire body, tightening, tightening. The ceiling slowly dissolved into a black cloud shot through with crimson flashes.

He passed out.

22

Raymond angled the Winchester upward at Raider standing atop the timber pile having reduced it to half its original height and pausing to catch his breath.

"Boy, of all the bent pricks I ever come up against in my life, you got to be the one I'd get the most pleasure outta dropping. What do you say you and me have us a little accident?"

"What if your aunt digs into my partner a little too deep?" asked Raider, turning back to his work, picking up a timber and tossing it down to the left side. "And kills him? What'll you do then for hostages?"

"You saying you think I won't pull this trigger? Is that what you think? You want me to? No, you don't. You know if I hit you I'll kill you, just like we done the three . . ." He stopped, clamping his mouth shut. He turned away. "Shit."

"What was that?" asked Raider. "What three?"

"None o' your goddamn business."

"The three fellas who were living inside when you got here? Somebody was. Maybe not working the mine, but living back in the shack. Right?"

"Seriously, how'd you like me to blow your head off?"

"Be patient, you'll get your chance. Ben promised you, remember?"

"How could I forget?"

Raider was tired, too tired to care what fell out of his mouth, up to and including outright insults. Fuck it all, he thought, let him shoot. It was bound to come down to this one day anyway. A man can't go riding up, down, and around the territories gunning after bad people and not expect the worm to turn one day. If he doesn't, he's a damn fool. It was funny, though, how you could get pushed and pushed and pushed until you toppled over the

edge into I-don't-care. He'd asked for this, in the line of
duty to be sure, but asked for it all the same. Doc and he
sure hadn't turned it down. Allan Pinkerton and his sons
and his General Manager Wagner frowned on that sort of
conduct. It was unbecoming an operative, unprofessional.
A Pinkerton had to be half dead or three-quarters out of
his skull to turn down any assignment. Easy cases, snaps,
tough ones, dangerous ones, the hairiest of the hairy,
any operative with the salt in his blood accepted and went
to work. The assignment was his and with it the chance
that he might be signing his own death certificate before
the last entry found its way into the Case Journal, it was
closed and filed, the last photograph taken and stuck
away, the expense sheet argued over with that penny-
pinching son of a Scotsman, and . . . next case.

Raider was so tired he could not prevent himself from
yawning, nor his eyelids from flickering and threatening
to close. The last halfway decent night's sleep he'd had
had been back at Boisé. And the punishment and stren-
uous exertion he'd sure put body and mind through added
to the nervous strain that was promising to exceed his
capacity to withstand the onslaught. All the same, he had
little right to gripe when he thought about Doc and the
ordeal he was being put through at the moment. The
trouble was that the slug *had* to come out. What it boiled
down to was either the old woman killed him or the slug
did.

No, she wouldn't kill him. Not yet. For the same reason
Raymond hesitated to gun Raider down.

He finished unpiling the wood, and Raymond ordered
him to unhitch Judith from his partner's wagon and back
her down one side of the other wagon's pole and, fasten-
ing her reins to it, pull the wagon clear of the rocks. She
did so and was returned to her shafts. The apothecary
wagon had been completely emptied of Doc's merchandise, the canvas bonnet proclaiming "Acme Overland
Apothecary. If you're ill, if you ail, AOA will never fail"
now spread out on the ground on the far side of the opening through the cliffs and the wagon's bows removed.
Obviously the old woman preferred a nondescript look
for Doc's wagon rather than chance running into anyone
who might recognize the advertising on the bonnet on

the long trek south. Her reasons were of small interest to Raider. He was far more concerned with the impending departure. Up to the present his and Doc's luck had been uniformly bad—save for overpowering Charley—completely bad. And even Charley, and getting away as they had, had backfired on them. Thinking about it, Raider had to concede that it was a medium-sized miracle that the two of them are still alive . . . all credit due to Albertina.

"Haul ass, Pinkerton, we're heading back."

Raider shrugged and, entering the mine, started down the passageway, Raymond following, one-handing the rifle.

"Would you mind clearing up one thing for me, Raymond? Which one o' these stopes leads to the secret way out?"

"You just passed it on the left. It opens up big, a natural cavern. It comes out about half a mile up the way."

"No wonder you boys got ahead o' me so easy."

"Want to go back and take a look? You might like it; you might even try to make a run for it. That I'd like."

"I'll pass to the dealer, thanks."

They continued on through to the knoll and the shack, Raider stifling yawn after yawn, doing his best to hide his exhaustion from Raymond, unwilling to give him the opportunity to ridicule him. Entering the shack they came upon a scene that all but froze the marrow in Raider's spine.

Doc was lying in the rocker unconscious, his chin on his chest, his head tilted to one side; he was stripped to the waist. Ben stood over him holding a spider filled with sizzling coals. Resting against the edge of the spider was what appeared to be a stove lid handle, the end of it buried amongst the coals. As Raider looked on in horror, Mrs. Greenleaf, her hands covered with blood, finishing wrapping a rag around the right one, lifted the holder glowing red-hot at the end out of the spider, blew on it, and jammed it against the wound. An ominous hissing, a slender wisp of smoke rising, and the stink of burning flesh. Raider lunged forward.

"For chrissakes, that's enough! Take it away!"

He almost got to her arm to grab it, but Dewey-Blair

and Lydell got hold of him and pushed him back. Mrs. Greenleaf ignored him. Slowly she took away the holder and leaning in close to the wound inspected it.

"That'll do fine."

"Jesus Christ, look what you've done!" snapped Raider. "Burned away half his shoulder . . ."

"Nothing o' the kind," she said mildly, turning to him and dropping the handle back into the skillet. "Ben, take it back to the kitchen. It was a bad wound, deep; it had to be cauterized. Lydell."

"Yes, Maw?"

"Let loose o' him and go and fetch an old sheet outta the bottom drawer o' the chiffonier." Nodding he went into her room.

"We got the wagon out," said Raymond. "Both of 'em are all set to load."

"Good," she said, "we'll get at it. First take this one out to the barn and give him a pick and shovel." She eyed Raider malevolently. "You're to dig my son's grave. It seems fitting."

Ben and Lydell both returned, Lydell coming up to his mother's elbow and grinning broadly.

"Gee, maw, We sure are gonna wind up with a passel o' bodies in that barn."

"Shut your mouth!" He did, his grin vanishing. "Make yourself useful, get a saddle on your horse, and ride on over to the Tilbys and get the four mares. When you get back here, get 'em ready and hitched up. And don't take all day."

She turned back to Raider. "You got no cause to worry 'bout your friend, he'll live. I owed him, that's the only reason I fixed him up. He did well by Bertie, getting her better from the scarlet fever; I did well by him. That makes us even. Get him outta my sight, Raymond."

Doc groaned. She glanced at him, then stooping, searching about the rug, found the slug, picking it up, holding it so everybody could see. It had hit bone and was flattened at an angle like the kepis of the guards at Boisé, reflected Raider, looking back over his shoulder as Raymond shoved him out the door.

They walked toward the barn and moments later, with

Charley's corpse lying in its coffin set on a bale of hay close by, Raider began swinging a pick.

"Not there!" snapped Raymond. Then his expression softened and he laughed. "That spot's already what you might call taken."

"Where then?"

"Over in the corner." He indicated. And shook his head. "Why she wants him buried in here at all I don't know. But I ain't about to question it. Go ahead, get busy."

He left Raider, who immediately sat down on the nearest bale to get off his feet for a minute or so. Doc's shoulder had looked awful, he thought, as if a two-pound shell had plowed its way through. He wouldn't put it past her to deliberately gouge it, work the hole around it four times as big as was necessary to get at the slug, knowing that when he woke up the pain would be excruciating. And the wound would take six days longer to heal. She was right to cauterize it, but the leer of satisfaction on her face, the gleam in her eyes as she did so, gave her away. She was in her glory; she fancied she was branding him, rather than cauterizing him.

He could only hope she had sense enough to bandage it properly, in an ascending spica. It was the only type of bandage he knew that forcibly limited movement. However she bandaged it, for the next four weeks Doc's left arm would be useless, glued to his side like one carved out of wood. It would take at least a month before he'd even know for certain that he'd be able to use it again. And how well was questionable. For the rest of his life he'd know when it was going to rain, that was for sure.

Loosening the dirt with the pick, Raider began digging. It was hard work, the blade striking stone after stone that needed the pick to free them. It took him almost an hour to get down four feet. With a roof over his head, he decided, Charley wouldn't need six.

23

Just before noon the Greenleafs and their hostages set forth, heading southwest for Carlin and Crescent Valley beyond, leaving everything Doc had in the world, including his expensive wardrobe, scattered on the ground outside of the entrance to the New Glory. He lay in the rocking chair in his wagon suffering brutally. He voiced no complaint, but every time a wheel struck a rock or rut and the wagon jounced, however slightly, he would wince and tighten the muscles of his jaw so that Raider marveled his teeth didn't shatter.

Raider had been handed Judith's reins and instructed to stay twenty feet behind the family's wagon, Lydell sharing the driver's seat of the apothecary wagon with him.

Albertina hung over Doc, inundating him with sympathy and affection, the two of them surrounded by household goods stolen from the shack. The two water barrels had been topped off, the contribution of the well behind the barn. The coffin had been lashed to the side of the family's wagon and discretely covered with the canvas bonnet from Doc's rig.

Charles Wilbur Carroll, Jr., had gone under the lid of the other coffin, hammered in place by a tearful Dewey-Blair. Charley was buried with a few words out of Mrs. Greenleaf's Bible intoned by Ben as his mother and Albertina carried on just exactly as Raider expected them to. As the coffin was about to be let down Mrs. Greenleaf threw herself across it screaming: "My boy, my darling boy . . . my first born!"

Her performance made Raider almost as sick to his stomach as the sight of his partner's complexion. Doc looked as if every drop of blood he carried had come out of his wound.

Now, with the hideout well behind them and the sun burning into the ridge of the Independence Mountains to the west, the four-mare wagon picked up the pace and Raider urged Judith to keep step. By the route they were following the Mexican border lay at least 650 miles away. At 30 to 35 miles a day tops, it would take them the better part of three weeks.

They had stopped once in the middle of the afternoon to water the horses and Judith, everyone with the exception of Doc getting down to stretch legs. Ben and Dewey-Blair had double-checked their packing. An hour after sunset Mrs. Greenleaf directed Dewey-Blair at the reins of the lead wagon off the road and into a clearing amid the sagebrush. Within a couple of days, mused Raider, yucca and cacti would begin to replace the sagebrush; the ground would turn sandier and saltier. He did not want to be around to witness this transition. The further they traveled from the Idaho border, the tougher it would be for him to get back, round up help, and return. On second thought, at this stage why bother heading that far north? Why not settle for Cameron? Or anyplace that showed a telegraph pole.

Settle for nothing; he was kidding himself. He couldn't desert Doc, not in his present condition. They'd kill him the way he'd feared they would have killed Judith earlier, out of pure spite. Even Albertina wouldn't be able to save him from her mother's wrath. What a fix! What a goddamn bind!

A prisoner of his rocker, Doc had to be fed. Raider climbed up to do so, with hot beans and cornbread and coffee, while Dewey-Blair set up a small tent for his mother and sister. Albertina had meanwhile deserted her "doctor" to help her mother move their bedclothes inside the tent. Raider took full advantage of the girl's temporary absence from Doc's side.

"How are you making it?" he asked.

"Okay," said Doc softly.

"You sound great. What you need is about six steaks to build your blood supply back up. Goddamn beans and bread aren't worth nothing."

"What are you getting so persnickity about? I'll live."

Doc forced a smile, the moonlight bluing his pallor, lending his face the look of a corpse. "Listen to me . . ."

"What?"

"You've got to get out."

"Forget it."

"I'm serious, Rade."

"Me, too. Don't you think I've thought about it? Do you think there's anything else been on my mind, other than you, since we pulled out? If I leave you, if I get away, they'll put two right through your head."

"What's the difference?" Raider stared, unable to believe his ears. "If you stay we both get it down over the border. If you got away, got help, got back on their trail and caught up with 'em . . ."

"Doc, they'd kill you."

"They wouldn't. You, yes; me, not before Sonoita, not with Albertina around."

"I wouldn't stake my life on that lamebrain."

"I would; she's crazy about me."

"Yeah, and her old lady's crazy period."

Doc sighed in exasperation. Raider listened reluctantly while he voiced appeal to reason. Just the thought of leaving him, deserting him, gave Raider a feeling in the pit of his stomach akin to that inspired by swallowing rotten meat. He hated even discussing it; but in his heart he knew that Doc was right. And finally he came around to agreeing.

"Don't try it tonight," cautioned Doc.

"Why not tonight?"

"They'll be looking for it. Nor tomorrow night. Maybe the next. In the meantime hang around me, fuss over me every chance you get. You know, make it look like a herd of oxen couldn't tear you away."

"Friends to the end." Raider groaned wearily.

"Something like that. What's the matter, doesn't being nice to me appeal to you?"

"It's not that, it's the whole shootin' match. Every bucket we pick up, the bottom drops out. Shit, we're here now because that damn Diamondback conked out on me. And you and that shoulder; Doc, he shot you with your own gun!"

"And you shot him with his, what was rightfully his. His relative's up near Pearl."

"Pink!" It was Ben standing with his mother and sister. He gestured to Raider. "Cut the conspiring and get on down here."

"Not tonight," whispered Doc, "not tomorrow; the next night. I'll be starting to get my strength back by then, too."

"You hear me?"

"Coming." Raider got down and walked over to Ben. Mrs. Greenleaf eyed him.

"If you think you're gonna skin outta here, you'd best think again," she said.

Raymond came up smirking. "Ben, remember what you promised when we was bringing him back?"

Ben nodded. "Raymond figures on account O'Toole shot him, he should be the one to do him in."

Mrs. Greenleaf shook her head emphatically. "I'm sorry, Raymond."

The redhead's red face fell. "Geez . . ."

"No. It has to be one o' the immediate family. We're the ones been injured and deprived by this vermin, not you Clapps. With Charles gone to join his daddy in Abraham's bosom, Lydell becomes the oldest. It'll be his pleasure."

"I'll sell you my pleasure for five dollars," said Lydell grinning, coming up to them.

"You will do no such thing, you dimwit!"

"I was only funnin', Maw."

"You don't fun about cold-blooded murder."

Taking it all in, Raider groaned quietly. Maybe hanging around until the night after the next dovetailed with Doc's logic, but it promised to be a long forty-eight hours. Had he his druthers, even with them looking for him to get out, he would chance it tonight.

They settled down for the night, Raider was bound and bedded down between Dewey-Blair and Lydell. The horses and Judith were hobbled about fifty feet away under the shadow of a rise of a couple of hundred feet well covered with vegetation. Raider slept. He was awakened what seemed half the night later by a shrill voice, a very familiar voice. He and both Dewey-Blair and Lydell. It was Mrs. Greenleaf. She was walking slowly in a circle around the dying campfire. Flinging her arms out, tossing her head and haranguing the moon.

". . . the wicked know who they are. Deliver me, O God, out of their hands, out of the hand of the unrighteous and cruel man. Hear me, hear me. I have cleansed my heart in vain, and washed my hands in innocency. And yet am I made to suffer."

She stopped, lowered her arms, and stared at Dewey-Blair, up on one elbow watching her aghast.

"Maw . . ."

Ben woke. Getting to his feet, he started toward her, reaching out for her. But her glance was fixed on Dewey-Blair.

"Charles, get up. We've waited long enough for Daddy. Saddle up, ride into town, find him, and fetch him back here."

"Maw, I can't . . ."

She bristled, striding up to him, planting her fists on her hips. "You dare to disobey your mother?"

"He's Dewey-Blair, Maw," said Ben, "not Charley."

"Don't contradict me, Benjamin Carroll!" She whirled to face him. "One more word and I'll hide you within an inch o' your life. Where's my stick? Where?"

She twisted about searching. Raider watched in silence. Doc was right, as if he needed convincing; she was over the edge. Doc was lucky she hadn't jammed the knife into his heart. All three sons were grouped around her now, quietly pleading with her.

"O God, O God, O God, why cast us off forever? Why doth thine anger smoke against the sheep of thy pasture? He disobeys me, God, my boy, my Charles Wilbur. Punish him, show him thy wrath as I show my own. You'll pay for this, all of you. Just you wait till your daddy gets back!"

She continued to rant and rave, threatening, then lowering her voice to a mumble, abandoning her scriptural mumbo-jumbo in favor of insults, berating each one in turn. Albertina woke, emerging from the tent sniffling, the tears rolling down her puffy cheeks. The place was becoming bedlam, everybody talking at once, nobody listening. Raider glanced at the apothecary wagon; Doc's head and shoulders were silhouetted against the sky. He appeared to be asleep, though how he managed that when nobody else was able to was beyond Raider.

The men finally got the woman calmed down and pulled back to reality. Everyone went back to sleep.

24

The next two days passed without incident. In spite of the rigors of the journey, Doc was fast improving, able to quit his rocker and take his turn at the reins alongside Lydell. His color began coming back and his strength and spirit. There was little to be gained by concealing his recovery, playing invalid; Raider was the one who planned to leave. Unfortunately the Greenleafs continued to bind him, wrists and ankles, before bedding him down for the night between Lydell and Dewey-Blair. But on the morning of the third day Doc succeeded in passing him the pocketknife, dropping it into the breast pocket of his shirt. Before being tied up that night, Raider planned to conceal the knife in his mouth.

Even securely tied he had managed to catch up on his sleep, so this was to be it; when the moon was high and the night halfway to morning he would make his break for it. A full gun, a mount to bareback, and luck would be all he'd need. They wouldn't dare send only one man to chase him, not knowing he was armed. And they could hardly spare two, not in this God-forsaken part of the country, not without assurance as to just how long they'd be chasing.

But the best-laid plans are frequently upset by events beyond the control of the planners. Moving along in the late afternoon under the shadow of the Shoshone Mountains the Greenleafs and their "guests" ran into trouble. It came at them preceded by a dense cloud of dust rolling over the alkali flats.

"Company," said Doc, up on the seat alongside Lydell, Judith's reins in hand.

"It's the goddamn law!" snapped Lydell. "Pull over, you, and climb down."

The wagon ahead had already stopped, Ben and

144

Dewey-Blair getting down, hauling out their rifles. Standing on the seat, Mrs. Greenleaf took charge, waving her arms and yelling instructions.

"Take cover, boys, you too, Pinkertons. Get him down, Lydell."

"What about you, Maw?" asked Ben.

"Do as I tell you. Albertina . . ."

"Maw, what's gonna happen? Maw? Doctor? Mawwww?" She had been sitting in Doc's rocker, singing to herself and browsing through a picture book. Her eyes were round with fear and her thumb deserted her mouth as she appealed to her mother for explanation.

"Hush, precious," said Mrs. Greenleaf. "Nothing to fret over. Take cover, boys . . . move! Albertina, stir your stumps, climb up on the seat like a good girl and take those reins like you been driving all along."

"Maw . . ."

"Do it, Goddamnit!" Mrs. Greenleaf hesitated until certain that her commands were being obeyed, then turned about and sat down. Her sons and Raymond, Raider, and Doc meanwhile had bellied down in a dusty gully about thirty yards away to the left and slightly ahead of the wagons.

It was not the law. No such luck, reflected Raider dourly. Out of the boiling billowing cloud came Indians. Shoshones, fifteen of them. Raider's heart dropped two inches in his chest. No hunting party this; a party of a different sort. Their faces were striped with war paint and their ponies war-bridled, a single length of rope with two half hitches in the middle tightened around each animal's lower jaw rather than looped around its nose with the single rein running back to its rider. The Shoshones carried lances and Raider counted eleven Henrys, lever-action repeaters, "the rifle you load on Sunday and fire all week," in William Pinkerton's words. Sixteen shots to the clip.

They came barreling up, shaking Nevada, dragging their dust behind, short-legged, dark-skinned little men in antelope hides, their belts festooned with scalp locks and ermine, their headdresses eagle quills.

"Some rough-looking bunch," murmured Ben, sidling up alongside Lydell. "We shouldn'ta left Maw and Albertina out there."

"Maw said to," Dewey-Blair reminded him.

"Who they after, Ben?" asked Lydell.

"How the hell should I know? Maybe Sioux?"

"More likely Cheyenne down around here," said Raider evenly.

"Oh? You know that for a fact?" asked Ben in a mortally offended tone. "You're smart as the doctor, aren't you, Pink? You just got that God-awful habit o' outsmarting yourself. Okay, boys, get ready to let 'em have it. When I give you . . ."

"Hold it, hold it for chrissakes!" burst Raider. "That's your mother and sister out there. They got you three to one. Maybe you can knock out a few, even half, but the rest'll massacre you—and take the women."

"What do we do?" asked Dewey-Blair.

Ben erupted. "What in hell you asking him for? He's our goddamn prisoner, he ain't in charge. I'm givin' the orders!"

"So give," said Raymond quietly.

"Why don't you parley with them?" inquired Doc evenly, deliberately setting himself up as a target for another outburst—in preference to a bullet through the head and the loss of his scalp after the fact.

"He's right," said Raider. He glanced at Doc, who, for some unfathomable reason, appeared amused by the Indians' appearance and the Greenleafs' inability to deal with it.

"What in hell are they doing off the reservation?" asked Lydell.

"Ask 'em, dimwit!" bellowed Ben. "Shit. . . . All right, let's get back up there and parlay. Maybe all they're lookin' for is ribbons and stuff."

Raider clucked softly and rolled his eyes at the sky. By the time the six of them had returned to the wagons the Indians had taken over, climbing up the sides, picking through the loads. Their leader, identified by his war bonnet as a subchief, rode up to Raider and the others. He was as stumpy and bandy-legged as any of his men, chicken-chested, a dried-up piece of rawhide of a man, but his face clearly betrayed an arrogance, a hewn-rock determination, that had to shake the confidence of anybody he confronted.

"Mancha-wa-keemo-wa."

"What's he say?" asked Ben of Raider.

"How should I know?"

Ben sneered. "You pretend you know everything else."

Unable to get a response, the subchief gave up talking in favor of sign language. Raider knew a little sign language. The subchief knelt and traced a ripple in the sand.

"He says they're Snakes," said Raider.

"What are they doing down from Idaho?" asked Ben.

Raider ignored the question, his attention glued to the Indian's hands. Much of the rest of what he had to sign was obvious. He wanted arms and ammunition; he wanted all their mounts. He would leave them the mares and Judith.

"That's damn big o' him," rasped Ben.

"Bennnnnn . . ." It was Albertina from the apothecary wagon seat. Two Indians had climbed into the back and opened her trunk. They were arguing over a calico dress, jerking it back and forth between them.

Ben spat, cursed, and whipped his rifle around, planting it against the subchief's midsection. Not a trace of reaction, not even a wink indicated that he even felt the metal touch his flesh.

"Easy, man," said Raider, backing off two steps. "I wouldn't do that if I were you."

"You ain't me. Tell him to tell his braves to leave our stuff be and get down. Pronto!" Ben tilted his rifle, bringing the muzzle upward against the soft flesh under the Indian's jaw.

There was no need to tell anybody anything. Seeing the rifle aimed at their leader the Shoshones got down from the wagons of their own accord, the two annoying Albertina dropping her dress and joining the others.

"Eee-cheebe-wa-na. Calla-apodeyah!" barked the subchief.

Every brave recovered his pony, climbed on, and stood fixed in place awaiting further orders.

"Kotaba . . ."

Off they rode.

"Yippy yay!" Lydell whipped off his hat and tossed it high.

"Hot damn, it worked!" burst Ben gleefully, lowering his rifle.

Raider stared at him. "It worked your ass; they'll be back."

"They come back here, I'll blow his head off."

"They'll still come back," said Doc.

Dewey-Blair edged forward, studying the Indian's face, his own seized with curiosity. "What are you gonna do with him, Ben?"

"What, Ben?" asked Doc.

"You shut up, Pink. I just might plug you and keep him for a hostage."

"You're kidding yourself," said Raider. "Look at his eyes; in his head he's making his peace with the Great Spirit. He's ready to die. You shoot him, you'll make him a hero. His people will heap great honors on him."

"Nobody's ready to die," said Ben scoffingly.

Raider shook his head. "No white man, but every Indian. They're always ready."

"Fuck all this bullshit. Lydell . . ."

"Yeah, Ben?"

"Put him up in your wagon with the Pinks. Albertina can ride up in the lead wagon with Maw. Keep your forty-five on this red bastard. You, Doctor, just drive. And both o' you pay no attention to anything goes on. Dewey . . ."

"What?"

"Tie his horse to the tailgate of the Pink's wagon. Lydell, keep your eyes peeled back o' your head. The first sign o' dust coming up behind, stand him up and put your gun to his head so's all his braves can see clear."

"You're outta your mind!" snapped Raider.

Ben's right caught him full in the side of the head, knocking him down.

"Get up and shut up like I told you afore. Let's go."

25

It was becoming a circus; all they needed were elephants and candy, mused Raider, they already had the clowns and the ugliest female in the world. The Shoshones did not follow. He would have been amazed if they had. Instead they circled back, climbed into the mountains, and raced on ahead.

"I can't see nobody up there," said Lydell, "but I can feel their eyes."

Raider and Doc scanned the ridge. There was no sign of life in among the piñon and juniper. But the dimwit was right, they were up there. If they ran true to form, they would follow their leader's captors until sundown; then, when they stopped for the night, they would circle the camp and come in screaming and shooting. He called up to Ben on the seat between his mother and sister in the lead wagon.

"He's speaking the plain truth, Ben. They got their eye on us."

Ben retorted without turning his head, without even a quick glance up at the ridge. "I don't see nothing up there but trees."

"Have it your way," said Doc, "for now. But come sunset you can bet they're going to have it their way."

"Let 'em come," said Lydell, unexpectedly imbued with a sudden burst of confidence. "We can take 'em."

Raider and Doc exchanged looks, both shaking their heads. Being killed because of the stupidity of others was not a particularly inviting way to go. The Shoshones may have been off the reservation, out of their territory, but like any Indians they had the talent for turning wherever they happened to be into familiar ground when the occasion demanded. Along with their Henrys and lances, they carried knives and tomahawks. And anger. Eyes and skins full of it, even before Ben had taken their leader. Raider guessed that they weren't out after anybody, Cheyenne, Sioux, or white-eyed troublemakers, but that they were running from some action, a more powerful adversary. Why else wander this far down into Nevada from the Snake River?

Their reasons for being there weren't important; the fact that they were, that Ben had stupidly grabbed their number one, and that they were spoiling for a massacre were all that counted. Their mouths must be watering over Raymond's red-thatched scalp.

Raider had seen a massacre years back in the Big Horn country, Crows against settlers. Down behind a creosote bush playing dead with an arrow in his ribs, he'd watched a kicked-in-their-bellies brave slice away most of a man's face, with one swipe of his Spontoon tomahawk. Charley's face, gore from ear to ear, had brought back memory of the Crow-killed man.

This bunch would kill him and Doc and the rest of the men, and likely Mrs. Greenleaf, who would raise such a ruckus one of them would fill her big mouth with lance. Ugly as she was, they'd nevertheless spare Albertina . . . for a time. They'd run her up into the hills, gang-fuck her until she threatened to split, then open her throat.

In the old days they would have taken her back to the tribe to work as a slave. This they couldn't get away with at Duck Valley. If, that was, they had anything to do with the reservation. A lot of die-hard Indians of every tribe shunned the white man's corral, even at this late date.

He considered the other side of the ledger; if indeed they had just come from an action they would likely be low on cartridges, maybe even tapped out completely. Not that that would lessen the danger to any degree. What they had left to fight with would only bring them in closer. There was only one way he could think of to keep them at bay. Find a natural fortification of some kind and sit up all night with hands wrapped around guns cocked and ready to blast.

Between Doc and himself they had Doc's penknife. When the shooting started they'd be helpless. They'd never be able to grab horses and run, or weapons. What they would be called upon to do would be to walk away without the Greenleafs spotting them through the attackers. The obvious uncomfortable fact of the matter was if they both didn't at least try to get out, the chances had to be fifty to one either would ever see another sunrise.

Raider's eyes drifted back up the mountainside to the top. The trees were thick, solid green cover. Even 200 feet up into them they'd have a good leg on escape, if Doc could make it. Up, up, and over the top, down the other side to the Reese River, cut north, and maybe make it up to Battle Mountain.

"What are you thinking about?" Doc asked Rade.

Lydell could not tear his eyes away from the mountains, but this didn't prevent him from interrupting. "He's thinking when they come at us you and him can make a break for it."

Raymond was sitting behind them near the tailgate. He turned and grinned. "I sure would like to see you try."

"What are your mother and sister gonna do?" asked Raider. "How are you gonna protect 'em when they come whooping up?"

"Don't you worry none about that." Lydell still was unable to tear his eyes away. "Ben's sitting up ahead there figuring it all out. He knows what he's doing."

"He knows shit!" Raider scoffed. "He's gonna get us all killed, faster than hell if he kills that subchief."

"We'll see," said Lydell mildly.

"Oh, hell yes, we'll see all right!"

Doc turned in the seat and caught Raider's eye. "Take it easy."

Raider ignored him. "Lydell, you too, Raymond. When the shooting starts you've got to give us guns. With us helping maybe we can hold 'em off, even beat 'em. There's a good chance . . ."

Raymond laughed. "You crazy in the head? We hand you iron and you'll give back lead. We're not stupid, you know."

"Assholes."

"Partner," said Doc, "calm down."

"Yeah, yeah, yeah . . ."

Doc winked and tapped his temple. Lydell, still studying the mountains anxious-eyed, and Raymond, looking back the way they had come for signs of the Shoshone, failed to notice. Raider caught his partner's sign and stopped bitching. But dredging his mind he couldn't figure a way in the world of wriggling out of this one.

Shortly before sundown, the sun actually long out of sight behind the mountains to their right, the shadows as thick as wool, the sky pale pink, they came upon a mass of boulders, rubble shed by the mountains millenniums ago. Ben led them over to the site, finding a low-lying ledge under which both wagons were parked. A lucky find, reflected Raider. Dug in, armed, and with plenty of ammunition, the three Greenleafs and Raymond could hold off triple fifteen Shoshones.

Ben was delighted with his find, climbing down all smiles, his nervousness vanished and with it his nastiness toward two of his three prisoners.

"We'll eat cold tonight," he announced. "No point in giving away our position with a fire."

Raider laughed. "You got to be kidding, you still think they're not watching us?"

"They are, Ben," said Lydell, "I can feel their eyes, honest."

"Let 'em watch. Even a redskin's got more sense than to attack these rocks."

"And are you planning on staying here?" asked Doc.

"If they don't come at us here, they'll come at us when we pull out!" sputtered Lydell.

"Oh, shut your dimwit mouth! I'm fed up with your bellyachin'."

"Hold your tongues, both o' you," interposed Mrs. Greenleaf, as Dewey-Blair helped her down. She pointed to the largest boulder. "Albertina, precious, you and I will stay ahind there. Boys, bring all your guns and all your ammunition to me. I'll divide what we got evenly among you."

Ben nodded at the subchief who stood motionless staring into space.

"What about him, Maw?"

Mrs. Greenleaf thought a moment. "Sit him out front of our rock where they can get a good look at him. After you gather wood and we build the cooking fire, you build a second fire alongside him."

"I don't think . . ." began Ben.

"Oh, hush up, Benjamin. The Pinkerton's right, they see us. No sense goin' without a fire. We'd likely freeze afore sunup."

"You're plumb right, Maw," said Lydell.

Ben muttered something and glared at him, then at Raider who couldn't resist grinning.

"You're making friends at a great rate," commented Doc in a low voice. "First the red-haired one, now your cellmate."

As the second hour ran its course and the world whirled forward and night settled over it like a velvet cloth over a crystal ball, the waiting gradually became pure torture. Both Pinkertons had long since given up any further efforts to persuade Maw and Ben of the wisdom of arming them. The woman was as bullheaded as her son. No one slept, no one dared to. As the night wore on it seemed to Raider to stretch itself to twice the length of the night between the Pulford farm and sunup beside the Bruneau River. The subchief, bound and set out by a small fire in front of the boulder concealing Mrs. Greenleaf and Albertina, did not budge for seven solid hours. Raider checked him out of the corner of one red eye every now and then. He seemed to have stopped breathing; he didn't even blink.

The sun came up over the Utah border flooding the Basin with ghostly whiteness, a curiously heatless sun, more like another planet shining with reflected light. And the Shoshones attacked, blazing away, lead ricocheting off the boulders, pinging loudly. Raider and Doc went flat and stayed that way, Doc moving with unaccustomed agility.

"That thing must be healing nicely," commented Raider.

"It's sore, but not bad, something like a week-old horse kick." Raising his head, Doc threw an anxious look in Judith's direction. The shooting, the war whoops, didn't appear to disturb her, not nearly as much as they did the wide-eyed horses, who whinnied and clopped about nervously in their hobbles. Ben could shoot and Raymond wasn't bad, wound and all. But Lydell and Dewey-

Blair were no great shakes. The latter, Raider quickly decided, was an outright waste of lead. Ben agreed.

"For chrissakes, aim afore you shoot!" he roared.

"I am, I am."

"Benjamin, mind your foul tongue!" shrilled his mother.

Jesus, thought Raider, *what a cast-iron bitch!*

The Greenleafs had plenty of ammunition; not so their attackers. Within minutes the Shoshones' firepower slackened off. The braves semicircling them out front all but quit entirely while the rest of their party, hidden in the trees overhead, angling their fire downward, were reduced to a shot or two every thirty seconds. Raider saw three Shoshones out front yell, jump, fall on their war paint, and die. Or pretend to. The third one was just hitting the ground when a shot from above plowed through the brim of Ben's hat, striking the rock he was crouching behind and whining away at an angle. Cursing, he finished reloading his rifle and, to Raider and Doc's astonishment, brought it up and pulled a shot cleanly through the subchief's temple. It shattered his skull in its skin and slammed him over like a ninepin, dead before his shoulder hit. Before either Pinkerton could react, a shot from high up caught Dewey-Blair full in the brisket. Albertina screamed, her mother echoed her, and together they scrambled to him. It was, Raider could see, a bad hit. First estimate out of the box he would give him fifteen minutes to bleed to death internally. Ten, if the women were stupid enough to pick him up to bring him under the protection of the ledge, where everybody should have been from shot one.

The Shoshones, though, seemed not in the least concerned with Dewey-Blair. Their leader's murder right before their eyes roused them to a blue frenzy; down from the trees and over the flat they came, dodging the Greenleafs' lead, taking hits that slowed but failed to stop them, coming with knives and tomahawks, and lances flying, clattering harmlessly off the boulders, falling short, one only reaching Raymond. It hit him in his wound, of all places, taking away shirt and bandage and scab, releasing a freshet of blood and setting him howling.

Ben and Lydell ignored him and Dewey-Blair, keeping up a steady fire, picking off the braves so close now that even Lydell couldn't miss. And dropping them like fence posts in a tornado, sending the two or three survivors coming down the mountain running back up for their lives.

All quiet. Except for Albertina's labored puling over Dewey-Blair.

"Benjamin!" Mrs. Greenleaf came staggering up wild-eyed, snatching a fistful of his shirtsleeve. "He's hurt bad." As quickly as she grabbed him she let go, searching about, finding Doc and hurrying up to him. "Real bad. You got to save him. I can't, it's in too deep."

Doc shook his head. "I'm sorry, Mrs. Greenleaf, I can't do anything either. I'm not a surgeon."

"Do something!"

"Even if I were, I don't have any instruments, I . . ."

"Benjamin! Get on your horse and ride. Get a doctor. Hurry!"

Ben protested. "But Maw, he's spitting up blood, he's . . ."

"Do as you're told!"

Ben heaved a great and tolerant sigh and turned to Raider. "What's closest?"

Raider pondered. "Stiles. Up the line about twenty miles." He pointed directly north.

Ben nodded and turned to Lydell, who came scrambling up.

"We done it, Ben, licked 'em proper. I knew we could."

"Shut up and listen. You keep your eyes on these two. If either of 'em tries anything, kill 'em both. I don't mean scare 'em, I mean shoot to kill. You, Doctor, get at Raymond and tend to him. Maw's too worked up to." Lydell started off. Ben's eyes wavered back and forth between Raider and Doc on his way to Raymond in the rear, closest to the trees. "Hold it, Lydell, I changed my mind. You ride up on to Stiles, I'll stay and watch these two. Make it fast. Ride like you never rode afore."

Lydell nodded, holstered his pistol, and ran to saddle his horse. Seconds later he came barreling by, whacking away at the animal's flank with his hat.

"Yippy yay! Yippy yay!"

156 J. D. HARDIN

Dewey-Blair coughed. Blood showed at the corner of his mouth and trickled slowly down his chin. Raider's glance wandered to the ledge, under it the family wagon with the second coffin slung to the side under its canvas. Dewey-Blair had built it. He, it appeared, was destined to sleep in it.

Doc stood behind Raymond. The redheaded one's neck where it joined his shoulder was a mass of raw, bleeding flesh. It looked as if somebody had gone to work on it with a knife. It had to be extremely painful, decided Raider, looking on. Raymond's face was contorted with pain. Doc ripped away what was left of his shirt, washed off the wound with drinking water from one of the barrels, and dressed it as best he could. He was almost done, fixing another sling across Raymond's chest designed to hold the pad in place when his patient broke into the semblance of a grin, all he could muster of one.

"You standing behind me like you are, you could reach down easy quiet-like and whip my gun clean outta my holster."

Ben flashed him a dirty look. "Cover up, damnit!"

Raymond dirty-looked him back. "Take it easy, Ben, it ain't reloaded."

"I appreciate your letting me know," said Doc.

Raymond's smile dropped into a frown. "You go to hell."

"You're most welcome, I'm sure," said Doc. "Somebody's got to tie this knot. I can't use my left hand."

"Albertina!" snapped Mrs. Greenleaf.

The girl, hanging over Dewey-Blair whining disgustingly, straightened up and still whining went to Raymond and began tying the knot. Mrs. Greenleaf held Dewey-Blair in her arms, patting his cheek, wiping the blood trickling from the corner of his mouth with the hem of her dress and babbling to him in an undertone. His eyes were taking on a glazed look as the life drained slowly out of him. Raider studied him; he was fighting for it, giving it everything he had left, but anyone could see that he was dying. Anyone but his mother.

Everybody, the Pinkertons included, stood or sat watching him, patently fascinated by the sight of life giving way to death, the transition gradual but clearly going on. His stomach had to be filling up with blood. He coughed and coughed again; now a mouthful of blood was spilling over his lower lip crimsoning his chin down to the dimple in the center of it, plopping drop after drop onto his mother's arm supporting him across the chest, keeping him from falling to his right. He sat staring into space, his eyes slowly filling with death, submerging his pupils. He didn't appear to be breathing, noticed Raider. His breath was so slight as to be imperceptible, like the way the subchief had breathed, effortlessly. The Indian now lay in the dust in front of the boulders, a red splotch the size of a silver dollar staining his temple, his eyes enormous, staring sightlessly up at the sun. Beyond him lay six of his men.

The rattle of death escaped Dewey-Blair's throat, his eyes brimmed with it, and he seemed to sink back into himself. His mother paid no attention to the signs, keeping up her muttering, comforting him, assuring him that a doctor was on the way. But Ben saw. He moved slowly over to his mother, gently gripping her arm still across the dead man's chest, pulling it back.

"It's no use, Maw, he's dead, bless his soul."

She stood up with surprising quickness, scowling at him ferociously. "He's not. He's sleeping. Can't you see? Are you stupid?"

Bending over, Ben closed Dewey-Blair's eyes. The body did not fall; it just sat there, the blood no longer issuing from the mouth, the chest sunken, the hands laid out beside the legs palms up, fingers slightly curled. Raider had never seen a deader man in all his years.

"I tell you he's dead, Maw! *Dead!*"

"Liar!" She slapped him; he recoiled, his free hand flying to his cheek. "You dare lie to your mother. He's alive. Lydell will bring the doctor back and he'll get the bullet out and make him well. Now shut your mouth."

"He's dead, Maw," persisted Ben, tears flooding his eyes. "Face it, you got to. We all got to."

"Ben . . ." called Albertina, standing alongside Doc off to one side of Raymond. "You musn't say that. It's mean. He's not dead, he's just sleeping. Maw knows, don't you, Maw? Dewey-Blair's asleep, isn't he? Maw? Maw? He is. Ben, honest he is. . . ."

"Albertina," began Ben, then sighed and gave it up. Raider couldn't take his eyes from him, didn't dare to. A change seemed to be coming over the man; it was almost as if he were aging a year every ten seconds, his face darkening as the fire of fury built itself up in his brain. His whole world was gradually crumbling and, realizing it, recognizing how helpless he was to prevent it, to restore his mother's sanity, his brothers' lives, his frustration was threatening to overwhelm him.

"This does it," he said hollowly, to no one in particular, or perhaps to the fates ganging up on him, pushing him into a tight corner. "There's gonna be a little change in the plan." He glared at Raider, then at Doc. "This, every bit of it, is on account you two interfered. Daddy, Charley, Dewey-Blair, Raymond there, even Maw. You made her addled; she never woulda started takin' on so if you hadn'ta showed up. We'da been long gone just the way we planned. But you two come snooping, sticking your noses into our business, giving us fits, delaying us, wrecking everything. We coulda been there by now, free as birds, no harm to nobody, just gone. To never come back; wipe the slate clean. You bastards, I'm gonna fix you, the two o' you. I been achin' all over to ever since we nailed you. We don't need you for hostages; we need you dead!"

Swinging his Winchester around, he levered a cartridge into the chamber, aimed at Doc, and fired. But levering and aiming took time enough for Albertina to spring into action. She had saved Doc's life once, she would save it again.

Flinging herself in front of him she screamed in protest. The bullet caught her below and between the shoulderblades, plowing into her heart.

"Noooo . . . " she wailed.

She sank limply to the ground. Dead.

Maw shrieked and hurled herself at Ben, pounding him with her fists, his rifle clattering to the ground as he tried to hold her off. Raider and Doc needed no second invitation. Both broke for the trees, Raider sprinting by the girl's body and the injured Raymond, grabbing Doc by his good arm and pulling him along. Mrs. Greenleaf was screaming hysterically, Ben yelling back, Raymond roaring.

"They're gettin' away, Ben. Ben! Ben!"

Raider could hear Raymond break his .45 and begin to reload, but they had reached the piñon pine by now and every step further up the mountainside put more trees between their backs and their captors' lead. It came, wild shots gouging tree trunks, scarring them.

"Faster, Doc. Just a little further. They can't see us."

Doc was puffing, his face as red as Raymond's, struggling to pull one leg up after the other.

"Easy, Rade, slow down."

"We can't!"

"We have to. If I don't, I'll pass out." Doc was fighting for breath like a winded horse, his chest heaving, lungs burning. He looked wobbly to Raider; he let go of his arm and slipping behind him, pushed him forward. Below them the yelling persisted, both Ben and Raymond shooting blindly. Doc sank to the ground.

"Give me a minute, Rade," he panted.

"Just a little further. They'll be coming up after us; we got to . . ." He paused. "Listen . . ."

The shooting and the men's yelling had stopped. But not Mrs. Greenleaf's. She continued to carry on uncontrollably. There was no sound, however, of anyone climbing up after them, no whipping branches, no loose stones dislodged and rolling back down.

Raider let Doc rest, then helped him to his feet, and they climbed higher.

"Where are we heading?" Doc asked.

"Let's talk about it."

"Stiles?"

"What for? Think about it, Doc, they haven't got us anymore, we got them. They're stuck, at least till Lydell gets back. And the way she's carrying on down there, Ben and Raymond won't be able to do anything with her for hours. Besides which they got bodies to bury."

"Albertina saved my life again, Rade."

"She saved both our lives." Raider shook his head. "This one has to be the craziest, most screwed-up assignment we've ever had. Bar none. I swear that whole brood is nuts, not just the mother."

"We still have to figure out the next move. We've no guns, no food, no horses. Judith's down there, and my wagon..."

"Judith's okay, let's not get started around that circle. She's..."

He stopped short, freezing; something was stirring in the trees above them.

"What is it?" whispered Doc.

"How the hell do I know?" Raider resumed the climb, pushing branches out of his way as the woods thickened. Ten steps up he pushed two branches left and right and came upon a pony tethered to a branch. "Doc!"

"What?"

"It's a Shoshone pony. Come on up."

Doc joined him, breaking into a broad beaming smile. "Her owner must have been killed."

"No kidding!"

"She can't be the only one up here; there's probably half a dozen."

"We only need one more, for you."

"This one's automatically yours, is that it?"

"Doc, take a look at yourself. You couldn't ride six miles in your condition." He snapped his fingers. "I got an idea. We don't want to lose what's left o' that bunch down there, but we still need help, right? At least arms and ammunition."

"Never mind the warmup, spit it out."

"We find another mount, sure, but you stick here."

"You mean just plump myself down in these woods and wait? For what, a toadstool to spring up under me?"

"When they pull out, you follow them. Meanwhile, I'll take this little girl on ahead."

"Where?"

"South, southeast now. Where else? They still got to be heading down. They're moving southwest now, they should be veering off to the southeast anytime. Down to Las Vegas, likely, to pick up the Colorado River, cross into California, then into Mexico."

"Sonoita."

"Maybe not, not now with us getting away. Better Mexicali or Tacate, even Tijuana."

"So now we're into a guessing game."

"No, damnit, not if you keep 'em in sight. Stay here, I'll find you a pony."

He did, in short order, a fine, feisty little *grulla* mare, all mane and muscle and wondered out loud why the surviving Shoshones had neglected to take all the mounts when they'd fled. But who could say why an Indian did or didn't do anything?

"Where exactly will you head?" asked Doc. "Straight for Las Vegas?"

"Sure, down on the Gallinas. If I'm right they'll be passing either through there or close by. They got to, it just makes sense, Doc."

"I don't know. They haven't made anything like sense up to now."

"They got to take the shortest route."

"How far is Las Vegas from here?"

"No stone's throw, you can bet. Maybe two hundred and fifty." He turned to rebridling the pony, removing its war bridle and halter bridling it around the neck and nose so that a vigorous jerk of the rein would cut its wind and bring it to a halt.

Mrs. Greenleaf was still performing below. Doc clapped Raider on the arm.

"Take care of yourself. Whatever you do, steer clear of any Indians. If they were to spot you . . ."

"I know, riding a pony. They'd figure I'd bushwhacked the rightful owner. I doubt I'll run into any on the way down. I'll be too far west for the Paiutes, maybe way down the Chemehuevi or the Cahuilla, but they're both peaceful sorts, nothing like these boys up here." They shook hands. "You sure you're okay now, not dizzy or anything?"

"I'm fine," said Doc. "As soon as you reach Las Vegas, contact William up in Denver. If we can get help coming down we'll be in good shape. When you're done, what'll you do, ride back up? Yes, that would make sense, it'd get us back together. Then, in case we don't get any help down here in time, we can make a try at stopping them."

"I could maybe get the law in Las Vegas to help us. Though if you stop to think about it there's just the two left and Raymond. He's not in the best o' shape. I'll get us some guns after I wire Denver."

"What do you plan to use for money?"

"I still got my operative's card in my boot. Willy can wire me what I need. Christ Almighty, if he won't do that much I'll wire him collect that we quit!"

"Don't, Rade, you're hitting a nerve."

Raider eyed him suspiciously. "You thinking about packing it in after this?"

"Yes and no. You and I are getting a trifle old for this fast a pace."

"We're neither one of us close to forty yet."

"Sometimes I feel twice that. You know, like now. I mean, how many times do you have to be shot before one shot hits a vital spot and good-bye?"

"We'll talk about it after we wrap things up, okay?"

Raider mounted the dun-colored pony, waved once, and charged up the mountain. Doc stiffened, half expecting gunfire from below at the noise of the horse climbing. But evidently Ben and Raymond had their hands so full of Mrs. Greenleaf they hadn't heard a sound.

Looping the *grulla*'s rope around the nearest limb, Doc crept stealthily back down to the concealment of a fairly large piñon. Bellying flat, he peered through an opening in the bushes. By angling his head left and right he could take in most of the open area to the left of the overhang. No one was back under it. Ben was still trying to calm his mother down and looked to be making some progress. It was either that or she was running out of breath. Raymond was up on his feet, grimacing with pain, staring down first at Albertina lying on her side, her dead eyes staring, then at Dewey-Blair. Had the girl's eyes been closed she would have looked as if she were asleep, so comfortable was her position.

Hoofbeats sounded back the way they had come. Lydell and the doctor? But only one horse . . . As it clopped into view, Ben deserted his mother, who had sunk down on her knees, and ran to it yelling to Raymond. Slung over the horse's back and tied on, wrists to ankles, was Lydell. Dead. The top of his head was a mass of red pulp, his brain protruding. Doc whistled softly and turned his eyes from the grisly sight. The three Shoshone survivors had fled the field, but had evidently stayed close enough to keep an eye on the family. That they might do so had never occurred to Ben. Or to Doc himself or Raider, he mused. No doubt because there had been so much else going on claiming everyone's attention.

No more "yippy yays" for Lydell. And now there were three. Three to bury three. The moment Ben ran out to catch his brother's horse, Raymond started for Mrs. Greenleaf, moving as fast as he could, suffering as he was, but reaching her too late to keep her from raising her head and seeing Lydell. For a long moment she apparently failed to realize who it was, unable as she was to see his face. When it dawned on her she shrieked once, the sound slicing up Doc's spine to his hackles, all but raising them straight up. Then she collapsed, covering her face and sobbing loudly.

Crabbing to his right Doc got up and went back up to the *grulla*, patting it fondly, as he wished he might Judith.

"Patience, little girl," he said to the pony. "It's going to be awhile before they move out."

27

Raider descended the mountain about two miles up from the scene of the carnage, coming down and picking up the Reese River where it wound its way through the Shoshone Mountains down onto the flat between them and the range of hills to the east leading into the Big Smoky Valley. If he was right, once the family began moving again, Ben would steer them southeast across the valley near Alkali Flat toward the Monitor Range.

He worried about Doc; his partner had no shortage of guts, but he was not in the best of shape. The short climb up the mountain confirmed that. Less than 200 feet, he himself could have climbed it backward without working up a decent sweat. But of course he'd had practice.

Funny, though, Doc telling him he'd hit a nerve when he'd tossed off his threat to quit the Agency if Willy Pinkerton failed to send him any money. Funny because there had been times lately when the thought of quitting had found refuge in a corner of his own mind. It wasn't the money. A job like this one, if it was money a man was after Allan Pinkerton couldn't come close to paying him enough. Couldn't and wouldn't, the tight-fisted bastard. So what was it that kept the two of them hanging onto their cards, catching every assignment Wagner and the old man tossed their way, absorbing the briefing and riding out. The thrill of the chase?

"Shit!"

What then? What else was there? For him there was Doc. In their four years together they had become as tight as two fingers, closer than friends, closer even than brothers. Bound together by something more than necessity, more than conscientious dedication to duty. Neither one had ever given that much thought to what too often happens to him who chooses to live by the gun. You think about that and you don't set foot out the door!

What? Who could say? Who cared? He knew in his heart he himself would never quit, no matter how hairy it got. Oh, he'd threatened to, more times than he could recollect, but it was always voiced in anger, just hot air. Doc the same. The two of them'd get discouraged, disgusted, fed up to the teeth with the old man's General Principles, the red tape, the haggling over expenses, and a dozen other built-in irritations. But what would either of them do if they did get out? What could they possibly find out here to equal all the juicy good things carrying an operative's card ensured? Strictly speaking, they were their own bosses, the freedom, the moving around, the new faces, new places, even the uncertainty had its value. But more than all these things there was the towering satisfaction that came with wrapping up a case. Part relief, to be sure, but mostly satisfaction. Tying up the strings and handing the package to Wagner. Tying up this one would make him feel twenty feet tall, pleased as parson's punch with himself. Doc the same way. In an instant, in that moment when both realized that it was all over, all the aches, all the pain, all the regrets and black memories would wash away in one huge wave of gratification. Maybe that was the core of the allure.

Very soon after coming down the mountain he pulled over to the Reese and watered the mare. She drank eagerly. Twice he had to pull her back to let what she'd swallowed settle a bit to keep her from getting cramps.

On he rode into the afternoon, getting hungry, wondering what he would do for dinner. Mrs. Greenleaf's beans heated up in one of those blue enameled pans and some of her bread or biscuits would do just fine. Funny how her crazy streak didn't seem to interfere with her cooking ability.

He rode into sundown, the mare perfectly willing to run and he to let her. She seemed tireless, her endurance phenomenal. In part he could thank the Shoshone who had broken her. The Indians were as hard on their ponies as they were on each other, not to mention their white foes. He was skirting Alkali Flat, midway through the valley, bringing closer Kawichk Peak rising nearly ten thousand feet into the purple sky, when the horse began to slow.

And brought her right forehoof straight down into a hole, pulling her down, smashing her neck against the ground and flinging Raider head over heels. For the second time in less than a week he was tossed lucky. Rising shakily to his knees and feeling for broken bones, he sighed deep with relief at finding none.

He heard a plaintive whinnying behind him. She was not as fortunate; her neck was badly wrenched, her right foreleg broken in two places, at the fetlock and higher up in the middle of the shank. Again she whinnied, looking up at him with her soulful eyes, pleading for help.

"Son of a bitch. Son of a bitch!"

Ripping off his Stetson, he flung it to the ground and kicked it fifteen feet through the air. She was in agony. He'd have to put her out of her misery. He couldn't, not looking down into those eyes. He'd shot a horse in such a circumstance before, back on the farm in Arkansas. He'd only been sixteen or seventeen at the time, but every so often he'd see its eyes again in a bad dream. And wake up suddenly, feeling rotten all over, reaching for a bottle if there happened to be one handy.

He did not have the luxury of a gun this time. Again he glanced down. Tears were rolling out of her eyes, spilling down over her muzzle.

"Sweet Jesus Christ!"

He cast about looking for a rock. There was none, not that he could see. Nothing but alkali and sandy soil as dry as old bones. He fanned his pockets, touched his breast pocket, felt the penknife, and took it out.

What a way to do it, he thought wearily, what a stinking cruel way. Maybe not; once her strength began ebbing away she'd begin to feel drowsy and gradually just float off into death. But why deep-think it? What choice did he have?

Kneeling, he patted her muzzle and spoke softly to her, reassuringly. But she was in too much pain to care. Rising, moving down her, he opened the little knife and bending over her belly, plunged it home, drawing it straight toward him, slicing the snakelike pulsating vein, releasing a rooster tail of blood.

28

It was like waiting for a stage that would never come, reflected Doc, sitting on the ground listening to the family carry on below. He had gone down to his window in the bushes twice since Lydell had come back minus his scalp. Mrs. Greenleaf gave no sign of letting up, but Ben and Raymond were rapidly running out of patience. Ben yelled at her, a slight tone of hysteria in his voice, as if he were catching it from her.

"We're not digging three graves, you hear me? Christ Almighty, we'll be stuck here all week!"

"We can dig 'em real shallow and mound 'em over," suggested Raymond.

"Get at it!" snapped Ben. "Nobody's stopping you."

"You could help, you know. They're all three closer to you than me."

"Fuck it! I say stick 'em back o' the ledge and just pile dirt and rocks on 'em. Look at this ground, will you? It's all over hard pan."

"We got the pick."

"So get busy!"

"Have a heart, Ben, I can't swing a pick with one arm. I'll dig, but you'll have to . . ."

"All right, all right."

"What about the redskin? What about all his dead?"

"Let 'em be where they lay, all of 'em. They won't start stinkin' till we're long gone."

Doc crept back down a third time. Mrs. Greenleaf was sitting on the ground, staring at her fingers, her face a disaster. She was muttering to herself, going off to the moon again, he thought. He shook his head; another hellfire sermon in gibberish coming up. Ben, too, looked to be losing hold, stalking about wild-eyed, ranting, glaring at

Raymond, who of the three appeared most in control of himself.

It couldn't happen to three nicer folks, mused Doc. He did feel sorry for the girl. She hadn't done either him or Raider any harm. On the contrary. She may have been jug-ugly, as intelligent as a rock, and imbued with all the per-sonality of a cactus, but now she was dead. At seventeen. Although what sort of life would she have had to look for-ward to in the company of her mother and brother? Not a very promising one. But to be dead at seventeen . . . Ben's conscience must be chewing him into bits. It was, it had to be.

It was getting dark out, and he was getting hungry. As was the little black *grulla*. Hungry and probably thirsty. From where he lay Doc could not see Judith, the wagons having been moved out from under the ledge to make room for the bodies. She was down there, all the same, out of sight with the family's horses down the way.

His thoughts flashed back to the hideout and a vision of his wares and belongings scattered about the grass by the mine. He'd bet every dollar he'd ever earned that his suits and canes and imported shoes would never make it on any expense voucher traveling under Allan Pinker-ton's eyes. The man never paid more than nine dollars for a suit in his life! Doc shook his head disgustedly and dis-missed all thought of his loss. The possibility of losing Judith was of considerably more importance.

Ride, Rade, like you've never ridden before, he thought; if lightning luck so long overdue them struck, they could stop the family and wind things up right here.

It was at least a twenty-mile trudge back to the ledge and the manmade mayhem centered there, maybe twenty-five. Much of it back to the Reese and cool water down his dusty throat. Sitting down, Raider took off his boots and his socks, turning the latter inside out to let them dry for a few minutes on the hot ground. He turned to mas-saging his feet. At first grip, back came a trace of the sore-ness inflicted by his long march over the Boisé Range to the Pulford farm. The prospect of another such test of en-durance all but sent a shudder up his spine. Turning his head, he looked at the pony for the first time since he'd cut her. The ground around her was black with blood and she lay still, dead. He glanced down the way toward Kawichk Peak rising, piercing the oncoming darkness. He would walk most of the night, through the chill and the ponderous silence of this empty bowl full of desolation, gain the Reese, and there catch an hour or two of sleep before completing his trek.

No. That wouldn't work. There'd be no sleeping tonight. He couldn't take the chance that the two wagons might roll right by him as he lay snoring. Jesus, he was tired though; every bone, every muscle cried out for relief, for rest. But there'd be none this night, nor anything, not even Boisé Range blueberries to appease his growling stomach.

Turning his socks rightside out, he put them on and his boots, his Pinkerton National Detective Agency operative's card #312 falling out onto the ground. He picked it up and eyed it briefly, then restored it to his left boot, putting both on. Getting up he started off. Maybe he wouldn't have to hike all the way back. By now they could be heading toward him, rattling along, leaving their dead in their wake, Doc trailing, one eye on Judith, the other on the brood.

He despised walking; up on a horse he felt comfortable. He could eat and sleep, do anything but piss, shit, and fuck up on a horse's back. His hand-tooled Middleton boots were built for stirrups, not for shanks mare. All the same, he had to be honest with himself, he couldn't assume he would meet the Greenleafs and Doc halfway. His partner was counting on his reaching Las Vegas; he had to get back to him, let him know that his horse had broken down and that Las Vegas and everything that went with it had to be shelved for the time being. This Doc had to know, his own strategy was dependent on it. Then too, back up the mountain overlooking the ledge and Camp Carnage there could easily be a third horse left behind by the fleeing Shoshones.

He walked the granite-hard ground until his feet began to swell, until his toes ached so it felt as if they would break away from their joints. His heels and soles felt like they were being probed by hot irons, the pain shooting up through them. And still he walked, until one more step threatened to topple him flat on his face. He plumped down hard and rested, taking off boots and socks and gingerly kneading his feet. No wonder people lost in the desert wound up crawling on all fours! Fifteen minutes passed, moving the moon chasing the earth, and he redressed his feet, stuffing them into his boots with some difficulty.

And resumed walking.

29

Doc slept lying flat at the opening, nodding, dropping off, to be awakened just before sunup by shouting drifting up from below. He lit up his last Old Virginia cheroot, drawing on it hungrily, sighting down its length, wishing it were edible, and watching fascinated as Raymond and Ben, necks bowed, jugulars jutting, faces two inches apart and both crimson, strained their lungs at each other. Mrs. Greenleaf was still sitting against her boulder, masked with madness, her hair unbound and hanging down straight making her look like some kind of hellhag come up out of the sea. She was mumbling to herself, studying her fingers, completely disregarding son and nephew. None of the bodies had been buried, although the bonnet from the apothecary wagon used to cover the coffin had been removed and now covered Albertina.

"Goddamn!" roared Raymond, "Can't you see I'm hurtin' terible bad! I can't swing no pick, I can't shovel, I can't hardly stand!"

"These corpses got to be buried! We can't go and leave em' like this! It ain't Christian, it ain't right. . . ."

"I know, I know, but I can't help it!" Raymond stood holding a shovel, his shoulder sagging awkwardly. He was suffering and speedily losing all patience with Ben, his reproaches and his persisting failure to recognize the realities of the situation.

He finally flung the shovel aside and started off.

"Where do you think you're goin'?"

"I'm leavin'."

"You can't!"

"The hell I can't! Who's gonna stop me? I say fuck the loot, fuck Mexico. I just want out. I'm headin' home."

"No you don't! You ain't leavin' me out here on the rim

o' nowheres with her like she is. Look at her, for chrissakes, she's bustin' up completely!"

"So are you, and me too." He check reined his anger,
his voice softening. "I'm sorry, Ben, I am, purely, but she's
your worry, not mine. I ain't direct kin to neither o' you."

"She's your blood aunt, you bastard!"

"Don't you call me bastard."

"You called me crazy."

"I didn't no such thing!"

"You did! Good as did. I don't like that, Raymond. Nobody calls me crazy. You can cuss me out, you can get mad
as a pinched hornet at me, but you don't call me crazy."

"Oh, for chrissakes, shut up!"

"I'm sayin' you don't!"

"I'm leavin', that's all there is to it!"

He flung out a hand dismissing the whole scene and
stalked off out of Doc's sight.

"Come back here. I mean it, Raymond. You hear?
You can't leave, I won't let you! *Raymond!*"

But Raymond was through talking; riding was all he
cared about, up on his horse and on his way back to Lubbock. Shed all this. Doc could hardly blame him. But Ben
did. Quaking with fury, his eyes bugging, he watched
him leave. Seething, calling after him and getting no response, he went wild, cursing vilely. Then, whirling
about, he snatched up his Winchester and fired twice.
Doc swallowed. Unbelievable! Incredible!

"Good morning, Benjamin," said his mother pleas-
antly, the noise of the shots apparently jarring her into
temporary sanity. "Did you sleep good?"

"Yeah. Maw . . ." He crossed to where she sat, leaning
the smoking rifle against the boulder and stooping, taking
hold of her shoulders. "Listen, Maw, listen real close.
We're not goin' on. It's too far, we'd never make it. We got
to turn around and head back. You need a doctor, Maw;
you're sick, you need help. There's that home over to
Reno on the Verdi River. They take care o' folks like you.
But first we'll head back, back to your bedroom, your
stove, everything, all the stuff you liked we had to leave
behind. We'll rest up a spell and see how you feel then, if
we still got to, we'll head west for Reno."

"Reno? Why Reno?"

"Aw, Maw . . . it just makes sense. Trust me. Now, you just sit here while I get us ready to pull out. We'll have a bite o' breakfast, I'll tie the jenny onto the tailgate of our rig, let her trail along behind with the other wagon. It ain't far, just three days and we'll be home."

Doc died a little. Beautiful! This was all he needed. With Raider on his way to Las Vegas, no doubt riding like the wind, there was no way in the world to contact him, except chase after him. Which would be insane. He'd never catch up, not with a fifty- or sixty-mile lead.

The alternative was just as unacceptable, but there seemed no way to avoid it. He'd have to follow mother and son back to the New Glory. And take them on the way, providing he could get his hands on some kind of gun to go up against Ben's arsenal. Take them on the way or back at the hideout. Better there, where they'd be removed from any possible interference, like uninvited Shoshones. Then, too, he'd be stuck with her; he'd have to take care of her until help arrived.

Ben made a fire and presently the mingled odors of bacon and coffee came wafting up to where Doc lay. He grumbled. The heartless bastard! He discarded the cheroot stub and pinched his nostrils to keep from smelling the delicious odors, almost tempted to jump to his feet and charge back down, knock Ben flat, and cram his face with everything edible in sight. He watched him try to feed her. She showed little interest in eating or in anything else, her mind slipping its traces once more, drifting away into the realm of make-believe.

"When Daddy comes back with Charles he'll be bringing money, my dears, lots and lots o' greenbacks. We're going to leave this place, we're going south to Utah, maybe to Salt Lake City. I've always wanted to live in Salt Lake City. You'll love it there. It's so beautiful. We'll have our own home at last, a big white house with a shingle roof, green shutters and lacy curtains. With a picket fence all around, and a yard for you to play in. There'll be trees and flowers too, all kinds, the prettiest flowers that grow. And we'll all be together, Daddy and Charles, Benjamin, Dewey-Blair, Lydell, and baby. Dear little dumpling darling, mother's precious. Come, precious, we'll have a tea party with your dolly. Laugh and clap your hands, twirl and twirl, my precious. When Daddy comes back with Charles he'll draw you a picture. And he'll bring money, children, lots of money. We're going to move, you see, down to Utah. . . ."

The sun cleared the mountains to the east tinting the valley gold, brightening the piñon and junipers' greens, sending rails of light down through the trees, one falling on the pony's flank setting it gleaming like polished onyx.

Ben checked over each wagon's load, hitched up the four mares and Judith, tied her to his tailgate with the rope he'd used for Raider's wrists and ankles at night, and having transferred the rocking chair from the apothecary wagon to the family's wagon, helped his mother up into it. Then he collected all the weapons and ammunition belonging to the dead, disregarding the Indians' empty Henrys. Lastly he strung Raymond's, Lydell's, Dewey-Blair's, and his own horse to the end of the apothecary wagon. Climbing up onto his seat, he swung the mares hard left and started back the way they had come.

Doc let him get half a mile away before venturing down to the site. He took the subchief's knife and two of the Henrys and, returning to his mount, began following the little caravan paralleling its progress, sticking to the slope and its cover—and replanning every step of the way. If he pushed his horse, he could beat Ben back by a day and a half. If he didn't push, he could still afford to detour to Stiles, trade the Henrys for a hot meal and some feed for the pony, maybe even a weapon, and still get to the New Glory before the wagons. And set up an ambush.

Riding with his back to the south, continuing to parallel the wagon road, he examined other options. He never looked back; he had no reason to. What was there to see? Only the corpses warming in the sun, the litter, the ashes of the cooking fire, and the black dot coming ever so slowly up the valley.

Ten minutes from the camp he deserted the slope in favor of the valley, reaching it and staying well behind the Greenleafs. If the Shoshones who had caught Lydell and returned him dead were still lingering in the area, he wanted to be able to see them at some distance before they saw him.

30

Raider made it to the ledge, pulling his way around Mrs. Greenleaf's boulder and sitting down hard. Glancing about he began counting . . . six, seven, eight, nine, ten, eleven corpses. No sign of Doc's, thank God. Nor the mother's or Ben's. Out front past the dead Shoshones he could see on the ground where the wagons had been turned around and headed back. To the hideout? Could be. Resting for a while, he then pulled off his boots with some difficulty and got up. He had no feeling in his feet, nothing but numbness, a million soft needles piercing just below each ankle. He'd never get his boots back on. Not today, maybe not tomorrow, maybe never. He felt constrained to sneak a peek down to assure himself that his feet had not swollen up and blown themselves to bits, or been sucked up into his legs.

There was no point in wasting steps checking the corpses; it wouldn't help him, it wouldn't help them. But there, on the ground not three feet away lay a slice of bread two-thirds the size of a dinner plate. One bite had been taken out of it. Snatching it up, shaking Nevada off it, he began picking little pieces and popping them into his mouth. Two pieces, three, then losing control, wadding the slice into a lump and cramming it into his mouth, biting, chomping briefly, and gulping it down. It had to be the most delicious bread he'd ever tasted! Whoever had taken the bite and discarded it had to be crazy.

Lifting his eyes, he surveyed the mountains. Somewhere up there under the foliage stood another pony. There had to be at least one. Leaving his boots by the still-warm fire, he started up the slope. The grass underfoot had give to it, unlike the Alkali Flat and the valley floor. He noticed a spot in passing where the grass had been trampled down in a circle about six feet across. At

175

an opening in the bushes. Peering through it, he got a good view of the deserted camp below. Further up he recognized the tree where Doc and he had tethered the ponies they'd found. Standing leaning against it to catch his breath and wipe the sweat from his forehead, he whistled. And listened. Nothing, save the soft murmur of the passing breeze. He whistled again, louder, facing south, facing west up the slope, then north. And listened. The whinny was barely audible, as if coming from a mile distant, muffled on its way by the trees and bushes.

He found the pony. It was a miserable-looking sheep of a mount, with legs like Sturges' churns, four inches of hair sticking out all over its body, a mane and tail that hadn't even been finger-combed since the day it was foaled, all tangled and matted, and wearing a face that compared unfavorably with the front of a locomotive.

"Pony, you are the most beautiful four-legs on the face of this earth."

It showed a belly full of grass, most of it green, decided Raider, studying the chewed-up ground. It had to be thirsty, but more than half a bucket of water spilled down its craw and it would blow up like a damn Pennsylvania lard hog.

He rode it back down to the camp, carefully. No broken shank for this one. He was still hungry and so beat-to-boots that if he didn't watch himself he'd sure enough doze off in the saddle somewhere between here and sundown and take a third header. Somehow, using just the right number of curses to intimidate them, he got his boots back on.

He picked up a couple of the Henrys and a knife that would make a Boker Tree Brand straight razor look dull by comparison.

Casting a last look around, sighting nothing else worth scrounging, he mounted his miserable-looking mustang and climbed back up the slope. He was still famished; the bread had been delicious, but a whole loaf would have been more like it. In the woods there had to be something worth the picking, there almost always was, even out in this desolation, blueberries, purslane for the seeds, maybe even breadroot, sweet like turnip, even unwashed as it would have to be unless he held out until he reached Pine Creek.

He wondered how Doc would work it. Follow them, get ahead of them at night? Stop at the first settlement and get a wire off to Willy Pinkerton? Raider fervently hoped his partner wouldn't attempt to take Ben without help. His, preferably.

He could cut away to Stiles and barter the Henrys for something substantial to fill him. But hungry though he was, food had to be secondary to a weapon; twin pearl-handled .44s would go nicely with the knife. Any hand gun would be better than collecting ammunition for the Henrys.

He rode on, dodging branches, concentrating on the plant life, listening to the juices noise about in his belly. He estimated he'd covered at least two miles with only half a handful of blueberries off a dying bush to show for it when the pony broke into a clearing. In the center was a dead fire. Two lances lay beside it. On the far side of the clearing stood two war-bridled *grullas*. Between them was a stumpy little Shoshone with skin the color of tobacco juice and not a tooth in his face. Blood stained the front of his hide apron, and tied to the cartridge belt around his waist was a fresh scalp. His right hand went for the holster by his hip, jerking out the .45, two-handing it, cocking. . . .

31

Doc elected to bypass Stiles, and when darkness fell and the Greenleafs pulled over for the night he rode wide around them and straight on toward Carlin. He could not possibly make it in one try; it would be too far for him and the pony. He loathed riding, especially bareback. Already the old aches were beginning to come back to life. By the time he reached the New Glory he'd be in marvelous shape.

Maybe, he thought, he should turn back and try to catch Ben by surprise. Possibly steal his rifle, unless he slept with it the way Raider did when necessary, buried shallow in the sand with just enough muzzle showing to grip, lying on top of it. He put aside the temptation; what it came down to actually was that he simply wasn't prepared for any confrontation. Better to get them back to the shack, the perfect layout for an ambush. If he slept a few hours he could probably make Carlin by midmorning, eat, arm himself, wire for help. It all seemed so routine. Why was it that it never turned out that way?

One undeniable fact hovered like a buzzard around the edge of his plans, the awareness that with Raider out of the picture and Denver better than 600 miles away east of Utah, even if he struck it rich and got a promise of help from someplace within a hundred-mile radius of the hideout, it still wouldn't reach him in time. Or rather he couldn't assume that it would. It all came down to the buzzard; like it or not, he'd have to wrap it up alone. A shrewd, wary, capable, and desperate man and his lunatic mother. Take him, kill him if it came down to that, but at all costs keep her from harm. Somebody had to survive to reveal the whereabouts of the silver. Was that a fact? Not really. Where else could it be but in their wagon, more than likely hidden someplace in the bed. Or the jockey box.

Still he had no driving ambition to kill either one; he wouldn't go in that direction unless there was no way to avoid it. There'd already been far too much killing—wanton slaughter described it better.

He was too hungry to sleep anything but fitfully. The sight of the pony casually munching grass set his mouth watering. He did regret running out of Old Virginias. A smoke would at least occupy his taste buds, until it raised his appetite one more notch.

He dragged into Carlin just before noon looking sorrier in the window of the barber shop than he had ever seen himself. His derby was caked with dust, his one-armed shirt and vest—the jacket to his suit long gone—and trousers so dusty the plaid was practically obscured. He could not understand why his hunger persisted, now that he had swallowed at least four pounds of the Big Smoky Valley and two of Crescent Valley beyond it.

First he would rid himself of the antique Henrys. The .44 bore had no use for 30-30s. Unfortunately it developed that nobody in Carlin seemed to have any use for the rifles.

The squat little scalper of Lydell Greenleaf committed two minor mistakes that together gave Raider time to react. The Shoshone wasted one second bringing his free left hand up to two-hand the pistol. And another holding off cocking until he had. Raider used this lapse as sagely as his instincts allowed, ducking behind his pony Comanche-style and in the same motion pulling the knife and letting it fly. It missed by a good two feet, but sight of it coming in his direction was enough to distract the Shoshone and move him one step to the right. Twisting his body, Raider slammed sideways against him, knocking him flat. The .45 squirted out of his hands, winding up in the bushes ten feet away. Both leaped for it; the Shoshone got it. Raider got him, by the wrist, hammering the ground with it.

But he wouldn't let go. He was a little more than half Raider's height and weight, but he was rawhide strong, not an ounce of whiskey fat on him. It was like trying to collect a spring jumping out of its housing, twisting, turning, whipping every which way. Raider finally got him around the chest, bear-hugging him, the two of them rolling a circle around the dead fire, the Shoshone's face mashed against Raider's throat.

Suddenly he felt warmth and wetness and a gripping sensation; the bastard had taken chew hold of his throat, biting hard, hurting like a son of a bitch! Raider roared pain. Toothless though the bastard may have been, his goddamn gums felt like a sprung trap!

Raider let go, reaching up between them and pushing as hard as he could to get through to his throat. Failing to, he hauled back his left smacking the Indian in the side of the head. He hung on. *Christ Jesus fuck,* he was gonna rip out his fucking, goddamn throat, apple and all! All but passing out from the pain, Raider tried one more play, certain it would be his last; straightening his index finger, he jammed it hard into the brave's ear.

He let go howling, grabbing his head with both hands, rolling about, kicking wildly. Blood spurted from his ear and at sight of it he howled louder. Raider threw himself by him, grabbing the gun, breaking it.

Empty! Up on his knees he raised it butt high and hammered the Shoshone silent. Before he hit the ground Raider was down on his knees at his cartridge belt.

"Ogaba!"

Still on his knees, he turned into sight of the other two Shoshones standing on the far side of the circle, their Henrys raised and aimed straight at him. He cursed and started to let go of the .45, then suddenly caught himself. Ten to one neither Henry was loaded, he thought. Ten to one. Great odds, almost as good as those against the man across the table trying to one-card two pair into a full house.

But that was poker, not life and death.

Ten to one.

They stood as motionless as two gate posts, the muzzles of their weapons two inches apart resembling empty eyesockets staring.

Ten to one. Fuck it!

Turning away from them he popped one cartridge from the unconscious man's belt, jammed it into a chamber, closed up and jumped to his feet. Leveling the gun at them.

They dropped theirs. Turning away from them, loading, and jumping up had consumed all of five seconds; five times Raider had winced as both Henrys boomed, firing straight at him. Five times he'd felt his whole side cave in; five times his heart had stopped; five times he'd died roaring. . . .

He sighed, his heart revolving in his chest, turning back over and settling into position.

"I will never do that again if I live to be ninety," he muttered to the world. "Okay, friends, back off."

They didn't understand. They understood the .45, though. He motioned with it and they backed off.

"Chi-mawga," said one.

"Shut up." Kneeling, he unbuckled the belt from around the unconscious man's waist and, clutching it close, laid it over his pony's back. Then moving behind the pony, never taking his eyes off the two, he laid the pistol down pointed at them and strapped the belt on. Searching briefly in the bushes he found the knife he'd thrown and jammed it along with the loser's knife into his belt. The two Henrys he'd been carrying which he'd let go of at first sight of the Indian still lay where he'd dropped them. Let 'em lay, he thought, the .45 was all he really needed. The Henrys would be dead weight, but the knives he could barter for food in Stiles, someplace.

It was clear to him now why the Indians had left the ponies tied in the woods above the camp. To carry their dead away after the wagons had moved out.

He mounted the pony. The two Shoshones still stood staring at him, their eyes brimming with hate. The other one groaned and stirred slightly.

"Serves you right, you son of a bitch," grumbled Raider, touching his injured throat cautiously. No blood showed on his fingertips, but his windpipe hurt like hell. It was a miracle it wasn't crushed and suffocating him. He had a good mind to give the Shoshone his knife back—right in the throat!

He charged off down the slope and into the valley heading north for Stiles. To hell with berries and breadroot; meat and potatoes was what he craved.

Glàncing back over his shoulder, he saw no sign of any pursuers. The two with the Henrys he'd embarrassed badly. But they'd get over it; they'd forget all about him once they got back to the ledge and set about collecting scalps.

In his mind's eye he pictured all three squabbling over Raymond's.

32

Doc departed Carlin with money in his pocket wired him by the Denver office. Help was "on the way," an all-too general assurance that he knew from experience could mean anywhere from ten days to two weeks. In Carlin he'd taken time for a hot meal and, although it took him some two hours, managed to swap one of the Henrys for some .44 ammunition for the other. The knife he'd taken from the subchief he preferred to keep. A souvenir. He got to the hideout late the following afternoon, exhausted and aching. Ignoring his merchandise strewn about where Raider had been ordered to toss it, closing his eyes to it, he walked watery-legged through the mine passage to the knoll and into the deserted shack. Lying down on a bunk, taking pains to select one other than Charley's, he fell asleep. He had plenty of time before the Greenleafs got back; he could afford to sleep, there was nothing he needed more.

He slept all night, awakening early the next morning. After washing up, he located a left-behind loaf of bread hard enough to stun someone, managed to break through the crust, and ate about half. This with coffee and some tinned Crawford yellow peaches brought from Carlin was all the breakfast he needed.

Outside on the knoll an eerie feeling came over him as he walked about trying to decide where it would be best to position himself to greet Ben and his mother. From around the corner of the building where Charley's corpse in its coffin had been set up to enjoy Raider's execution looked to be suitable. Recollection of the incident and Albertina's most welcome intercession brought back other memories; Mrs. Greenleaf digging the slug out of him, conspiring with Raider in the barn, taking Charley out front, meeting Ben and Raymond and Raider on the road north . . .

The breeze dipped groundward, snatched up a quantity of dust, and whipped it into a dervish whirling briefly, then vanishing. He walked to the barn. Maybe leaving one door slightly ajar and bellying down inside with the barrel of the Henry poking out would be better. No. One of Allan Pinkerton's General Principles affirmed that in any shootout—armed engagement, he termed it—an intelligent operative stayed clear of buildings, if it was possible. Any structure, particularly a wooden one could be too easily set on fire. The corner of the house would do.

Charley's grave inside the barn appeared undisturbed, as Doc expected. The flowers in the window boxes needed watering and he was about to tend to it when he decided that prolonging their prettiness wouldn't accomplish much. Once the case was wrapped up the place would be abandoned. Certainly no one was hanging about, holding his breath, waiting to move in.

He ventured out front and began poking through his wares. Most of the crates were sprung, but surprisingly, their contents were intact, with no more than a couple of dozen bottles broken. He set about piling everything up, keeping one eye out for his disguise box. It was nowhere to be found and he decided that it must still be in the box under the driver's seat. How it had escaped discovery by any of the Greenleafs he couldn't guess. But it had. The showdown with Charley in the alley in Cameron came back to him. Ripping off his mustache and van dyke. He couldn't recall any other case that produced quite as much physical pain as this one.

He test-fired the Henry. It kicked like Judith in a temper and pulled high and to the left. He'd have to be careful; hopefully, ideally, he'd be able to get the drop on Ben and there would be no reason to shoot. Hopefully, ideally, but not likely. When last he'd seen him, Ben had been moving down the same road his mother was taking —toward raving insanity.

Finishing stacking up his wares, a chilling thought occurred to him. How stupid could he get? Cleaning up the area had to be tantamount to climbing up above the mine

and loudly announcing to mother and son that he'd gotten
back ahead of them.

"Weatherbee, don't you ever think before you tackle
anything?"

He rested a few minutes, then set about recluttering
the area. Then he went back inside to wait.

33

Arriving in Stiles and getting three dollars in paper from the first man he approached in exchange for the two Shoshone knives, Raider was tempted to splurge one of the three dollars on a bottle of Tangleleg. But if he started drinking and couldn't stop, by the time he'd slept if off Doc could be down a well with two burros backed up to it getting ready to shit the man to death.

Standing in front of the Sagebrush Saloon he watched the pony drink from the trough and once more fought down the insistent urge to wet his own insides. He settled for coffee and a steak as tough as boot leather. Then went on his way, cutting eastward to pick up the wagons' trail before sundown.

The clouds flocking over the horizon ahead showed amethyst bellies, the breeze was up and cavorting about the valley, and sundown was still two full hours or more in front of him when far ahead he spied a sight that lifted his heart. Parked near a group of hills, sitting half in the shadow of the highest among them, were the two wagons. Pulling sharply to his right, he rode up to within 200 yards, dismounting and tying the mustang. Checking the .45, he began creeping up on the wagons, sticking close to the start of the slope as he did so, steering clear of sagebrush or anything else growing that bending and springing back noisily might betray his presence. He was within fifty feet of the apothecary wagon and the horses tied in a line to the tailgate when he noticed that Ben and his mother were nowhere about. Nowhere about the wagons, seemingly. But what about the hills. Up in them? Over them?

There was no sign of life up above, other than the birds. Listening for a long time, all he could hear were the birds and the breeze. Moving past the apothecary wagon, giving

Judith a friendly pat and a few words of affection as he did so, he slipped underneath the family's wagon. He examined the bed; it was solidly constructed, with no secret compartments, no hinges, nothing unusual. This neither surprised nor disappointed him. If there was a secret compartment it would be in one or the other four-square and hollow side supports. The difficulty with that was he'd have to unload the damned thing in order to get a good look. That could wait, he wasn't about to present a slowly moving target to the man up on the slope keeping a weather eye out for visitors.

Coming out from under the wagon into the shadows, Raider waited, listening. And thinking. The silver had to be in the wagon. There was no other place it could be. They certainly hadn't left it buried back on the knoll. Or entrusted it for safekeeping with anybody. The odds against that had to be a thousand to one. Reflecting on odds sent a slight shiver up his spine and his hand strayed to his holster, patting it.

Hearing nothing, seeing no sign of the two, he started back toward where he'd tied up the mustang, once more staying in the shadows as much as could. But coming up to a thick cluster of sagebrush, he was forced to move out and around it. As he had coming up, with no damage done.

He did so and was almost back into shadow when a shot rang out, the slug whining by so close to the knuckles of his right hand he could almost feel it scrape them.

"Goddamn!" Twisting about, he hurled himself up closer to the start of the slope.

Two more shots followed in quick succession. The clean crack, the familiar echo betrayed a Winchester. No question. Any question there could have been was promptly answered:

"O'Toole! Hey, Pink, I gotcha!"

Raider kept silent.

"You can't move, left or right or frontways."

Three more shots; Raider hit the ground and rolled over into the bushes onto his belly. And began snaking his way upward, .45 out and cocked, squinting ahead, surveying the hills. There was no piñon here like the Shoshone Mountains, few trees of any kind, but a lot of bushes, dwarfed by continual exposure but unusually thick.

He pulled himself upward with his forearms, at the same time pushing with his toes. They ached, but for some reason not as furiously as they might have. At the moment, at least, Ben and his eye and his Winchester were too close to permit him to worry about other things. The bushes provided good cover, but moving through them it was impossible to keep them from moving. Two more shots came down at him and a third and fourth, biting rock and whining away an inch from the heel of his left boot. He lay still as death, his heart banging away at the ground, climbing up his throat and into his mouth.

He was a sitting duck, practically! Why didn't the bastard keep shooting, spray the spot? Lifting his head slightly, Raider examined the lay of the land ahead. Rock jutted out about fifteen feet above, a small replica of the overhang under which the family had parked the wagons back at the battle site.

If he could get up under it, he could move to his right protected, circle up the rest of the way until he was above Ben. If he made it he'd have the edge he needed. The edge Ben had now.

Scrambling, pulling with all the strength he could muster, he made it to underneath the ledge, evading a round dozen wild shots, any one of which could have plowed through his back.

"Pink, hey, Pink. You're crazy, you know that? Pink?"

Not answering him was getting on the bastard's nerves; the rising inflection of his voice gave him away. Continuing to play dumb might even goad him into anger. Angry men get careless, make foolish mistakes, tactical errors. So Allan Pinkerton maintained. Raider himself had never noticed. He wondered if Allan Pinkerton's ideas on the subject had ever undergone practical testing.

Deserting the end of the ledge far over to the right of where Ben's shots seemed to be coming from, Raider circled slowly, carefully and wide up to the top, staying as low as possible every foot of the way. Ben continued talking, shooting blindly, getting more and more annoyed.

"I'm gonna kill you like you killed Charley—in the face. I'm gonna turn your damn head into a melon, all pulp all over. You hear, Pink? You're dead! And don't think I'm gonna bother to bury you, neither. The goddamn buzzards can pick you clean. I only wish to Christ I could kill you a thousand times. Hey, where'd your sidekick get to? Did the Shoshones get him? I sure hope . . ."

Raider raised up on all fours and peered down the slope. At first he saw nothing, but when Ben started cursing him, he strained his ears and his eyes and pinpointed the voice below behind a mass of small rocks. And spotted about six inches of the Winchester barrel poking out, pulling back and poking out again.

Damn! He'd have to get around in front of him to take him. There looked to be no way of doing it from this high up. He might just as well be sitting inside the mouth of a cave. He could be, at that.

Raider pondered the situation; if he started back down, Ben couldn't help hearing him. If he was stupid enough to show himself so as to be able to turn and fire up the slope, he'd have him cold. He'd gun him down before he could even go into his turn. One thing more was in his favor, thought Raider, Ben would have to be as surprised as hell to discover he'd gotten above him. Maybe that surprise and his itchy trigger finger would push him into a blunder. He might even come out of his hole shooting.

Up into a crouch Raider moved swiftly and quietly over to a position directly above Ben, about forty feet higher up the hill. He picked up a rock, and was about to throw it, see it land and, he hoped, roll down over the mouth of Ben's stone pocket and bring him out like a badger out of its hole, when he heard a sound behind him. Dropping the rock and going for his gun, he turned.

There stood Mrs. Greenleaf, her hair hanging down straight, her eyes wild and staring at him insanely. She was covered with wildflowers, a crown of them circling her head, a necklace of them and wristlets and loose ones hanging from practically every part of her. Around her waist was a belt of them six inches thick.

"Charles?"

A voice in the back of his head silently shouted warning. He turned away from her, spinning, raising the .45, coming around just in time to see Ben aiming upward at him, the grin of Satan spreading across his boyish face.

Then, in a split second, the grin vanished, the Winchester barrel dipping slightly.

"Maw, get outta the way. *Maw! Goddamnit!*"

Raider dropped flat, crabbing forward, swinging around a rock, getting him in his sights.

"Drop it, Ben!" He fired, deliberately missing. "The next one's for your heart!"

Ben started to drop, not his rifle, himself, pulling off wild shots as he lowered. Raider got off one shot only. It caught Ben full in the chest, toppling him over backward yelling, the rifle spinning up into the air and coming down on him.

Raider ran down. Ben lay on his back, arms spread, face blank, eyes staring at heaven. A spot of blood the size of a half dollar centered his chest. Raider sighed silently; he couldn't have placed it better if he'd been standing a foot away. Crouching, he closed his eyes and holstered the .45. Then took it out again to look at it. Lydell's gun.

He headed back up the hill to Mrs. Greenleaf. She was sitting down picking at her flowers, Indian paintbrush, little blue and white gillias, wild pinks, delicate columbines, a dozen varieties.

She smiled at him, then frowned, pouting. "Charles, where have you been, you naughty boy? You were supposed to watch baby Benjamin. You're a big boy now, almost eight years old. You musn't run off when Mommy needs you. Charles, don't just stand there, help me back down the hill."

"Sure."

"What?" She smiled and held up one finger chidingly.

"Sure, Maw."

34

The Greenleafs had left little behind, apart from Doc's merchandise, the beds, and most of the gear and the tools in the barn. The food he had brought with him from Carlin would suffice until they showed up. And there was hay in the barn for the pony. Calculating roughly, taking into account a morning and an afternoon stop each day of at least half-hour durations, Doc figured that Ben and his mother would arrive sometime between sundown and midnight of the following day. The last he'd seen of Ben he seemed to be in a grand rush to get her back, let her rest for a time, then take her to the asylum and place her under a doctor's care. Which was all he could do.

Doc put himself in the sole surviving Greenleaf brother's boots; Ben's plan would probably be to pay the asylum a lump sum out of the Adams & Company silver, then take what was left and head for Mexico. No wagons, no household goods, just a gun, a horse, and his saddlebags bulging.

At sundown Doc settled down to watchful waiting at the corner of the shack, the loaded Henry by his side. A thick counterpane of clouds obscured the moon and stars, and when darkness arrived it was like a great black bowl overturned and placed down onto the world. Sitting with his back against the side of the house looking upward, he had to squint to make out the ridge of peaks crowning the knoll, so black did it speedily become. The wind died and dampness filled the air setting his shoulder wound, healing and beginning to itch, aching dully.

The rain arrived two hours after nightfall, fat drops plopping onto the knoll, raising little puffs of dust and hammering his derby. There was nothing he might use for a poncho, his own being still in his wagon, so he went into the shack, leaving the front door wide open. Sitting in the one rocking chair left behind, he positioned it with its back to the kitchen door, well out of sight of anyone approaching from the mine. He would have to hold the Henry with one arm only; it weighed a ton, but he would manage. Angling his chair slightly, he could see across the knoll to the exit of the mine. Come sunrise he could see; at the moment he couldn't see ten feet beyond the doorway. But he could hear and, more important, whoever emerged from the exit would be unable to see him.

Shortly after eleven the rain let up, then stopped altogether; the clouds gradually dispersed and the moon and stars appeared, lighting up the knoll effectively. Sitting in his chair, the Henry laid across his knees, Doc could now easily make out the exit. The hour passed in silence, the only sound the occasional grinding of the rockers against the floor as he tipped back and forth. And dozed and awoke, sitting up stiffly, hefting the Henry, readying it.

Somebody was coming down the passageway, walking slowly, no doubt feeling his way along the wall. Coming closer, one set of steps. Ben! Jumping up, Doc stopped the chair from rocking and moved swiftly to the door, closing it to within three inches of the jamb. Then sitting with his knees drawn up, he rested the Henry on the dip between them aiming at the exit. At that moment a fragment of cloud left behind by the vanishing cover started across the face of the moon plunging the knoll into darkness. He strained his eyes. Ben emerged from the mine.

"Hold . . ."

A shot boomed, the sound trapped by the surrounding rock and magnified considerably. The slug hit the jamb two inches from Doc's left ear, splintering it. He fired back, the Henry sounding like a twelve-pounder. Squinting he strained to see through the blackness.

"Drop it, Ben! Come out with your hands up."

"Christ Almighty!"

Doc lowered the Henry and stepped out. Raider came toward him holding a .45 in his left hand, his right gripping his wrist.

"You stupid son of a bitch! You nearly blew my goddamn arm off." He held it up showing the ragged edge of his sleeve.

"Where in hell did you come from?" asked Doc in

astonishment. "Why didn't you call out? Identify your-self?"

"How am I supposed to know it's you?"

"Who else would it be, you idiot? Who?"

"I didn't mean to shoot, goddamnit; I had it out, nat-urally, but I . . . I pulled off before I realized it. I'm a little nerved up. What are you gaping at me like that for, goddamnit? You got to be as beat and as tightened up as I am."

"We could have killed one another so easily!"

"All right, all right, all right!"

"Did you pass . . ."

"Shut up and listen." Raider dropped down tiredly on his butt. "I tangled with Ben forty miles or so up the line from where we got away. He's dead, I buried him. Which was more than he did for his own. His mother's outside in the wagon; cracked up completely. She thinks I'm Charley. All the way back she's been babbling to me like I was nine years old."

"Get up. Let's go, we'll bring her back in here. She can lie down in her bed."

"What are we gonna do with her, Doc?"

"It's not for us to do anything." He shrugged. "Turn her over to the nearest doctor, I suppose. What else? They'll put her away. I don't know, I've never dealt with anything like this. I don't know what the book says, if it says anything."

"Screw the book, screw Allan Pinkerton. We haven't followed the book since the start, why should we worry about it at this stage?"

"Who's worrying?"

"All right, all right . . ."

Doc shook his head and studied the ground. "When you think back, she wasn't all that sane to start with. And with all that's happened these past few days, it doesn't surprise me she's cracked up completely."

Together they brought her back to the shack to put her into her bed, Doc finding linen and a straw pillow in the family wagon and making the bed. Fifteen minutes later she lay fully dressed under the covers, her wildflowers scattered all about where they had fallen off her. She had yet to utter a sound, not even a reaction to sight of her bedroom again.

"It's as if her mind's drifted off someplace and taken her voice with it," said Doc. "I think she's running a fever, too; she seems hot to me."

"How are we gonna get her to a doctor?"

"I wouldn't move her. You'll just have to ride to Cameron and bring one back here. He'll know what to do. How's Judith?"

"She's okay, all the animals are. It's all the people that are dead."

Mrs. Greenleaf had fallen asleep, breathing heavily, a contented smile playing about her lips. They left her in privacy, returning to the front room. Raider was in the midst of recounting what had happened on the slope and how Ben had been killed, when he suddenly broke off in mid-sentence.

"What's the matter?" asked Doc.

"Something's out there."

"I didn't hear anything."

Raider had moved to the open door. The moon, no longer hidden by the cloud, flooded the knoll with light. Raider motioned Doc to him.

"I . . ." began Doc.

"Sssssh!"

They stared at the exit. Steps were clicking faintly up the passageway, three, perhaps four men coming toward them.

"Stay here with your rifle," rasped Raider. "No, better I take it, you take this." He proferred Lydell's .45.

"Keep it. I can handle the rifle."

"Get flat on the floor." He himself swung around behind the corner of the shack. A man emerged from the exit, gun in hand, then two more behind him.

"Drop it!" snarled Raider, "Or I'll kill ya!"

The command was like a bomb dropped and about to explode in their midst, sending them flying to the sides, dropping flat and firing. The exchange was brief, Doc's Henry punctuating it, booming so loudly over their heads the three newcomers dropped their weapons as one and got up grumbling, hands high. Raider and Doc approached them.

"Who in hell are you? What do you want?" snapped Raider, slowly fanning the .45 back and forth at them.

"Raider! Weatherbee!" One of the men took a step forward.

"Oh, for God's sakes!" Doc's shoulders sagged and he broke into a weary smile. "Joe Fischer . . ."

"In the flesh," said the man, coming all the way up to him, his pale face softening into a relieved grin.

William Pinkerton's men, the "help" Doc had sent for from Carlin. Come not all the way from Denver, which would have taken them a week, but from Logan, just over the Utah border, explained Fischer.

"By train to Elko, by horse over to here," he went on.

"It's good to see you," interposed Raider, "but we're all wrapped up."

"Damn, I was afraid of that," said one of the others.

"We're not," said Doc airily, flashing a glance at Raider. "We still have to recover the silver."

Raider glared at him disdainfully. "We've as good as got it, Joe. It's in the wagon out front, the big one."

"So let's go get it."

"The hell with it. It's safe, it can wait till morning." Raider yawned. "I don't know about the rest o' you, but I'm beat to boots. Go dig it out if you want to, I'm turning in."

35

Mrs. Greenleaf seemed to be sleeping the sleep of her sons, her withered flowers filling the room with pleasant odors. The first to get up in the morning, Doc looked in on her. Then he roused the others, much to his partner's irritation. All five wandered out to the area at the entrance, and while Doc fed Judith, hay brought from the barn—regretfully he was out of oats—Raider, Fischer, and the other two Pinkertons set about unloading the family wagon. They examined the bed.

"No sign of any compartment," said Raider worriedly, down on his knees examining one side of the bed, then the other, pressing hard where the boards met. "Unless it's nailed up. From underneath."

"It's not," called Fischer from under the wagon. "It's as clean down here as up there. But there's supports running full length on both sides."

Doc thought a moment. "So there's no compartment, it still has to be in there somewhere."

"In these sides," said Fischer from underneath. "I don't see any new nails here. What they must have done was take down these bottom boards, stick the silver in, and put the boards back up. A bit awkward, maybe, but that's the way I'd do it. These hollow bracings run full length both sides."

"We can open 'em up from the top down," remarked Raider. "I think there's an ax in the barn."

He went back into the mine and moments later came back with a sledge hammer. Fischer had come out from under the wagon and, taking it from him, began smashing first one side of the bed, then the other.

There was nothing inside either.

"This is ridiculous," said Doc morosely, "it's got to be here."

"Nothing's ever *got* to be anything," observed Raider.

"This may be a silly question," said Fischer, "but did either one of you by chance happen to look under the seat or in the jockey box?"

Raider and Doc exchanged sad looks. Both places were inspected. There was no sign of the silver, nothing but tools and Doc's .38 Diamondback.

They stood off staring at the wagon.

Raider was fast running out of patience. "I say we burn it. Take it outside the rocks, throw some dead grass into it and light up. It's dry as dust, it'll go up like kindling."

"Sure." Doc nodded. "And if the silver is in there, it'll melt into one big glob. The Adams people would love that."

"It's not in there," said Raider defensively.

"Then why bother to burn it?" inquired Fischer.

While the others watched, Doc walked slowly around the wagon. Suddenly he stopped, snapping his fingers, his eyes brightening. "Oh boy, oh boy, oh boy . . . "

"What?" asked everybody in chorus, Raider excepted.

Doc beamed. "They moved it. Why not? They had every opportunity to. To my wagon. Ben was shrewd, so was his mother." He ran to the apothecary wagon and pulling himself up over the tailgate, jerked open his telegraph equipment compartment.

It was empty. So was the box under the seat and the one hanging from the tail end of the bed.

"Good going, Doc," said Raider, "I knew you'd locate it."

"You don't seem to be doing so famously! 'Burn it,' he says . . ."

"Go to hell on your mule, Weatherbee."

"All right," said Fischer tiredly, "let's not start. Doc, what about the mother? Is she totally gone?"

"She's crazy as a bedbug," said Raider.

"All the same, it wouldn't do any harm to question her, would it?"

"I don't think it'll do any good." Doc shook his head. "If she were all there she wouldn't tell you; why should she if she isn't?"

"Why don't we make sure?" Fischer gestured palms upward.

Raider, Fischer and the others trudged back through the mine to the shack, congregating in the bedroom. Mrs. Greenleaf was still asleep. Raider felt her forehead. It was cool. If she had been feverish, whatever had caused it seemed to have disappeared. He shook her gently by the shoulder.

"Maw . . . Maw . . ."

She woke up slowly, her eyelids fluttering, an Indian paintbrush blossom falling from her necklace of flowers onto the sheet.

"Charles . . ." She smiled wanly.

"Maw, listen real close." Raider sat down on the edge of the bed, the others grouping themselves behind him.

"Who are those men, Charles?"

"Just friends. Maw, listen. I can't remember where we hid the silver. We've been looking high and low."

"Silverware?"

"No, no, the money. The Adams money, the eighty thousand."

She didn't understand. She was twenty-five years back in time and hadn't the remotest idea what he was talking about. Still he pressed her. Until Fischer intervened, clapping a hand on his shoulder.

"Give it up, Rade, you're just not getting through."

"Damnit!" Raider jumped up and smashed his fist against his palm. "This is bullshit! All these people dead, all these near misses, Doc out there with half his shoulder blown away, no food, no sleep, goddamn Shoshones . . ."

"Take it easy," said Fischer as they left the bedroom, the last man closing the door.

"Take it easy, my ass! We're fucking screwed, don't you see? Everybody else who knows where it is, is dead!"

Fischer tried to calm him down as they went back outside. They were heading for the exit when Doc emerged, all smiles.

"What are you all looking so glum for? Come and see what I found."

36

Doc had found no silver. There was none, not a penny's worth. What he had found was paper money, greenbacks, twenties and fifties, mostly. All neatly rolled up and stuffed down every other spoke in both back wheels of the family's wagon. The elm spokes had been carefully and meticulously reamed out eight to ten inches from the hub ends up, from the wheel ends down. A skilled carpenter would have had to do the job. Dewey-Blair?

The find added up to ninety-three dollars short of the eighty thousand.

Two days later, with Mrs. Greenleaf under a doctor's care and on her way to the Insane Asylum at Blac'-foot, Idaho, Raider and Doc repaired to Burley, down the line from Blackfoot, to rest, catch up on sleep and n. h-ment, fill out their report, and forward it to William Pinkerton in the Denver office along with their individual expense sheets. The report, which would provide the substance of the Case Journal, would be sent on to Chicago, to 89 Washington Street, the home offices of the Pinkerton National Detective Agency where Chief Allan Pinkerton and his General Manager Wagner would evaluate it and meet with officers of Adams & Company.

As he always did, Raider left the actual paperwork to his partner. He had culminated their wrapup conference convened by Doc with Joe Fischer and his men at a table in the Burley House Saloon over a pair of bottles of Taos Lightning. Excusing himself, Raider had gone straight across the street to Madame Felicity's brothel, there to set about shedding all recollection of the past few days in the company of a young and voluptuous female whose moral standards roughly paralleled his own and who, for the princely sum of one dollar, would permit him to take liberties with her which could never be described in the Greenleaf–Adams & Company Case Journal.

They lay naked on top of a jasmine-scented double bed with twin cherubs gazing down on them from the top of the headboard, an incense burner spreading the odor of jasmine to the corners of the room and a banquet lamp with birds flying all over the globe surrounding the chimney sitting on the nightstand, sending out a faint yellowish-red glow that softened the shadows and altered the lady's skin tone from ivory white to flamingo. Raider, having already been twice laid, reveled in relaxation, stretching, chasing the last traces of weariness out of his long and lean body, his thoughts slipping back to the night before upon his and Doc's arrival in town. Following a hot meal and half a bottle of Rookus Juice, he had immersed himself in a steaming plunge bath to scrub off Nevada and sweat out the exhaustion that had taken possession of him body and mind.

Now he lay on his back studying the peeling, crack-laced ceiling, mulling over the events of the week behind him. The sight of Mrs. Greenleaf standing on the slope decked in wildflowers had somehow served to cap the whole bizarre experience, personifying it. In all his travels he had never come upon a human being so bitter, so staunchly and unswervingly dedicated to vengeance. With, as Doc had pointed out, so little justification for such an attitude.

He wondered if she would ever recover her sanity. Probably not, according to his partner. Doc's feeling was that she would not because she had no reason to, He, Raider, hadn't quite understood what he meant by that until Doc explained that she had nothing to come back to, no family, no happy memories, certainly not recent ones, nothing but heartache and disappointment, shattered hopes and plans. Sonoita and all it had stood for, underscored by Lydell's yippy-yay, remained as out of reach as the moon.

"Whatcha thinkin' about?" asked the girl. Her name was Annie. She had hair the color of Raymond Clapp's, fire-red upstairs and down, and she loved to fuck. The only thing she seemed to like better was to suck.

"Nothing important," said Raider solemnly.

Her hand stole across his thigh to his loins and his cock, as soft as a fistful of feathers, enjoying a well-deserved respite. Gripping it lightly, she began to play with him, but was unable to induce erection.

"Can't you get hard?"

"Can't you get me hard?"

"Are you funning? I could make a snowman . . ."

Up on her knees, her plump breasts swinging like giant peaches on a bough in the breeze, she lowered her head and took his cock between her wet lips, ringing it to hold it upright, then slapping the head lightly with the tip of her tongue. Raider's balls rumbled silently, rousing themselves and beginning to fill. His cock slowly straightened; she filled her mouth with it, ringing it down to the root, angling the head flush against the roof of her mouth down past her palate into her warm throat.

"Easy . . ." he murmured.

"Mmmmm, yummy, yummy."

Her head bobbed faster now, like the pump rod on a steam engine. Harder and harder his cock grew, hard as bone, hard as oak, hard as iron, throbbing, filling, stiffening so he feared it would explode even before his balls could refill completely and release their load.

A knock rattled the door; her head stopped abruptly mid-stroke.

"Hey, don't stop!"

She resumed. A second knock.

"Mr. O'Toole?" It was a woman's voice, Madame Felicity. No mistaking the deep, gravelly tone. "O'Toole!"

"Beat it, can'tcha?"

Smoke came shooting under the door, rising into the room.

"Come out! Come out! The house is on fire!"

Annie blanched, letting go of his cock, straightening up. "Oh my God . . ."

Bouncing out of bed, she snatched up her Chinese dressing gown.

"Hey, for chrissakes, where you going? What the hell . . ."

"Can't you hear?"

More smoke poured under the door.

"Hurry!" yelled Madame Felicity.

Sitting up, bracing himself with his hands flat behind him, Raider gazed down at his cock, beginning to soften and bend.

"Jesus Christ, son of a bitch!"

Annie was into her robe and out the door, brushing past the hulking sequined and flowered silk presence of Madame Felicity and hurrying down the hallway. The madame stared.

"Into your drawers, man, hurry!"

And with this, she slammed the door.

"What in hell!" Raider fumbled with his belt, buckling it, grabbing his boots. "What are you shutting the damned door for?"

More smoke poured into the room. Something was wrong, he thought. Whipping the door open, he found her vanished, her heavy step pounding down the stairs to the left. Flashing a glance in the opposite direction he scowled and cursed vilely.

"Forget your shirt, Rade, save your ass." Doc leered at him from behind an Old Virginia cheroot, smoke climbing from its end.

"You bastard! You son of a bitch! I oughta strangle you! How much did you give her?"

"Dollar."

"Heartless prick. Bastard!"

"You said that."

"Fire . . ."

"Did we interrupt anything important?"

"Doc, some day you're gonna do this once too often."

"Inside, partner, got something to show you."

"Couldn't it wait?"

"Would I interrupt your visit to paradise if it could? Would I be that inconsiderate, that sadistic?"

"Shut up."

Doc laughed and handed him a telegram, a long one, two full sheets and part of a third:

INFORMATION RECEIVED AND EVALUATED STOP WAS SO MUCH BLOODSHED NECESSARY TO SOLUTION OF CASE STOP COULD ANY LOSS OF LIFE HAVE BEEN PREVENTED THROUGH

MORE DILIGENT EFFORTS ON YOUR PART STOP
CAN YOU PROVIDE THIS OFFICE ANY PHOTO-
GRAPHS AT ALL STOP NONE FORWARDED
STOP PROFILES OF ACCUSED APPEAR SKETCHY
STOP INCOMPLETE STOP THIS OFFICE UN-
ABLE TO CLOSE FILE WITHOUT INCLUSION
ADDITIONAL VITAL STATISTICS STOP ASSUME
COMPLETE INFORMATION TO FOLLOW STOP
COULD DESTRUCTION CONTENTS APOTHECARY
WAGON BEEN PREVENTED STOP SINGLETON
ESTIMATES THIS LOSS AT 220 STOP CLIENTS
STOLEN FUNDS RECOVERED APPEARS 93 DOL-
LARS SHORT STOP ACCOUNT FOR DISCREPENCY
STOP COMPLAINT RECEIVED THIS OFFICE
FROM WARDEN BOISE PRISON REGARDING
DESTRUCTION TERRITORIAL PROPERTY STOP
GATE STOP WALLS STOP CELL BARS STOP
EXPLAIN FAILURE TO NOTE SAME IN REPORT
STOP REPORT APPEARS INCOMPLETE OTHER
REGARDS STOP REASSESS INFORMATION AND
CONTACT THIS OFFICE ASAP STOP EXPENSE
TOTALS ACCOMPANYING REPORT APPEAR OUT
OF LINE STOP REIMBURSEMENT FOR LOSS OR
DAMAGE PERSONAL PROPERTY BASED ON AGE
AND CONDITION OF SAID PROPERTY NOT ON
PURCHASE PRICE STOP OPERATIVE W EX-
PLAIN MALFUNCTION 38 STOP WAS WEAPON
TESTFIRED WEEKLY IN ACCORDANCE GENERAL
PRINCIPLES 9B 17 REGARDING CARE AND
KEEPING FIREARMS STOP INDIAN AGENT
DUCK VALLEY FILED COMPLAINT OVER
DEATHS SHOSHONES ACCOSTED BY YOU STOP
ADDITIONAL REPORT RE THIS MUST BE FOR-
WARDED HIM TO JUSTIFY ACTIONS IN INCI-
DENT IN QUESTION STOP ANTICIPATED COST
REPAIRING CAMERA LISTED EXPENSE SHEET
EXORBITANT STOP SUGGEST WEATHERBEE EN-
DEAVOR REPAIR STOP PRACTICING ECONOMY
WHERE WHEN WE CAN ASSURES BLACK INK
STOP TWO MONTHS PAY DUE YOU STOP
MONEY WILL BE FORWARDED WHEN ABOVE
QUESTIONS ANSWERED AND ACCEPTABLE EX-

PLANATIONS EVERY ASPECT CASE FORTHCOM-
ING STOP AGENCY POLICY AS STIPULATED
GENERAL PRINCIPLES 20A 2 CLEARLY STATES
CASE MAY ONLY BE CLOSED UPON COMPLE-
TION HISTORY IN ALL AVAILABLE DETAILS
STOP REPORT DENVER UPON RECEIPT THIS
COMMUNICATION FOR IMMEDIATE REASSIGN-
MENT STOP CONGRATULATIONS JOB WELL
DONE STOP

W

Raider slowly lowered the yellow papers, staring at
Doc in silence. Then he ventured a comment:

"Shit."

"We'd better get a move on," rejoined his partner.

"Shit."

"Rade . . ."

"I quit." Crumpling the wire, balling it tightly, he
handed it back. "Send it back to Wagner, my compli-
ments. 'Shove up ass stop.'"

"You're not quitting."

"Watch me."

Swinging about he walked off down the hall. "Annie,
hey . . . Annie?"

Doc drew long on his cheroot, tilting his head back and
spreading smoke above him. Chuckling. He addressed
the cheroot.

"Not to worry, the day he quits is the same day I do.
The day we catch it."

WE HOPE YOU ENJOYED THIS BOOK

If you'd like a free list
of other books available from
PLAYBOY PRESS PAPERBACKS,
just send your request to:

PLAYBOY PRESS PAPERBACKS
Book Mailing Service
P.O. Box 690
Rockville Centre, New York 11570

INTRODUCING A BRAND-NEW SERIES OF ADULT WESTERNS

J.D. HARDIN

"THE MOST EXCITING WESTERN WRITER SINCE LOUIS L'AMOUR"—JAKE LOGAN

Meet Doc and Raider, two Pinkerton agents whose daredevil and lusty escapades will capture your imagination from the very first page. Here is rip-roarin' gun-toting Western fare at its finest. Order the first two books in this series today and watch for more wherever paperbacks are sold.

___ 16563 **THE GOOD, THE BAD, AND THE DEADLY** $1.50

A wild chase through the Texas Big Thicket has Pinkerton agents Doc and Raider breaking jails and jaws.

___ 16556 **BLOOD, SWEAT AND GOLD** $1.50

Using a specially built freight car, Doc and Raider highball 12 million dollars' worth of gold from San Francisco to Kansas City.

PLAYBOY PRESS PAPERBACKS
Book Mailing Service
P.O. Box 690 Rockville Centre, New York 11570

NAME_____

ADDRESS_____

CITY_____STATE_____ZIP_____

Please enclose 50¢ for postage and handling if one book is ordered; 25¢ for each additional book. $1.50 maximum postage and handling charge. No cash, CODs or stamps. Send check or money order.

Total amount enclosed: $_____

GREAT YARNS FROM
ONE OF THE FASTEST-SELLING
WESTERN WRITERS TODAY

JAKE LOGAN

_____	16281	**RIDE, SLOCUM, RIDE**	$1.25
_____	16590	**SLOCUM AND THE WIDOW KATE**	$1.50
_____	16293	**ACROSS THE RIO GRANDE**	$1.25
_____	16575	**THE COMANCHE'S WOMAN**	$1.50
_____	16595	**SLOCUM'S GOLD**	$1.50
_____	16570	**BLOODY TRAIL TO TEXAS**	$1.50
_____	16619	**NORTH TO DAKOTA**	$1.50
_____	16600	**SLOCUM'S WOMAN**	$1.50
_____	16648	**WHITE HELL**	$1.50
_____	16416	**OUTLAW BLOOD**	$1.25
_____	16434	**MONTANA SHOWDOWN**	$1.25
_____	16458	**SEE TEXAS AND DIE**	$1.25
_____	16475	**IRON MUSTANG**	$1.25
_____	16493	**SLOCUM'S BLOOD**	$1.25
_____	16507	**SLOCUM'S FIRE**	$1.25
_____	16526	**SLOCUM'S REVENGE**	$1.50
_____	16565	**SLOCUM'S HELL**	$1.50

PLAYBOY PRESS PAPERBACKS
Book Mailing Service
P.O. Box 690 Rockville Centre, New York 11570

NAME_____

ADDRESS_____

CITY_____STATE_____ZIP_____

Please enclose 50¢ for postage and handling if one book is ordered;
25¢ for each additional book. $1.50 maximum postage and handling
charge. No cash, CODs or stamps. Send check or money order.

Total amount enclosed: $_____

THE BEST
PAPERBACK BAR GUIDE
AVAILABLE

PLAYBOY'S
BAR GUIDE
BY THOMAS MARIO

A perennial best seller, <u>Playboy's Bar Guide</u> is the authority on every kind of drink from aperitifs to after-dinner concoctions. Complete with more than 700 recipes for the most exciting potations, <u>Playboy's Bar Guide</u> is a perfect party companion for every festive occasion.

16449 $1.95

PLAYBOY PRESS PAPERBACKS
Book Mailing Service
P.O. Box 690 Rockville Centre, New York 11570

NAME_____

ADDRESS_____

CITY_____STATE_____ZIP_____

Please enclose 50¢ for postage and handling if one book is ordered; 25¢ for each additional book. $1.50 maximum postage and handling charge. No cash, CODs or stamps. Send check or money order.

Total amount enclosed: $_____